KENTUCKY DRAGON

MICHAEL PARK

FOX POINT BOOKS

Kentucky Dragon

Print edition ISBN: 9780999771525

Published by Fox Point Books; foxpointbooks.com

Copyright © 2025 by Michael Park

All rights reserved.

The story, all names, characters, and incidents portrayed in this production are fictitious. No identification with actual persons (living or deceased), places, buildings, and products is intended or should be inferred.

ALSO BY MICHAEL PARK

The Glass-Face Man
Good to Grave: Why Some Human Hosts Succeed and Others Burn

For Harlan

PART ONE

"So slowly, slowly she got up,
And slowly she came to him,
And all she said when she came there,
'Young man, I think you are dying.'"

Barbara Allen, traditional folk song

CHAPTER ONE

The first time I remember seeing the chicken man, I was eleven years old. It was 1998, and we had just moved into the house on Tyler Lane. My new bedroom was crowded with boxes, and my dog, Calvin—a fat, black lab—was already sprawled on my bed. He wagged his tail, probably waiting to see if he could get away with staying. *Yep, you know the routine.* Even in this new house, 'lights out' meant my room was fair game, as long as Calvin didn't hog the covers. In pajamas, I was unpacking my books, Power Rangers, and Star Wars figures in the closet, when someone knocked on the front door.

Calvin jumped off the bed and pawed my bedroom door, whimpering. I heard footsteps in the living room off to the right. My older brother Don's room was across the hall, and Mom and Dad were farther down on my left, past the bathroom. This new 'Tyler Lane House'—Don and I called the red-brick, one-story ranch that, like it was a resort—wasn't big, but neither was our 'Whitman Drive House' back in Schaumburg.

I grabbed Calvin's collar and opened my door. Mom and Dad were at the front door, chatting with someone on the outside porch. Don's door stayed shut. *Was he watching out his window?* My window just showed the dark trees in the back. Much less interesting.

Keeping my hand tight on Calvin's collar, I edged along the hall until I had a better view. A blonde woman wearing too much makeup was outside, offering my parents a plate of brownies. Dad was already eating one, and Mom gestured in, probably offering the blonde lady a drink.

There were still dirty streaks on the living room carpet from the movers. Past our couch and Dad's worn leather recliner, the whiskey lamp in the front window glowed yellow. First thing Dad did when we got here was position the lamp in the windowsill. Really, it was just an old, unlabeled whiskey bottle with the bottom cut off. The whiskey lamp was mounted on a wooden stand with a small, bare lightbulb inside, rigged with a green cord. The bottle was scored, blackened with flecks of I-don't-know-what in curls that radiated around the light, as if the bulb were slowly burning the glass. Maybe it was.

Mom and Dad took brownies, they all shook hands, and then Dad shut the door again. Beside me, Calvin didn't move, growling. What was wrong with him? His body was tense. Mom and Dad headed through the living room into the kitchen.

"Calvin," I whispered. "Come on, boy. No brownies for you."

But he was still watching the closed front door.

"Show's over."

He barked once, too loud. The sound made me jump, as if someone had clapped right by my ear. *Thanks a lot.*

Don's door opened. "What's Calvin barking at?"

He looked tired, like maybe he wasn't watching out the window and had actually been trying to sleep. Don was a head taller than me, but slouching now, rubbing his face.

"I don't know. He was chasing something earlier. Rabbits, I think. It's a cool backyard, really big."

Don gave me a 'I-got-out-of bed-for-*this*' look. "Don't be dumb, Mark. It doesn't matter how big our backyard is. I know *you* didn't have any friends in Illinois, but I did. And now what? *Poof.* They're all gone, so we can be here for Dad's *Kentucky fried job*."

Dad's new job here in Louisville had something to do with health care, or maybe it was insurance. I didn't know exactly, but he wasn't a doctor. I tried not to think about what Don said, about me having no friends.

"I heard you can get a driver's license at 15 here, so next year you could go visit," I said.

"You can get a *permit* at 15, dumbass. It's 16 for a license, almost two years from now for me. By then ..." He stopped himself. "Sorry, it's just bullshit. This isn't your fault. I'm not mad at you. I'm pissed at Dad. I would never do this to my family. You and I are just along for the ride."

We were in it together. Cool. There were other reasons for the move, and it was more complicated than Dad being selfish, but the two of us were a secret team. When was the last time we talked like this—*had* we ever talked like this? He was popular, always perfect grades, and he'd had three close friends since kindergarten who did everything together. I was only included when they had room for an extra player on James Bond on the Nintendo 64 or if they needed someone for dodgeball, usually not. I never had friends like that. I don't know why.

There was another knock.

My stomach didn't feel right, like I'd swallowed moldy bread.

Dad was still eating a brownie, calling back to Mom as he went to answer the front door again. He opened it and froze.

Don stepped past me, closer to the living room. I followed with Calvin until I could see. A thin man in a gray suit waited on the front porch, smiling. He had a receding hairline, veiny neck and hands, and was carrying a black duffel bag. I couldn't hear what Dad and the thin man were saying, but Dad was stiff, his hand fixed on the front door. There was a different rhythm to his movements, like he was apologizing.

But that was silly. *The thin man is a stranger. Probably another neighbor, just without brownies.*

The man stepped past Dad into the entryway, then saw Don and me.

"These are your boys?" he asked. "Perfect. Don and Mark, is that right? And you're Don?"

Don nodded.

Calvin shook, and I smelled something acrid sweet. I looked down. He pissed on the floor. *What the hell?* "No, Calvin! Bad dog."

Dad should have shouted, and Mom should have come running in from the kitchen, angry that I was out of bed. Except Dad didn't notice, just kept watching the thin man. No sign of Mom.

The man gestured to Don. "You go by 'Don,' right, not 'Donald'? I want to show you something, Don."

Dad was still holding the front door, as though he needed it for balance.

Why isn't he coming back in?

"Please," Dad said, "let him go back to bed."

The stranger kept his eyes on my brother. "Don, come here."

"Do as he says," Dad said quietly.

Don stepped closer to the man, and he set down his duffel bag, unzipping it to look inside. His fingers were lumpy joints that ended in dark purple fingernails. He couldn't have been *that* old, but his hands were withered, like Grandma Elizabeth's, Dad's mom, when we saw her at the nursing home over the summer. Her husband, Dad's dad, died before I was born. Grandma Elizabeth was 76 years old, though. The man looked about Dad's age.

Dad closed his eyes and seemed to be talking to himself. Where was Mom? The stranger guided Don around so he blocked my view of the bag.

"Do you see this, Don?" the man asked. "Do you know who that is? Do you know how many *parts* of her there are?"

Don shook his head, didn't speak.

The man glanced at Dad. "Really? A prayer? I thought we were past that."

When Dad opened his eyes, they were glassy.

"Please stop," Dad said. "Please."

The man returned his attention to Don and took out a foot-long needle blade that resembled an icepick.

"Sometimes people get sad. So sad they can't see colors or get out of bed. So sad they can't eat or think or *want* anymore. Do you know the kind of sad I'm talking about?" Still holding the needle blade, the thin man raised a small metal hammer. "And do you know if you put a knife into the eyeball right here ..."

With his finger, the stranger touched the inside of Don's right eye, where it met his nose. Don blinked the finger away but didn't step back, still staring at the bag. *What did he see?*

"... you can slide a blade in and in *and in*, and then give it a nice tap with a hammer, move it around a little in the brain, and pull it back out again without causing any pain at all. Or *nearly* any pain. And you can do that with both eyes. Tap, tap, tap into the brain," the man said, "just gently into the gray and pink, circle it around, very carefully, and then slowly back out again. And do you know what you find? The sadness is gone. No more tears."

"Can we talk outside?" Dad finally let go of the door, approached the man.

He smiled, friendly and casual. "Of course. When you asked me to leave a moment ago, I thought maybe you were confused. Your *lamp* is too bright in the window, by the way. Try turning it off once in awhile."

Dad pointed to Don. "Get back in bed."

When Don started to go, the man said, "It was very nice to meet you, Don."

I tried to catch Don's eye, but he just looked at the carpet, his face slack and distant. I'd never seen him like that, and it made my stomach clench tighter. I might throw up, still smelled Calvin's piss. He was hunched, knowing he was in trouble.

"Where is she?" Don asked, almost too quiet for me to hear.

The man nodded. "Good question. Not 'who,' not 'why,' but *where*. Very practical. The nicest thing I can tell you—and this is me being a reasonable guy, because you've been polite—the nicest way to put it is: *she's gone.*"

Dad said, "Don ..."

Don faced the man and clenched his fists.

"It was very nice to meet you," Don told the man. "What should I call you?"

That's weird. Not 'what is your name' but 'what should I call you.' Why did he say it like that?

"I'm the chicken man."

The what? Who uses a name like that? Was this a joke?

Don shook his head, muttered, "Whatever," and went past me to his room. If it were a joke, he should have smiled, not stared at the carpet with his jaw clenched.

The chicken man noticed Calvin and me standing in the hall. He winked. Then, he put away his needle blade and hammer and followed Dad onto the front porch.

I was shivery, my stomach still too tight, as I brought Calvin into Don's room. A narrow path led back through mounds of suitcases and boxes to his bed. Without the light on, I could only see his shadow on his bed, even when I sat beside him.

"What did he show you? What was in his bag?"

"Go away," he said. "We can talk in the morning."

Tell me it's okay. That this was all some sort of elaborate joke.

"He said something about a girl," I said. "You asked where she was."

"Stop it, Mark." But he didn't sound angry or frightened, just drained. He curled away from me and shuddered. Then, a soft, strained sound. What was that?

He was crying, covering his face.

I put a hand on his back. But he didn't stop crying for a long time.

Don't think about it.

But I remembered the way the chicken man winked at me. Like he knew things I didn't. Whatever this weird joke was about, it upset Don. So why didn't Mom and Dad explain it?

The front door opened and closed again. It could have been five minutes or five hours later. Calvin went to check it out, and I followed him. Maybe I would get in trouble, but the chicken man was just a neighbor or one of Dad's friends, wasn't he? Mom and Dad would say so. We would laugh and talk tomorrow like we always did.

Mom sat at the kitchen table, holding a plastic cup of red wine, with the bottle open in front of her. Dad stood at the counter. He looked unkept and distracted. In here, the cabinets were all open, boxes full of newspaper-wrapped dishes lined up on the floor, waiting to be unpacked. Mom and Dad went quiet when they saw me.

"Mark," Dad said, "did you hear all that?"

Mom got up. "It's late. Back to bed."

"Mark was in the hall, he should—"

"No." She gave Dad a hard look that I knew meant she was ready to fight. Whatever this was, I wouldn't hear about it.

Dad stared out the window at the house next door. "Good night, Mark."

Mom walked me back to bed, stepping over the pee stain in the hall carpet without a word.

In my room, I let her tuck me in, and Calvin curled up on the floor. Why wouldn't the nervous pull in my stomach go away? It would be okay.

"Crazy night, huh?" Mom asked. "Listen, I know you probably saw and heard things that didn't make sense. Just trust us, okay. You don't need to worry about it."

"Okay. Sorry I got out of bed."

She kissed my forehead.

"We love you and your brother so much. Your father is under a lot of pressure, and moving is always stressful. Don't worry ... about a thing." She smiled. It was part of a song that she'd sung to Don and me since we were babies. Sometimes Dad joined in and switched up the words, adding funny lines about all the things we shouldn't worry about. *Don't worry ... about the chicken man ...* "Get some sleep."

When Mom left, Calvin climbed onto my feet. I didn't push him off, and a moment later, he was snoring. *Just go to sleep. All back to normal tomorrow.* But I was wide awake when my bedroom door slowly creaked open. Outside my room, it was dark. Mom and Dad were in bed, the chicken man was long gone, and the house was cold and black. I felt my pulse in the side of my neck. *What now?*

Someone stood in my doorway. Calvin sat up, but he stayed quiet. I held my breath, heard my heartbeat in both ears. If it were a stranger, Calvin would have barked, wouldn't he? Whoever it was ...

"Mark?" A whisper.

Don.

"Yeah?"

He came over to the bed, crouched beside me.

"I think we can find her." He was breathing fast, talking in quick, urgent breaths. "She's hurt, but ... she's real. I don't want to leave her like that."

"Who?"

"Our dead sister."

Chapter Two

When I was four years old, my older sister Abby vanished. I didn't really remember, but it's what I pieced together over the next seven years from Mom and Dad, and from Don. He's three years older than me, and Abby had been two years ahead of him, nine when she disappeared. They grew up together, when I was still the baby. I had vague, fuzzy toddler memories, though. Flashes of a pretty girl with dark hair, confident and loud. I remembered roller skates. She pulled me onto a slippery roller-skating rink, when I was still too small to balance. Another memory of her shoving Don on our old driveway, and he skinned his knee, cried, and then she convinced him not to tell Mom and Dad, if she gave him her GameBoy for the entire weekend. He liked Tetris and Mario Brothers, and it was *hers*. He stopped crying in two seconds.

Really, though, these might have been stories I heard, not things I actually witnessed. I had only just turned four when she disappeared. I remembered the next two years, when Mom and Dad fought. We knew they might get a divorce. And it wasn't until Abby had been gone for almost three years that Mom picked us up from school early. She brought us home to sit in our old living room, so Dad could say that Abby had "passed away." Our older sister, who I barely remembered, had *passed away*. Mom had been strangely quiet, not crying, as if she were angry with Dad for talking about it.

We sat for a long time asking questions that Mom and Dad refused to answer. "How did she die?" "Where was she all this time?" "Can we see her?"

There was a strange funeral service with a closed casket. We never saw her body. Now that I was eleven, Abby had been gone for seven years and dead for at least the last five. She would have been sixteen today. Except she wasn't.

"She's dead," I said.

"I know. That's why I called her 'our dead sister.'" Don was still crouched by my bed.

Calvin's ears perked up. My dog was comfy on my feet.

"Do you think someone can be dead *and* hurt at the same time?" Don asked.

What does that mean? I imagined a body in a coffin screaming, willed the thought away.

"I don't understand. Like a ghost?"

"I don't know, like a person, maybe a ghost, but a person who can still feel things after they die."

I sat up more in bed to face him. He still looked pale from whatever he saw in the chicken man's bag, but I couldn't tell if his eyes were puffy from crying. Even this close, my room was too dark.

"What did the chicken man show you?" I asked.

"It was her."

"He showed you pictures? Is that what you saw?"

"It was *her*, Mark. She's..." He shifted, watching the door. "We have to find her."

This didn't make sense.

"You think she's alive? Mom and Dad talked about that. They were sure she ..."

Passed away. Why couldn't I say it?

"She can be dead *and* hurt," he said, louder. "Jesus, I don't know why this is so hard for you to understand. I'm telling you, she needs us. We have to do something."

"Okay, sorry. Like what?"

"We have to find out about this chicken man. We need to know what happened to Abby."

No. That would be like scratching a wound that might not close again. Instead, we can go back to normal. Please.

I rolled onto my back and covered my eyes with one arm. Maybe this whole thing would disappear somehow if I didn't look. "Mom said they're taking care of things."

"In the bag, he had ..." Don grabbed my hand hard, and I looked at him again. "If you were there, if he had you, I would come for you, okay? And if the chicken man took me, would you find me?"

He squeezed so tight I couldn't feel my fingers. With all the boxes and unfamiliar shadows on the bare walls, this didn't feel like my room. This felt like a stranger's house that we'd snuck into in the middle of the night. Or maybe a dream, and we'd wandered here and gotten lost. Except the pressure in my fingers from him squeezing made it real. *Not a dream. This is happening.*

"Would you let him take me, Mark? Would you be okay, if *I* disappeared and then three years later Mom and Dad told you that I wasn't alive anymore? I wouldn't let that happen to you," he said. "I promise."

Don't think about what he's saying. "I promise too."

Don nodded, as if that decided it. The shadows shifted in his jaw, as he clenched his teeth, then relaxed again. "We didn't know to make this promise with Abby, but that happened."

I saw a coffin again in my mind, with someone trapped inside, deep underground. *How could someone be dead and still hurt?* In the daylight, this would make sense. *Just get through this now. Don't think about it.*

He let go of my hand, and my fingers throbbed. There would be a mark in the morning.

Don said, "I love you."

I don't think he'd ever said that to me before when it was just the two of us alone, maybe years ago. I couldn't remember. "I love you too."

***

The next morning, Dad still hadn't shaved, but he looked more like himself than last night. His eyes were pinched and tired-looking, but normal again. Everything was fine.

Mom brought over a pan with scrambled eggs, buried under a thick, gooey layer of cheddar cheese. She started to scoop some onto Don's plate.

"I'm not hungry," he said. "Can we set up the TV?"

Why was he being like this? I tried to think of something to say.

"No, eat your breakfast first," Mom said.

"Come on, Don." Dad stood with his coffee. "I'll help you set it up."

"The eggs will get cold." Mom glared at him.

Dad shrugged. "Then we'll eat them cold. How's that?"

As Don followed Dad into the living room, Mom finished serving and sat across from me. Usually, she cleaned up the pan right away, but not this time.

"How are the eggs?" Mom asked me.

"Really good."

Don had said we needed to learn about the chicken man and Abby, but what I really wanted was to just talk about breakfast, unpacking boxes, and the school supplies I needed for next week. Normal stuff. I would start 6th grade mid-year at a Catholic private school called Holy Cross. Don would be in 8th grade, even though he was three years older than me. I wanted to ask why we were going to Catholic school. We had never been very religious. Mom and Dad were both Christian, but the only times we went to church were around Christmas or Easter, when Grandma Elizabeth felt well enough to visit.

A click and electronic buzz came from the living room, then the sound of a woman talking, a character in a sitcom.

"Success," Dad said.

"Congratulations, you plugged in a TV," Mom called. "Now will you finish your breakfast?"

"Just a minute."

Mom was breathing faster, not really eating. She stirred the eggs on her plate into a lumpy mash, like she couldn't decide what to do.

Dad came back in, and Don followed.

"One of the connectors for their video game broke on the drive," Dad said. "I'm going to run out and get a new one. You boys want to come?"

Don said, "Yes."

Mom pointed to his plate, told him he had to eat. Don looked at Dad, who rolled his eyes and shrugged.

"Do what your mother says."

Don ate without even sitting.

Dad didn't bother to touch his plate or newspaper again. "Coming, Mark?"

I hesitated. I was almost done, too, but going along with Dad or staying here felt like picking a side in their argument.

"Go ahead," Mom said. "You don't have to stay home with me."

I went along. I got into the lumpy backseat of Dad's green Ford. Don was up front.

Our house matched the other suburban, brick houses here, all set back away from the road in the shadows of big oak trees that were probably older than the neighborhood. In the summer, when all the leaves were back, their branches probably crowded out the sky. Now, they looked skeletal and thin. No fences anywhere, but evergreen hedges marked off one yard from the next.

We turned onto a busier main road with gas stations and strips malls, passed a church and a high school, a bank, and a shopping center with a bookstore in the middle, called *Hawley-Cooke Booksellers.*

From the front seat, Dad said, "You don't need to be afraid of that man last night."

And we were back in it, all of it real. I couldn't see Don's face, but Dad watched me in the rearview mirror.

"Did you know him?" I asked.

"Of course he knew him," Don muttered.

"Yes, I know him. He just has a bad sense of humor, understand?"

I could imagine Don's thoughts: *great, now we won't learn any-thing.* By saying the chicken man was a normal person, this conversation was supposed to put the whole thing to rest. Dad had done this before, when I asked about a news story on the radio he didn't want to talk about, like missing children or global warming. This was his way to pretend to discuss it—with a short 'nothing statement.' This might also be our only real chance to ask about the chicken man.

"Can I ask a question?" Don asked.

Oh no. He was going to mention *her*, wasn't he? Mom and Dad didn't like to talk about Abby, except on the anniversary and her birthday. We lit candles sometimes, other times they told us stories. Mostly, they were extra nice and clingy, as if worried we might get snatched away too.

"Sure," Dad said. "Shoot."

"Have you seen what's in his bag?"

Dad switched lanes and pointed to a lot across the street. "Bingo. Radio Shack, here we come."

We pulled into the parking lot, and Dad got out, led us into a store full of TVs, VCRs, and radios, antennas, wires, batteries, walkie talkies, stuff like that. Dad never asked for help in stores, so we spent a long time looking at the wrong connecting cords, until Don found the right one in the next aisle. After Dad paid, we got back in the car, and he switched on the radio to oldies music. A Bob Dylan song about hard rain. Appropriate, at least, since the sky was dark and shadowy now. *Maybe we should press Dad again.* But the flicker of memory—the chicken man winking—made my stomach turn. I tasted the scrambled eggs on the back of my tongue, closed my eyes. What was wrong with my body? It was an impulse I couldn't control, like how Calvin peed in the hall. *Don't think about it.* Don and I didn't speak or look at each other as we drove home.

The rest of the day, I unpacked, and Don played video games. Mom and Dad weren't really talking either, and when they did, a door slammed or a box crashed from being thrown in their bedroom. Then their silent treatment split into muffled shouting and a hushed back-and-forth. This kept up for days, so that when school finally started, it was a relief.

By that first week, our house was mostly unpacked, thanks to Mom. She hadn't started working, and Dad was gone until late every day. We had to keep pushing dinnertime back, first to 6:30, then 7:00, and on Thursday we ate at 8:00. Every conversation between Mom and Dad was a low-level sarcastic fight. "Oh, I didn't have time to pick up more milk. I'm sorry. I was just working to pay for the food we're eating right now." "Food that just magically hopped up and cooked itself, I guess."

On Saturday, when we were all home together, I took Calvin out to the backyard and threw a tennis ball for him. He'd been whimpering and pestering more than usual all week. The quiet tension inside was getting to him, too.

We wandered the pine needle paths out back for a while. It was raining, but the trees kept me mostly dry. Near a thick hedge at the far end of the yard, Calvin had already started digging holes, and now he went at it again, uncovering mounds of black dirt and roots, with his front paws. At the old house, he usually only did this after Mom yelled at him. *We're all in it together, boy. Things will be okay.*

When I eventually called Calvin to go back inside, he ignored me and kept digging. After my third try, I went back to grab his collar and coax him out of the hole. There was mist at the bottom, rising from the dirt. *Or was that steam? Weird.* In different light, I might not have noticed it, but the earth was just dark enough that when the rain puttered in the hole, the droplets kicked up little bursts of white steam. It wasn't happening anywhere else, but most of the yard was also covered in pine needles and dead leaves. I leaned in closer and touched the back of my hand to the dirt. Sure enough, it was warm, much warmer than the ground on the surface. Not hot enough to do that with the rain, but there it was, a faint steam-mist rising from the hole.

I took Calvin inside and got Don. Eventually, he agreed to pause his video game to come see.

Don examined the steam and crossed his arms. "Okay. So?"

That was it? Our yard was literally *smoking*.

"Should we tell Mom and Dad?"

"Not right now. It's probably just heat from the sewer or something, not *that* strange." He looked away from the hole, then grabbed a long stick and stabbed it in the air. "Tomorrow, I think we should go to the library and tell Mom and Dad it's for school."

What? Not this again. We'd gone all week without it.

"Why?" I asked.

"Not to find out about *him*," Don said. "For Abby. Maybe we can look up what happened to her in the newspapers or something. We can at least get started. You promised, Mark."

We'd never done anything like this. Mom and Dad would find out, and now, in the rainy gray light, it was possible—almost—to forget about the other night altogether. *Maybe Don didn't creep into my room, and there was no chicken man ... if we just stopped talking about.*

"And the lamp," he said.

"What?"

Don pointed at the house with his stick. I could see in through the kitchen door, almost to the living room, where the whiskey lamp was probably lit in the front window, like always.

"Did you see Dad's face when the chicken man mentioned the lamp?" Don asked. "I've been thinking about that. He has something to do with the lamp. Remember, it was in the front window at the Whitman Drive House, too."

He was right. I had never paid much attention to it before. The whiskey lamp was just always there, like a mailbox or Mom's potted plants on the front porch, a fixture of our home.

"Dad's protective of that lamp," Don said. "I think it belonged to Grandpa, his dad. We should look at it, really study it, tonight, after they go to bed."

"Why do we have to do it at night? You just want to make it creepier."

He snapped the stick in one motion over his knee, and I jumped.

"It's a *lamp*, Mark. Besides, Dad won't want us to mess with it at all, especially not now. 10:30."

That shouldn't have settled anything, but Don tossed his sticks and went back in, before I could think of what to say.

At dinner, Don floated the idea that we might need to be dropped off at the city library tomorrow for a school project. If Mom and Dad had paid attention, they might have picked apart Don's phony story, but they were still too busy fighting and trying to hide it from us. Spaghetti and meatballs was one of Don's favorites, but he hadn't eaten anything. At the old house, Mom would have made him finish it, but here, Don scraped it into the trash.

In bed with Calvin a few hours later, I watched my bedside alarm clock hit 10:30, then checked the hall and quietly padded to the living room. The house was completely dark and quiet. No sign of Don yet, so I sat on the couch. The only light was a soft glow from the whiskey lamp but facing out so it lit the window glass, not the room.

Where was Don? I didn't have a watch, and there was no clock in here, but there was a clock on the microwave in the kitchen.

I waited in silence for a little longer, trying not to stare at myself in the TV. It didn't look like me. More like a shadow at the bottom of a pond, like the one across the street from our new school. It wouldn't stay in focus. When I looked for too long, my outline got blotchy around the edges. I was breathing faster, could feel my heartbeat.

If Mom and Dad saw me, I would say I had gotten up to get a drink of water. Where was Don? Maybe I *should* get a glass of water, that way, if they saw me, I would have it.

I went into the kitchen. The microwave clock read: 10:35. So it had only been five minutes. Fine. Don would probably be here any second.

In the darkness, I got out a glass, poured in tap water, and then found a flashlight in the top drawer near the stove. Back in the living room, I stood beside the whiskey lamp. When I turned it, the light angled back inside, casting long shadows on the carpet. Calvin was on the couch watching me. The bottle was old and unmarked, pretty normal-looking actually, except the bottom had been cut off to turn it into a lamp. The lamp stand was wooden, with a base and upright part that were both covered in leather on one side and bare wood on the other. Carefully, I lifted it to inspect the bottom. No markings or labels on the wooden base anywhere around a hole that had been cut out so the lightbulb cord could go through, into the bottle on top. It really looked homemade, not like something you would see in a store. Why did we have this?

"Mark!"

I jumped, smashing my water glass into the wall. Don grabbed my shoulder, laughing.

"Asshole!" I said. "What's wrong with you?"

The glass had broken, but I still had the lamp. My arms were shaking, and I was breathing fast, trying to slow down. *Just Don.*

"I'm sorry," he said. "You were so freaked out, I thought … oh shit."

Sharp glass had gashed the back of my left hand, not bad, but there was a long line of blood already oozing onto my knuckles and palm. It didn't hurt, but I felt a warm tingling. When I turned the flashlight on the floor, the carpet sparkled, glass slivers and little flecks everywhere.

"I'm not cleaning this up," I said. "And the lamp is just a stupid whiskey bottle with a lightbulb in it. It's nothing special."

"Okay, okay. Not so loud." He was getting paper towels from the kitchen and came back with a plastic garbage bag to pick up glass. "I didn't know you had a glass of water."

My pulse was calming down, my arms steady again. *So stupid. Why did he do that?* I set the whiskey lamp back in the windowsill, careful to arrange it exactly how it was. Except now there were red smudges on the outside.

"Look." I showed him. "We have to clean this off too. There's nothing special about the lamp. I'm going to wash this off and go to bed."

My hand was still bleeding, and now, as I held a paper towel on the wound, it started to throb. Not deep, but it pinched. Slowly, I unhooked the whiskey bottle from the base. We shouldn't get the leather wet. That might mess it up.

I switched the light on over the kitchen sink. If Don wanted to sneak around in the dark, let him. I needed to check my hand and the whiskey bottle. There was a lot of blood on the glass, so I turned on the faucet and lowered the bottle in. Don should do this. His fault, not mine, jumping at me in the dark like that.

"Don, I think I need a bandage, you might have to ..."

He was staring at the ground near the lamp. With the kitchen counter blocking my view, I couldn't see what he was looking at. I kept washing the lamp bottle.

"Mark?" Don asked.

The whole house was still, as if little pieces of plaster or wood had been rattling and blowing around in the walls before that I hadn't noticed—stopped now.

"What?"

"Mark?"

I went back into the living room. "Can you clean the bottle, while ..."

I was dead on the floor.

Chapter Three

I saw myself lying flat on the carpet, eyes closed. Not me, *another* me. A chill tingled my toes and fingertips, and I shivered, rubbing both arms. Don grabbed me—the other me, the body on the floor—by the shoulders, shaking him.

"Shit, no," he said. "Mark, wake up. Mom! Dad!"

The room was getting darker. No, it was my vision. When I turned my head, even a little, black smudges crept in from the edges.

I heard music outside, steady and rhythmic: a high-pitched voice singing over a guitar and flutes. Like one of Dad's folk songs, but I didn't recognize it. I had heard about this, an out-of-body experience. Looking at yourself when you're dead but not dead. Last year, Dad made us watch a cheesy documentary about a swimmer who cracked her head on the bottom of a pool and was brain dead. But when she woke, she remembered seeing herself and a white light at the end of a tunnel.

I was still holding the whiskey-lamp bottle. I felt emotion behind my eyes, in my sinuses, like I was going to cry. This wasn't real. I was losing feeling in my feet, and my eyesight smeared darker. I went over to touch Don. *Would my hand go through him, like a ghost?* No, it stopped. I felt his back, but he didn't react.

"Don, I'm here."

"Mom! Dad!"

The hall light came on behind me, and Mom and Dad rushed in, shouting. Dad pushed on my chest, breathing into my mouth, asking Don fast, serious questions. Mom grabbed the kitchen phone from the counter, dialed 9-1-1.

My vision was a smaller, closing circle. Everything else was blurring black. This wasn't a tunnel. There was no white light. This was like the opposite. *Not real.* Tears slid down my cheeks. I couldn't control them. *I'm going to die—no, this isn't happening.* In another moment, it would all go dark.

The song was getting louder. It seemed to come from a car on the street outside with the radio turned up too loud.

"... for the love of Barbara Allen!"

It was a steady song, with strange, sad words. But the singer was laughing, his voice too high pitched, like an old-timey recording from the 1920s. I could still feel the whiskey bottle in my hand but barely see the room.

"And all she said when she got there: 'Young man, I think you're dying ..."

Now my legs were going numb.

What if this is the last thing I ever hear?

My vision was almost black.

Fingers touched my cheek, pulled me close, and I smelled mint aftershave. Mint.

The front door opened, and now the singing was in the house: *"Oh yes, I'm sick and very low, and death is on me dwellin'..."*

"You did this with your blood," someone whispered, and then another word I could barely hear: "–un!"

Run.

"No better shall I ever be, if I don't get Barbara Allen!"

My vision a pinprick, I closed my eyes and swung the bottle and …

… and sat up, gasping. Dad and Don were over me, Mom on the phone behind them. She rushed over and grabbed me, crying.

"Oh God," Dad said. "Oh my God."

Don cradled my hand. "It's okay. I'll clean it up."

I looked down. The whiskey bottle had smashed all over my fingers, as if it had just exploded in my grip. Dad wasn't looking at me. He stared at the broken glass. Funny, it wasn't in my skin. I should have been all cut up, but I wasn't. Mom pulled my hand away from the glass shards to inspect it. Nothing from the whiskey bottle.

"What happened?" I asked.

Don picked up glass pieces and put them in a trash bag, while Mom pressed on my chest and checked my pulse. Dad was frozen, staring at the broken bottle. *See. It wasn't real.* I took a slow breath that steadied my heart. My left hand stung, but I was fine. Nothing wrong.

"You broke a water glass," Don said. "Then you were going to clean off the lamp, except you must have touched a live wire on the bulb, and … you weren't breathing."

Except I remembered everything. Seeing myself, the song, my vision closing, and someone, who smelled like mint, touching my face. *Hallucinations or whatever, over now.*

"You're okay, Mark," Mom said. "I called the paramedics. How do you feel?"

They were all still huddled around me.

"I think I had like an out-of-body experience," I said.

Don perked up, and now even Dad watched me, not the broken bottle. Finally, something more interesting than his stupid busted whiskey lamp. He'd been staring at it the whole time, hadn't he?

"Like what?" Don asked. "Like in a movie when somebody dies and they go toward the light?"

"Your brother is fine." Mom squeezed my shoulder, almost too hard. "Nobody is *dying*. He just gave us a shock, and I guess he got one too."

She forced a smile at her own joke. *Shock. Get it? Super funny.*

"Did that really happen, Mark?" Dad asked quietly.

"Not like a white light or anything, but I was here and could see all of you."

I started to tell them—about the song and the blackness—but the memory made the room lurch. My chest tightened, and I closed my eyes. *Slow breath.*

"Someone touched my face," I said. "And I smelled something like mint."

Dad got up abruptly and went to the front window. He peered out the closed shades, then came back, unplugged the lamp, and took the leather-wood base into the kitchen.

"We can get a new bottle," he said. "It'll be okay. We'll fix this."

Why wasn't Mom snapping at him? She should tell him how stupid it was to worry about the whiskey lamp, when his son had clearly almost died. Except she didn't. Instead, she rubbed my arm and told me to try to relax until the paramedics got here.

Wait.

"Where's Calvin?" I asked.

In the chaos, I'd forgotten about him. My dog wasn't here. He'd been on the couch, right there.

"I'm sure he's around," Mom said. "He's probably still in your room."

"No, he was with me."

"The dog doesn't matter," Dad called from the kitchen. "For Christ's sake, your heart just stopped. Don't worry about the damn dog right now."

Mom glared at him. "Your father's right. Calvin's fine. I'm sure."

Flashing lights appeared outside. Dad met the paramedics at the front door, and the night turned into a stretcher, exams, a bumpy ride to the hospital, machines, more exams. Mom and Dad complained about the paperwork and had a long discussion about how soon I should go to school (Monday), and what I shouldn't do (lots).

By 4:45 a.m., we were back home.

Walking up our front lawn, the sky was a deep black behind snarls of pale tree branches. No stars anywhere. That probably meant the morning sun was about to burst up. It couldn't really get darker than this, could it?

A yellow, handwritten sticky note stuck to the front door. Dad pocketed it without letting anybody else see. It was late, and so what if there was a note? Probably from one of the neighbors, offering to help. In the entryway, I called Calvin, but he didn't come. He wasn't in my room.

When I opened the door off the kitchen to call for him in the backyard, Mom rubbed my shoulders.

"Honey, I'm sure he's sleeping out there. He was probably just upset by all the excitement. You have to sleep too."

Except the back door had been closed, locked. Calvin couldn't be outside, and besides, I'd seen him on the couch when I first started messing with the lamp. So where was he hiding?

I finally gave up, said good night, and went to my room. Don was sitting on the foot of my bed, hands folded on his lap. The overhead light made his eyes look shrunken and accented the jut of his collarbone and shoulders, as if he'd lost twenty pounds in the last few hours. *No, it's just late.*

"We have to get started tomorrow, at the library," he said. "We're still doing that. Even if Mom and Dad say no, even if they try to use all this stuff as an excuse or something. Deal?"

I kicked off my shoes. Maybe if I got ready for bed, he'd leave. Why was he obsessed with the library, when our dog was missing?

"Fine, deal," I said. "Calvin is gone. Where could he be?"

"I don't know. What else happened when you were … wherever you were?"

I went to my dresser to look for pajamas. Don had a grim expression. *He won't go until I spill it, will he?* So I made him close the door, and then I told him.

"But that's it." I waved my pajamas at the door. "I don't want to talk about that place anymore or that music. It was like … like my death was funny. Like I didn't matter at all."

"It wasn't real. You're not dead." He punched my shoulder hard. "See? I couldn't do that to a dead boy."

Asshole. But even the dull pain in my shoulder felt good, because it also made the other place feel less plausible. This was real, not that.

Don went to open the door, stopped.

"I'm glad you're okay, Mark. I knew you would be," he said. "Don't worry. We'll find Calvin."

Except we didn't—at least not the next morning. Instead, Don reminded Mom and Dad about the library. There was basically no argument, and Mom drove us over.

"Better than going to church," she said.

The library looked like a converted old southern mansion. White columns on the wrap-around porch rose past a second-floor balcony to hold up an arching roof and chimneys. Old, rectangular windows, big enough for people to walk through, were all blocked up by tinted glass and boxy air conditioners. Set back from the sidewalk and surrounded by a pointy-topped fence, the library looked totally out of place in this rundown neighborhood of trash, weeds, and paint-peeling apartments. At the end of the block, a trio of men in hoodies were smoking and watching us outside the barred windows of a convenience store with a big *Kentucky Lotto* sign flashing above them.

Was Mom really going to let us out here? She didn't even comment on the surroundings and told us she'd be back in a couple hours. Don didn't care either, and I followed him through the fence to the front library steps, where a wooden sign read:

Louisville Metropolitan Library
Founded 1906
Pilcher House, c.1862

We went in and stopped at a main desk and security turnstile that blocked off a wide, quiet room of study tables and bookshelves. The whole place had a foreign, mildewy smell, not from the books—those mostly looked new—but from the walls. Maybe the old plaster and wide floorboards were rotting. *We shouldn't be here.*

"We're looking for information about a disappearance and death," Don said.

The librarian at the main desk was a short-haired, friendly woman wearing a sweater with reindeer on it. Back at our old house, Calvin tore up my sweater like that, but I didn't tell anyone, pretended I couldn't find it. If Mom and Dad knew, always a chance they might ban him from my room. *Don't think about Calvin. He's probably hiding in the backyard. You'll find him.*

"Explain please," the librarian said to Don. She wanted answers: What was this about? A girl who disappeared? Name? And *why* did we want to look this up? What was it for?

"It's for nothing," Don said. "She was our sister." And no, Don told her, we weren't going to ask our parents for permission, could she please help us?

Miraculously she did. The librarian walked us through the turnstile and back to an archaic microfilm reader in the far corner that reminded me of the X-Ray machine at the dentist, except even less fun. She showed Don how to use reader, then brought us to drawers full of little square microfiche boxes, organized by newspaper and date. We needed the date of the disappearance. Maybe start with Abby's death? There might be an obituary, right? Then work back. Maybe the obituary would reference the disappearance.

There was also a computer closer to the front desk with a search function that checked the books the library held. It couldn't do anything with the newspapers, and as far as I knew, nobody had ever written about Abby. Don sorted through drawers with old editions of *The Chicago Tribune*. I typed her name into the search computer: *Abby Morris.*

No results. It seemed to be searching the names and subjects of books. I tried: *chicken man.*

Sixteen results. All cookbooks.

I didn't want to root through microfilm. I'd heard the librarian explain how the machine worked, and all that winding and scrolling sounded tedious. Probably pointless too. I didn't say it, but Mom and Dad probably didn't even write an obituary for Abby. Still, Don searched through the microfiche boxes. Pretty soon, he'd tell me I had to help too, unless I found something else to research.

I tried: *whiskey lamp.*

Nothing.

What about: *out of body ...*

Three-hundred-and-fifty-seven results. That was way too many books to mess around with, and besides, what would I even be looking for?

Out of the corner of my eye, I saw Don fasten a microfiche roll on the machine. He glanced at me, probably to make sure I was working, and then scrolled through old newspapers on the screen.

I was forgetting something. If we were trying to find out about Abby and the chicken man, then everything from the night he visited was important. What about the things he said? The creepy conversation about jamming a knife into someone's brain. Wasn't that a lobotomy? Like a crude version of what he was describing.

I tried: *early lobotomy*

Ten results. That was more than I expected. I clicked through the results, stopped. *Shit.*

Case study in transorbital lobotomy, orbitoclast, Elizabeth Morris.

It wasn't a book, more like a report, 18 pages long and published in 1954.

They had a copy at the library. I found a call slip and copied down the info. The librarian looked at the slip, at me, at the slip, and then cleared her throat in a real slow, *hiccupy* way.

"This is not a children's book," she said.

"I know."

"This isn't even a book. It's a medical report."

Tell her it's for a school project? Tell her Elizabeth Morris is my grandmother and I'd seen her just a couple months ago at her nursing home near Chicago? That was true, but would it help?

"It's important," I said.

"Important how?"

What else could I say?

"It's ... she's my grandmother."

The librarian nodded, holding the call slip between her thumb and forefingers, as if it were delicate.

"I'm sorry," she said. "You need a grown up to sign for this."

A grown up? What am I, five years old? She told me how the file was in the 'stacks' anyway, not out on the shelves, and so it would take a long time to call up, especially on a Sunday.

"My dad will check it out when he gets here," I said. "I'm getting it for him. He works in health care."

She hesitated. "If your father wants to check this out, he'll need to request it himself."

Hopeless. I went back to the library computer without arguing.

In the back corner, Don was deep in thought, concentrating on the newspapers swiveling up across his microfilm screen.

I looked up the case study info again: *Elizabeth Morris, 1954.* I wrote it down on the back of a new call slip, a bunch of numbers and letters that didn't mean anything to me. They probably indicated where it was shelved in 'the stacks,' whatever that was. Then I went looking for the bathroom, except I really wanted to find an *Employees Only* door, something like that.

At the back wall, a directory told me the bathrooms were in the basement, down a wide staircase, with wooden steps sunken with age. This building wasn't always a library, was it? That was what the sign outside meant. It was built a long time before, in 1862, then turned into this.

Downstairs, a short hall led to water fountains, bathrooms, and a door labeled *Stacks—Restricted*. Even better. The door wasn't locked, and inside, long rows of crowded bookshelves extended back forever into darkness. There were several carts piled with more books, all with call slips sticking out of them, and an empty work desk next to the door. Whoever normally worked here liked cats and the *St. Louis Cardinals*. Maybe they weren't here because it was a Sunday?

Past the desk, the place was dark, and I reached for an ancient light switch on the wall. *Wait. What if somebody comes down? I probably shouldn't. Maybe there is a flashlight or something.* I approached the desk. This was beyond stupid now. But I opened the drawers to root around anyway: papers, yellow legal pads, and a sliding bottom drawer full of books, rolling batteries, rubber bands, and little black-and-red St. Louis Cardinal flashlights, two of them. I checked one to make sure it worked. Yep, the light was narrow and too white but good enough.

As I clicked it on and started back into the room, my pulse quickened, and I felt clingy sweat on my lower back. What was I doing? With the flashlight, this was absurd, felt like a robbery but crazy exciting, too. Almost like I was watching someone else. I walked into one of the dark book aisles. There were no windows, and the air tasted like dust and old paper, the specific, sweet smell of ink and slow rot. Also more familiar than whatever I smelled upstairs. Books were books, no big deal.

I compared the numbers on my call slip with the labels at the end of the rows of books, but they didn't line up. It wasn't just the sequencing, the amount of numbers was wrong—I had too many. There was some kind of system here, but I didn't understand it. I should go back.

This was illegal or something, too, wasn't it? What would happen if they caught me down here?

Stop it.

I walked a little ways, checking more numbers and letters on stack shelves, trying to find something that matched. The flashlight cast long, spikey shadows on the concrete floor. Nothing here fit. And why should it? I checked some of the books. This seemed like the fiction section, mostly mysteries and thrillers. So where were the *grown up* medical case studies?

I wandered deeper into the stacks. Blackness behind me. I couldn't see the entry door anymore. *What if the flashlight goes out? Don't be silly. Why would that happen?* But the longer I was down here, the more jittery I got. Why did I grab one, not both flashlights? How long had I been searching already? Five minutes? Thirty minutes? What if Don was looking for me?

I wasn't getting any closer to figuring out the filing system, when I reached the outer wall. Here, there were even more shelves, all with slimmer volumes, like binders and reports. And they matched. I had to follow the wall around, even deeper into the room, then backtrack after I accidentally passed it, but I found the case study.

A plastic folder with three rings through a photocopied report. The original had been done on a typewriter.

I started to head back, when a door banged open. I clicked off the flashlight and crept along the outer wall, away from the noise. This whole room was disorienting. I heard the whine of wheels from one of the book carts, and someone coughed. But I couldn't see anything past the blocky shadows of shelves immediately around me. It was still dark. Whoever was in here hadn't turned on a light.

I found a spot that felt far enough away from the entrance, and I sat between two of the bookshelves so anyone walking along the wall wouldn't spot me. They'd only find me if they looked directly up this aisle. Then, with the bulb-end pressed to my palm, I clicked on the flashlight again, so it lit up my hand in a yellow-red veiny glow.

I'd never done anything like this. What was driving me now? I felt an anxious rush. Excitement. I checked the blackness far down the aisle on my right. Was that a sound? Like a mouse maybe? *Hurry up. Just what is in this thing that's so important?*

I opened the report and angled the flashlight away from my hand so I could read. Hopefully, it wasn't bright enough anyone would notice. The beginning was a 'Summary' that started:

Subject 349, Elizabeth Morris (32), administration of transorbital lobotomy procedure successful in resolving psychotic behavior. Follow up indicates partial deterioration of general motor functions. Subject 349 consented to circulation of this outcome in consultation with Sister Maria Theresa.

A footnote told me that Sister Maria Theresa could be reached at The Motherhouse of the Sisters of the Holy Cross in Louisville, Kentucky. *What the hell?*

I flipped inside the report.

Background: Procedure was agreed upon after consultation with Subject 349 [Ilse 'Elizabeth' Müller, née Helfried; hereafter "subject"], her husband [Karl Müller (35)], both of Dudweiler, Germany, and Sister Maria Theresa. Subject and her husband immigrated to the United States in 1947 to Ohio, Kentucky, Missouri, and eventually settled near Chicago, Illinois. At the time of immigration, the family surname of Müller was altered to Morris. Subject's sister, a U.S. citizen already residing in the area, supported their immigration.

Prior to the procedure, subject gave birth to two male children in the United States: Donald Morris (b. 1950) and William Morris (b. 1952). Following the birth of William, subject began to exhibit symptoms of severe depression and hysteria, characterized by schizophrenic psychotic episodes.

I stopped for a second. To my right, down the aisle, I heard something. I didn't move the light, just watched the darkness. Totally quiet. I'd never heard Grandma Elizabeth called Ilse, but that was probably just her name in Germany—like their last name of Müller—not a big deal. William was Dad's name, except he didn't have any siblings. There was no uncle Donald. Did Mom and Dad name my brother Don after this imaginary person? Did something happen to Dad's brother? Why didn't we know about this? I should stop reading and walk away, leave the report on the floor. But I didn't.

Psychotic episodes included obsession with a supposed schuldeneintreiber, possibly as a result of trauma suffered during wartime. From 1937-1945, subject's husband served in the German army. Subject is believed to have resided in or near Dudweiler for the duration of the war. The fact that psychotic episodes have centered on an individual of German descent are suggestive but not conclusive.

I scribbled down that word, *'schuldeneintreiber,'* on my note but kept reading.

Subject was identified as a candidate for transorbital lobotomy by Sister Maria Theresa as a result of the course of schizophrenic psychosis. Subject's religious affiliation played a significant role, both in the pattern of episodes, and in the subject's decision to seek therapeutic procedures.

What was this saying? Grandma Elizabeth went crazy after Dad was born, and she knew this person, Sister Maria Theresa, who recommended she get a lobotomy? Seriously? It was written so stodgy, but that was it, wasn't it?

Subject was aware and signed written consent documentation regarding risks of the procedure, which include death, undesirable personality changes, postoperative convulsions, and relapse. Psychosurgery was therefore administered at Holy Cross facilities on June 14, 1954.

They were talking about my new school. There was a place on that campus where this happened. Did Mom and Dad know about this? Is that why we were going to school there?

Someone watched me from farther down the aisle on my right, standing in total darkness. He just stood there. Even without moving the flashlight, I could see his white face hovering, with small eyes and too far away to really make out.

I scrambled up and backed away. He wasn't there anymore. He was never there. As soon as I started to move, he was gone. *Get out of here.* Staring at the report in this dark place was a bad idea. No, I was okay. Nothing there. I didn't sit back down, though.

Procedure was initiated by inserting orbitoclast (ice pick)...

Chapter Four

I t actually said 'ice pick.' *Jesus Christ.* That was the thing the chicken man had. The aisle was still empty. My mind was playing tricks.

... orbitoclast (ice pick) behind subject's left eye socket with the application of hammer, before swinging orbitoclast in a medial and lateral motion.

Somebody stuck the orbito-whatever, the *ice pick*, into her head and moved it around. This was what the chicken man was talking about. He wasn't making it up. This was real. Maybe he did it. No, that was ridiculous. This happened 44 years ago, maybe even before the chicken man was born.

There was more about the procedure. *Don't read it. That's not important right now.* I flipped past it. What was I even looking for?

Post-operative visit, partial transcript
August 5, 1954

Dr. Waller: Good morning, can you tell me about yourself? What's your name?

I wrote that name down: *'Doctor Waller.'*

Subject 349: My name is Ilse. You shouldn't smoke in here. My mother says it will ruin the furniture.

Dr. Waller: Can I speak to your mother? Where is she?

Subject 349: I don't know. What do you want? [laughter] Are you one of those boys who wants to play with my knees, like this?

Dr. Waller: Ilse, can you ... please, stop. Thank you. How old you are?

Subject 349: I'll be 12 in December.

Dr. Waller: You're 11 years old now, Ilse?

Subject 349: No, I'm not. My name is Elizabeth, not Ilse—nobody calls me that anymore. Are you crazy? Look at me. I have two children. I'm 32. Karl, who is this man?

Dr. Waller: Elizabeth, my name is Doctor Waller. Do you remember me? I am friends with Sister Maria Theresa.

Subject 349: She's not my sister anymore. Anyway, he's going to open her up and feed her her own liver. He told me. He said he's going to make things out of her, like a drum or a coat. A Maria coat. [laughter] I sometimes think I'm 11 years old. Isn't that strange? Except I'm also very old and in a place for people like me. But I still know I'm 11. The world still looks and feels that way. How would I know if it's real or not? He told me that the skinny lamp can't stay on all the time, not in Germany or the Caribbean or even here. He told me Donald ...

[At this point, the subject began to speak in a form of provincial German, until the subject's husband was allowed to mediate and return the conversation to English.]

Dr. Waller: How do you feel?

Subject 349: Do you want to fuck me? Is this what you want?

[Again, the subject's husband intervened to calm the subject. A sedative was not yet administered.]

Subject 349: Why did my Karl agree to any of it? I don't understand.

Dr. Waller: You sound confused, Elizabeth.

Subject 349: Yes. Why don't you want me? Why doesn't anyone want me? Even he *won't take me. He says I'm not supposed to go with him. That's not the debt. My sister wasn't supposed to bring you here. She and the priest broke the rules. That's why he gets to take them to the kohlenmine. Maybe I'll go to the sunken lady. Maybe she wants me. If I were 11 and hearing this …*

I looked up from the report. The stacks were totally still and dark. My heartbeat thumped in my ears. This was just a report. No, this was what she said, all those years ago after they did that to her. And she *knew* that it would be recorded and kept.

What if she knew I'd read it someday?

That was insane. *Close the report and get out of here.* Don was probably looking for me by now. There was no one watching me from down the aisle. No more noise from the book carts. *Take the report and read it later.* No, it probably had an alarm thingy to stop people from stealing it. It was a binder with some paper in it. There was no hidden security device. *Take it and leave.*

But I didn't. I stood there in the quiet basement and read.

… if I were 11 and hearing this, how would I know I wasn't old and dying in a hospital somewhere? How would I know the people around me weren't just playing along?

Dr. Waller: Are you worried about that?

Subject 349: Are you worried, Dr. Waller? You're too close. He'll notice you.

Dr. Waller: What do you mean? I don't understand.

Subject 349: I was supposed to breed. That's all. I wasn't supposed to have a broken brain. He just collects for the leeres loch in der welt. You and my sister and the priest, he told me what will happen.

Dr. Waller: I would like to talk about how you're feeling.

Subject 349: You'll lose your son in a car accident this winter. It won't be an accident. Then, your wife will divorce you for her new boss, the one with the silver hair, the widower. And then he will meet you on a bridge in Connecticut. That's what he told me. He will let you play the game, the only game, and take you to der drache. Down to the hungry ones, while they sleep.

Dr. Waller: What you're saying right now is upsetting, Elizabeth. Who told you say all this?

Subject 349: The schuldeneintreiber. Dr. Waller, you can play the game. My husband won't play. He's happy with our debt and his arrangement, but what happens after he fucking dies?

Dr. Waller: Please stop using language like that.

Subject 349: Language? At least that has rules, like the game. Don't try to fight or he'll take more than just your erstgeborenes kind. Why do you think we have that lamp? Where do you think we got that? Karl, tell him. Tell him how you made that. Tell him what it is. Here, look at it. Don't you fucking touch me. Get your hand off!

[The psychotic episode escalated until sedatives were administered.]

End of transcript

There were still several pages in the report, but I heard footsteps along the inner wall on the other side of the basement. Should I hide?

A light came on in the distance, then another, tracking the footsteps as they came closer. I ducked behind a bookshelf to face the outer wall.

I held my breath and waited. There was something on the wall, a little farther down, sticking out. That was away from the footsteps anyway, so I crept closer. It was a bull's head: a taxidermy bull's head, complete with huge horns and glass eyes was mounted on the wall, its brown fur dusty, with mold growing around the corners of its mouth. I shined the flashlight on a little copper box below it that read:

Saarbrüken, 1920

So weird. On the floor, there was a white marble square with words engraved in it, totally out of place from the other old floorboards. Now that I got a better look, the wooden boards everywhere else were wide and ancient-looking, with misshapen nails sticking out. But that piece of marble was bright and smooth. Why was it here? It was engraved in another language, maybe Latin:

Quod Erat Demonstrandum

I wrote that down, along with a note about the bull plaque, and then went back through the report transcript and copied words I didn't recognize that were probably German. *Translate them later.*

I smelled rubbing alcohol and mint.

The scent made me stop writing. I still heard footsteps, but they seemed farther away. That was the same smell. The bull's head was watching me. No, it was a dead animal. I pressed the pencil again, but when I tried to write, the words were too scribbly. My hand shook. The same smell as when I was dead.

Not dead, when I saw myself on the floor. This was that smell. No one around. I was alone here. It was just a library basement.

That stupid bull's head. I started to go back, but my legs weren't moving. I had to go. My feet wouldn't budge. *Stop it. Get out of here. Forget the report and whoever is walking around down here. Just go back to the stairs and leave.*

The bull's eyes were black marbles with flecks of brown and red deep inside. It was watching me.

I really couldn't move. This wasn't just me being scared. My legs were locked. My right hand still held the mini-golf pencil and flashlight, and with my left hand, I had my call slip for notetaking positioned on one of the pages inside the report. My toes went cold. I was warm down here, and I had a jacket on. I felt my chest tighten. *Stop it.*

What was happening?

The red and brown flecks in the bull's eyes shifted, glimmering back and forth in the darkness. That was just the flashlight shadows.

Footsteps closer behind me.

I couldn't look away from the bull's eyes. My feet were going numb.

What if *I* was in a nursing home right now? What if Don wasn't Don? What if he was a nurse who worked there? What if when we moved to Kentucky, it was really just me being transferred from one facility to another? If everyone were playing along, if I was old and dying, how would I know?

All I saw were the dead animal's eyes. The rest of the basement was less solid, like it was drifting away.

That was why I couldn't move. That was why my feet were freezing. Because I was in a bed somewhere. My real hands were wrinkled and gray. My real feet were tingly or numb most of the time. This was all

...

"Is someone down here?"

The short-haired librarian stepped around the bookshelf on my left and saw the report in my hand. She snatched it and the flashlight away, then grabbed my wrist. Suddenly, I was moving again, away from the bull. *Don't look back.* She was saying how irresponsible this was, taking me at a fast clip back upstairs. My mother was worried sick and what was I thinking coming down here alone? The bull's eyes... *Don't worry about it.* I hid my call slip notes in my pocket.

Upstairs, Mom and Don waited by the exit. The librarian made a big to-do about finding me, how my library privileges were revoked, and if she found any damage, we would hear about it.

Mom apologized quietly. She was getting angrier and angrier. She had just been arguing with Don when we came up. He was watching me with a half-smile, probably impatient to hear what I had found. We shouldn't have come here. This was stupid, all of it.

Finally, after the librarian took back my library card and put Grandma Elizabeth's medical case study on a high shelf behind the front desk, Mom hustled us outside. She was parked right in front.

"You're both lucky your father isn't the one picking you up. Do you think this is a joke? Is that what your sister's death is to you?" Don started to answer, and she waved that away. "No, I don't want to hear it."

Nobody else around on the street, and now I tasted a burnt industrial smell. There must be a factory or a power plant nearby. Mom made us sit in the backseat.

"With everything going on right now, why would you do this?" she asked, when she was driving. "What's the matter with you two? We're trying to start over here."

"I'm sorry," I said. Not because I was, but because I felt like it might make her feel better.

"Don't mention any of this to your father," she said. "Do you understand me?"

What were she and Don arguing about? What part were we supposed to hide? Dad already knew we went to the library. Don stared out the window at passing warehouses and more distant office towers, lined up near the rusty iron bridges of the Ohio River.

"All right," Mom said. "I have to know, Mark. The other night, you said you smelled mint."

"I did," I said. "It was like mint-alcohol cleaner, like aftershave or something."

"Did you really smell that? Tell me the truth."

"What's the big deal?" Don asked.

We slowed down in traffic, closer to a highway ramp that would get us home. Mom watched the road, didn't look at us.

"Your grandfather, Dad's dad, Karl, used to always wear mint aftershave. He bought it special from Europe. It was disgusting." She laughed a little. "But even when he was older, he wouldn't let the nurses use a different aftershave. He always insisted on that same mint stuff. We spent years ordering it for him. Do you remember us talking about any of that?"

Of course not. Neither of us said anything.

"Maybe there's *more,* and maybe you were there." She laughed again, as if she didn't believe that—but wouldn't it be a riot if it were true? "Maybe we should all go to church."

When I closed my eyes, I saw the bull. It was starting to fade, but it was like the sun if I'd been staring at it for too long, so there were black marks burned into my vision. With every minute that passed, it got a little better, but it was still there.

When we got home, it was snowing. Not a lot, just flurries. The soft currents of snow in the air reminded me of our old house. Snow transformed neighborhoods into someplace new. Not really, of course. Snow was just icy water or whatever, but in Schaumburg, when it covered all the houses and trees, piling deep on the lawns and in high banks along the roads, it was magical. The geography of a place totally changed, even if only for a season.

Inside, Dad watched the news.

"Can you believe it? They may cancel school tomorrow because of this, one to three inches." He shook his head.

Don and I started toward his room but paused in the hallway, so Mom and Dad would think we weren't listening. Were they going to argue about the library? Were we in trouble?

"Another note?" Mom asked.

"No, I told you there wouldn't be. The lamp is fixed."

I hadn't noticed, when we came in. *Check the next time. Keep track of it.* Did Dad replace the bottle on the whiskey lamp? And so what? Was that the same thing Grandma Elizabeth called the "skinny lamp?" Strange name for it.

Mom's voice was almost too quiet to hear: "... to do something, don't we? Can you promise? I mean, can you?"

I leaned against the hall, watching the carpet. Calvin's pee stain was still there, a gray blotch that might never go away. It was here, even if Calvin wasn't.

"Yes. Okay?" Dad asked. "Jesus, you're acting crazy."

I heard Mom walking closer to us. "Go fuck yourself."

Dad laughed. "I just might."

Don and I slipped into his room, and he closed the door. Mom passed by, and their bedroom door slammed. Dad was still in the living room watching TV.

"So?" Don asked. "What did you find?"

I showed him my call slip notes: lots of almost illegible writing, mostly in German. He frowned. I described the report and the basement 'stacks.' But I left out Dad's imaginary brother, Donald, and how I'd imagined being old and in a hospital with dementia. I told him about the bull head, though, and the Latin on the floor. Just not its eyes.

He paced, while I sat on an unopened box.

"We have to find out what all that means," he said.

Mom and Dad had a computer in their room, but it was pretty much just for Dad's work. Neither of us had ever used it. But there were computers at Holy Cross. Maybe we could look up more at school.

"You're sure it was the same Holy Cross?" Don asked.

"How many can there be? Sister Maria Theresa, I guess she was a nun or something."

"And that word seems important: *schuldeneintreiber*." Don moved several boxes to find a notebook and cup full of pens, then he made a copy of my notes. "I didn't find anything in the microfilm. Nothing. And then when Mom got there, I asked if they did an obituary for Abby. Mom got mad. I think they're in some kind of trouble."

I watched Don finish writing and took back my note. "What do you mean?"

He knocked the notebook in the air, as he paced. *Calm down*. His short movements looked desperate, like a trapped tiger at the zoo, stalking back and forth along the cage bars.

"Think about it," he said. "Is it a coincidence we're at the same school where that happened to Grandma Elizabeth? And you said she talked about a 'skinny lamp.' Maybe that was Dad's whiskey lamp. Maybe it's worth money or something, and the chicken man wants it. He obviously knew about that report."

Because he was there. But that was stupid. It was too long ago. I got up, but Don kept pacing, blocking the door.

"At school, we'll figure out the translations for all of this," Don said. "And we can ask about the nun. Maybe she's still there, even."

"Grandma Elizabeth said the nun was going to die, that somebody was going to—"

"I know, take out her liver." He stopped and shrugged, like this was the most ordinary thing in the world. Except his eyes were a little too wide, and he was still bouncing the notebook against his side, the way he shook his leg involuntarily when I knew he was worried. "We can still check it out. It's just words, though, Mark. It's not real."

I went to the door.

"I know." But I didn't.

The next day, school wasn't cancelled, even though the lawn outside was frosted with a couple inches. It all melted on the roads. And in patches of grass. All the way to school, the bare spots bothered me, and at lunch, I mentioned it to Rachel, who sat beside me. She was blonde and sweet, and had shown me around on my first day, introducing me to people. At the time, I guessed the teachers made her do it, but now, we still sat together, so maybe not.

"It happens every year," she said. "You don't know about the coal mine? You might be living on top of part of it. My mom's house is over it. We don't get snow there, unless it's super deep. I have to go to my dad's to build a snowman."

That didn't make sense. The cafeteria was loud and echoey. Maybe I wasn't hearing her right, or she was lying. But Rachel had lots of friends. She was the kind of person who would share a pencil or point out wrong homework answers before school—like she had that morning before homeroom. Not someone who would make up stories about melting snow.

"Why would it do that, though?" I took a bite of my cheese pizza. It was too hot and tasted like greasy cardboard, but I was hungry.

"It's from the mine." She grabbed one of my cookies, split it in half, and kept the smaller part. "They dug it like a hundred years ago, and then stopped using it. I guess it ran out of coal or limestone or was too expensive or something. Anyway, it got blocked off, but there was a fire. And it's been burning ever since."

That was ridiculous. This must be some kind of joke to play on the new kid. Weird one, too.

What about Calvin's hole in the backyard? It had been warm but still. And where was my dog? Anytime I thought about him, I felt a nervous tug in my chest. What if he was lost or hurt and couldn't walk? He was probably thinking of me, couldn't understand why I wasn't there to help him. I took another bite of pizza and tried not to think about it. Didn't work.

After school, Rachel asked if I wanted to walk her home. She lived close by, on the other side of the buildings at the opposite end of campus, past the pond. On the back steps, I found Don and told him I needed to check out something. Without really lying, I tried to make him think it had to do with Grandma Elizabeth. He said he would find me when Mom got there to pick us up. Besides, he wanted to find a German–English dictionary in the school library anyway.

Then I found Rachel chatting with her friends near the carpool line. When they saw me, they smiled and peeled off. Rachel gestured across the street to a path that looped around the pond into a stand of snowy trees.

"It's that way," she said.

When we crossed the street, her shoulder brushed against me, maybe an accident, but I felt a shock of blood in my chest, ears, and between my legs. Rachel was already wearing a bra. I could see the outline of the white straps under her collared white shirt and open blue button-down vest. She didn't look at me, just led us along the path toward a line of stone buildings farther ahead, past more trees and a recently plowed parking lot. Even from here, I could tell those buildings had ornate curls around their windows and rooftops, walls covered with stringy ivy that probably thickened with leaves in the spring. Much more interesting than our utilitarian brick school building behind me.

We approached a shrine at the far end of the pond, with a stone statue of a woman—I guessed it was the Virgin Mary—folding her hands in prayer and looking up. There was a green plaque below:

In memory of those who swam home to the Lord.
Ama—Pond of Nun'Yunu'Wi

"What's that?" I asked.

"I don't know, a memorial."

A memorial to what? We kept going, alongside a curl of bare brown leaves by the pond. Maybe melted from the water—or coal fire.

No girl had ever asked me to walk with her after school, even if it was only across the street. Rachel probably saw how nervous I was. She was so pretty I felt like words might catch and jumble together, if I spoke. We talked all the time at school but were quiet now.

"Do you want to do something this weekend?" she asked. "You can come over to my dad's house, if you want to."

What did that mean? Like friends or was she talking about more than that? Past the shrine, we approached the parking lot. More missing snow over here, too, on a low rise along the right side of the path. Rachel kept watching the ground, impossible to guess what she was thinking. I'd never had a girlfriend or even kissed. *What should I do?*

"Sure," I said. "Saturday?"

We reached the buildings, and Rachel pointed to steps that led through dense trees and up a hill to a residential street with big, wooded houses behind the campus. I'd never been back there, only seen from school.

"Thanks for walking with me," she said.

I said I'd call her, and she left up the stairs, pale legs below her skirt and her blonde hair tossing. Rachel waved from the top, then disappeared into the neighborhood. I felt jumpy, strange—but good-strange.

I'd liked girls before, but this was different. I knew if I told Don, he would roll his eyes and maybe even tease me. Then he'd probably want to check those stone buildings to find out about Sister Maria Theresa and Grandma Elizabeth. But so what? None of that mattered. Let Don worry about it. I walked back, scooped up snow and packed it into a perfect snowball. The icy bite of the snow felt good on the back of my left hand, where the cut from the other night was already almost healed, just a pink lump below my knuckles. Mom worried it would scar, but that sounded kind of cool, like a character from a video game. That was all that night was anyway. Stories and memories that weren't real. I started smiling and couldn't stop. Until I got to the shrine.

The chicken man was leaning against it, still dressed in the same gray suit.

Chapter Five

No duffel bag this time, he was lighting a cigarette with a red flip lighter.

"Woah," the chicken man said. "That's a dangerous weapon you have there, Mark."

I stopped. He remembered my name. My stomach clenched, and I forced myself to take a breath. *Weapon—what's he talking about?* He nodded to my hands, the snowball. I let it drop.

"I'd like to talk, if you don't mind," he said. "I'll be quick."

When I didn't move, he blew smoke and pushed off the shrine to approach me. I had the strangest feeling he was an animal walking upright, not a man. Nothing specific was wrong about the way he walked, but it was as if those weren't legs—or he wasn't accustomed to using them this way. The twisting in my belly got worse.

"Mark, do you know what Serbian puppet theater is? Well, you know what *regular* puppet theater is, right? Like a Punch and Judy show? They make a big box, a miniature stage, and then puppeteers dance their puppets around to tell a story, while they're hidden below or behind the stage. The whole thing works with simple gears and ropes and wires."

He came over to me and tapped out some of his cigarette. *Run past him. Don't listen.*

"Do you mind if I smoke?" he asked. "I know it causes cancer, but what *doesn't* cause cancer, right? Anyway, Serbian puppet theater. There was a war in that part of the world, and this is actually an old tradition. War and puppets. They do shows with puppets to entertain the troops, to boost morale. You can imagine how lonely soldiers get. And war can be messy, especially there. That's why I always thought it was funny to call it *cleansing*. Get it?"

Walk away. He was blocking the path, but I could step around, back toward school. What would be do? Grab me?

"So the difference between regular puppet theater and Serbian puppet theater is—you guessed it—the puppets. In that kind of a war, there are always people who get in the way. Some fight back or cause problems, others just have some valuables. Honestly, nine times out of ten, it's because a general is bored and worried about soldiers misbehaving. So they take these people, the families who might not like the army, and they make them into puppets."

Don't listen. But, I couldn't look away from the yellow glow at the end of his cigarette. I smelled that chemical-smoke reek. *I'm not afraid.* My stomach bunched, but I didn't move.

"They're good at it," he said. "So good that they can do it while the people are still alive, Mark. They string wires through their arms and legs, their heads, necks, up and down the torso, almost like another muscular system, you understand? It's remarkable to see. And then they make them dance."

I sagged a little, my legs weak. My breathing was getting faster. *Stop. Just stop.*

"If there's a young girl in the family, let's say a pretty blonde girl with a boyfriend, they'll take both of them. Strip them naked, of course, and wire them up. Then they'll act out all kinds of things with these puppets. Usually, unless they want it to be loud, they'll wire their mouths shut or just use a simple gag. Whatever's easiest, really. You can imagine the stories they tell with these puppets, can't you?"

All I could smell was the cigarette smoke. If I tried to talk, I was afraid of what my voice would sound like. My tongue felt alien in my mouth. My shirt was clingy and cold on my lower back. I was sweating, felt it in my armpits, too.

"I don't like this place." He gestured at the campus around us. "I don't like having to come here, and I don't like having a conversation like this with you. I'm a nice guy, believe it or not. But this isn't about me. I need you to talk to your dad for me. Can you do that? Tell him he has a choice, but he doesn't have a lot of time. Tell him it'll be better for him, if he comes to me, so I can tell my boss your dad knows the rules. He chose to play the game, and it isn't over. Can you remember that?"

My stomach pinched and started to heave. *No. Stay calm.* But still, I wasn't sure I could speak. I nodded.

"Good. You seem like a smart kid. Let's not do this again, okay?" When I didn't answer, he lowered his voice. *"Okay?"*

I murmured, "Okay."

The chicken man tossed his cigarette and smiled. "If I had a nickel for every time I've seen that expression. Thanks, Mark."

He walked past me, the way I'd just come. *Oh God, where's he going?* If he went up the stairs that Rachel took ... He didn't. The chicken man hopped into an ordinary off-white car and pulled out, slowing to roll down his window as he drove by. An instrumental song played from inside his car, all guitars and flutes. My stomach cramped tighter, and I tasted bile, willed it back down. The ground swayed, like I was on a beam, trying to balance.

"Oh *Barbara*," he called, half-singing. "I've had this song stuck in my head for ... well, a long time. It's *the* classic, though. Gets you right there, doesn't it?"

He winked, just like at the house, and drove off.

I stood there, trembling. *Walk.* I pulled up one leg, then the other, going back to the shrine. I didn't look at the trees around the pond or the water, as I followed footprints—mine and Rachel's—back to school. Mom still wasn't here. *Good, okay.* Don was waiting for me on the steps, a notebook and German-English dictionary in one hand. He tapped his notebook, excited. *Stop it. Just, please, Don ...*

"I found it," he said, without waiting, "*schuldeneintreiber* means 'debt collector.' And the rest of it, look at this."

He shoved his notebook at me, flipping to a neat list of translations he'd copied down the page. All the things I'd found in the medical report. I held the notebook but couldn't make my eyes focus on it.

"I saw him again."

"I double-checked the translations," Don said. "Saw who?"

I looked him in the eyes, and his energy sapped down. His face went tight, cheeks hollow, and I noticed how skinny his neck suddenly seemed. I could see the veins and cords of tendons up his throat. Had he always looked like that?

"Really?" he asked. *"Here?"*

"Over there, by the pond. He wanted me to tell Dad that he's playing some kind of game, that he doesn't have much time. He also said he has a boss ..."

Don took back his notebook and stood, banging it against his side again in a nervous rhythm. "We'll talk about this later."

He looked past me as Mom pulled up.

We got in, and I tried to focus on her ordinary conversation. How was our day? Did roast chicken sound good for dinner? She apologized for being late and said she got lost—new city, new streets. I watched the hilly, wooded lawns of Rachel's neighborhood out my window. What name did he say: *Barbara?* I still heard the guitar and flute of the song from his car, like an echo in my eardrums that was skipping on a loop. It wasn't a scary song exactly, just sad and very simple. Maybe it was the skeleton for other, more complicated music. Other instruments and vocals growing around *Barbara* like organs and flesh. No, it was only an ordinary song. But Grandpa's mint aftershave was connected to the chicken man's song. That didn't make sense. None of it did.

"Mark, is everything okay?" Mom asked.

Why can't I just see Rachel? I scanned the houses set back above the road, much bigger than our new house. Which one was hers? Impossible to see much. They were surrounded by dense foliage, would have been completely hidden in the summer. Now, the houses were exposed, like lungs through a ribcage. *Stop it.*

But what if she was on a stage somewhere, her arms and legs stretched out by wires? I imagined Rachel's terrified eyes, flushed cheeks, and lips sewn shut, trying to scream as her limbs jerked and danced from pulleys overhead, like a puppet.

I was crying. I felt tears burning my eyes, tried to hide them with one hand. I couldn't control it, so I closed my eyes.

"Mark?" Mom asked again. "Look at me."

Rachel was fine. I opened my eyes, knew they were still red.

Mom watched me in the rearview mirror as she drove. "Did something happen at school?"

I wiped my face. "I have to talk to Dad."

Don't ask about it.

"You can tell me. What happened?"

"After school, I saw him again."

Mom stiffened, and her hands tightened on the steering wheel. "Who?"

She knew who. We all did.

When we pulled up to our house, the first thing I saw was the soft yellow light of the whiskey lamp in the front window. Sure enough, Dad had fixed it, replacing the old broken bottle with a new one. He had peeled off the label, but the glass was still embedded with the words, *Knob Creek.* Somehow, he cut off the bottom and mounted it right where the old bottle had been, still using the same old leather-wood stand.

If I let Don rope me into talking, I might start crying again. Needed something else—anything. Normally, I would have thrown a ball outside for Calvin, but instead, I settled on the living room couch with Don to play video games, James Bond. It was a first-person shooter, and we were both wandering the halls of a military base, trying to plug one another. With only two players, I watched what Don was doing on the lower half of the screen, while he tracked me too.

"There *is* a nunnery or sisterhood or whatever you call it on campus," Don said. "The librarian told me. It's back at the opposite end, past the pond."

Right where I had walked with Rachel. Those stone buildings. *Not now.* The game was settling my stomach, helping me to block out what the chicken man said.

"Do you know about the coal fire?" I asked.

He didn't, so as we played, I told him what I'd heard at lunch.

"That sounds like BS," Don said, and onscreen, he ran around a corner, his machine gun already blasting.

My screen on the top half of the TV went red, then black.

"Come on. Let me show you what I found," he said.

No hiding from this, so I followed Don into his room and sat beside him on his bed. He showed me his notebook: on the left side of the page were the bits I had written down, with Don's translations and notes lined up on the right:

schuldeneintreiber—"debt collector"

Dudweiler—Dudweiler, a city in Germany

kohlenmine—"coal mine"

leeres loch in der welt—"empty hole in the world"

der drache—"the dragon"

erstgeborenes kind –"firstborn child"

Saarbrüken—Saarbrüken, another city in Germany, near Dudweiler

Quod Erat Demonstrandum (?)

A coal mine, an empty hole in the world, a dragon, a firstborn child.

"That last one is Latin," he said. "I don't know what it means yet."

"*Erstgeborenes kind*," I said. "That means 'firstborn child'?"

"That's right, like Abby."

And Donald, Dad's brother, from the lobotomy transcript. I still hadn't told Don about that.

He was studying me, his body tense. "I think the chicken man is like a debt collector, *schuldeneintreiber* or whatever. And he's using what happened to Abby to scare Mom and Dad."

Maybe that made sense, but it barely explained anything. What about the transcript or the melting snow or how gaunt Don's cheeks looked now? I didn't want to think about any of this, except he really was losing weight.

"Don, are you feeling okay?"

He was squeezing the notebook page too hard, still on his bed.

"What he did today was illegal, I think," Don said. "But I don't believe the medical report has anything to do with him. That was just Grandma Elizabeth being crazy after her surgery."

He wasn't going to talk about how he felt or why he wasn't eating, was he?

"You have to tell Dad," he said.

I didn't argue, and that night, Don and Mom and I ate chicken and baked potatoes and steamed broccoli, while we waited for Dad to get home. We talked about school and the snow, until headlights shined through the front windows. I would have to tell Dad, make it real again. Maybe I could say I didn't feel well and go to bed, before Dad sat down. Calvin always used to run around barking, his tail slapping the walls, when he heard Mom or Dad come home. Not anymore.

Dad came in, and Mom and Don got up. Dad looked tired but relieved to be home, his nose pink from the cold outside.

"I have a plate waiting for you in the oven." Mom kissed him quickly, the way someone might wave a greeting.

Dad noticed me still sitting at the table and tossed his coat on the living room couch, even though we all knew Mom hated that. "Mark, what's up? Something wrong?"

I stared at my plate. Don's was still full of food he had been pushing around, not eating.

"The chicken man came back," Don said.

Dad held the back of his chair and watched me. "Is that true? You saw that man again?"

I looked at him, my mouth dry, even though I'd just been eating, could still taste the chicken and potatoes. "After school. By the pond across the street. He tried to scare me. He said you need to play some kind of game, and there isn't much time left."

Dad's jaw clenched, and he shook his head, breathing harder. "What else did he say?"

"I don't really remember." *He said Rachel would have wires looped inside her body and be hung on a stage like a toy.* My palms were slippery, as I stirred my plate and watched him. "I'm sorry, Dad."

Not because I was sorry, because this shouldn't be happening. *Calm down. Maybe it will just go away.*

Mom came in with Dad's food, but he didn't move.

"I'm going to kill him," Dad said.

Mom said, "Why don't the boys go—"

"I swear to God," Dad said, his voice too quiet. "This is crossing a line."

Was he asking Mom for permission? She just told him to sit for a moment and eat something. Couldn't we all have dinner as a family, even if it was late? Dad looked like he was about to storm out. But he didn't. He sat, and then Mom and Don did too. Dad dug into the chicken and chopped up his potato like he was gutting a small animal.

"I told the boys about your father's mint aftershave," Mom said. "Remember, the one we always used to order. I thought they would find it interesting after Mark's dream the other night."

My dream? Is that what we were calling it now?

Dad nodded, eating fast. "Pain in the ass. Took three weeks to get here, and almost twenty dollars a bottle, *before* all the shipping charges and taxes. He didn't get less stubborn as he got older. That's for sure."

We sat in silence as Dad ate. Mom and I were finished, and Don just mushed up his food more to cover the plate. Why wasn't he eating? When Dad finished, he rose and grabbed his coat off the couch.

"What's wrong?" Mom asked. "You're not going back out?"

"Yep. Don't worry. I won't do anything stupid. I just ..." He looked from Don to me, then smiled at Mom. "I'll be right back."

"You're being irrational," Mom said.

Dad was already headed for the door.

"Rationality is over-rated," he called back. "Get some sleep, boys. I'll see you in the morning."

Then he was out the front door. The car started up again and he drove away.

Without really talking, we helped Mom clean up. She didn't seem to notice Don's full plate, and she didn't say anything about Dad. She just cleaned the dishes and put the leftovers into Tupperware in careful, repetitive movements. Mom kissed us on the forehead, told us to brush our teeth, and then shut herself in her bedroom. I started to ask Don about dinner—wasn't he hungry? But he hurried to his room, too, said, "Good night, Mark," and shut the door.

As I changed into pajamas, I tried not to think about where Dad might be going or what Don was planning, then stopped, holding a pair of ripped socks. They were white, with blue stripes, and totally shredded at the toes. Calvin. When he was a puppy, he used to sneak into my old room and raid my closet. The year we got him, Mom also bought fancy, patterned cloth napkins. That was back when Calvin was an eager, little fluff ball, bounding around every afternoon after school like he couldn't believe he got to see me again. And one evening, when we were all in the living room watching TV, Don dropped popcorn, said he was sure Calvin would eat it—except, wait, where was the new dog? We found him sprawled under the kitchen table surrounded by beautiful napkin shreds, like flower petals. Mom started to shout, and Calvin licked her fingers, until Mom's face went from bright red to smiling. Just like that. "Ridiculous dog," she'd said.

Ridiculous, yeah. I held the socks for a long moment in my new room. It was still my *new* room, because letting it get too comfortable also meant being comfortable without Calvin. If he were here,

I wouldn't have to listen for nighttime noises. He knew when I was ready to get a snack or go outside, even before I did. Where was he? *Calvin is fine.* Except what if he wasn't? He couldn't have gotten outside. The door was closed. I forced myself to put the torn socks away. Maybe I'd let Calvin have them again when he came back, even though our vet said I shouldn't.

I got in bed and didn't hear Dad come home that night, but he drove Don and me to school the next day, same as usual. In homeroom, Rachel was smiling and casual, as if the chicken man never happened. For her, he hadn't, of course. While we waited for the first bell in homeroom, she told me about a concert coming up next month, said maybe we could still get tickets. But as she described the music, I imagined a guitar and flute playing, while naked puppet-people danced with wires in their skins.

"Mark?" Rachel was watching me, must have noticed how quiet I was.

"I don't feel well."

And the whole day, it got worse. All I could think about was Rachel and the chicken man and the German words in Don's notebook. I couldn't remember all the context for them. Why hadn't I copied more of it? No chance I would ever be allowed to read that report again. I had a library class for sixth period, right after lunch. We had a quiz on the Dewey decimal system and were supposed to study for other classes after. The teacher was a young guy with a red beard who always fidgeted and seemed totally out of place in a school library.

When I handed in my quiz, he said, "Your brother was in here yesterday after school. He checked out a dictionary and also wanted to know about the Sisters of the Holy Cross. He said your parents are friends with one of the sisters but don't know how to contact her."

Smart, Don. I almost believed it too.

"Right," I said. "Sister Maria Theresa."

"I called over. They're not affiliated with the school, you know. This is a different institution, the Motherhouse. And they usually ask us not to take classes over there. From what I understand, they're very busy. They don't allow visitors, is what I'm saying. But I did get this for you." He handed me a folded slip of paper:

Sister Maria Theresa
Brescia Hall, East Wing, Room 3E
3:00 PM

"I don't have your brother in class today. Can you give this to him?" he asked. "They're expecting him at 3:00."

I thanked the teacher, took the note, and went back to my seat at the library table. The school library was basically a long room with reference volumes and kids' books, a couple computer stations, and tables arranged in the middle. Nothing like downtown.

In the transcript, Grandma Elizabeth had been angry with Sister Maria Theresa. Who was this person? What did Don expect us to find?

The rest of the day dragged, but eventually it ended. Don found me on the school steps. I showed him the note from the librarian, and he lit up.

"Can't believe that worked. This is awesome," he said. "Let's go."

He ran across the street between the carpool line of cars.

Still on the steps, I called, "Mom will be here soon!"

"Then wait there. She's usually late anyway."

He was right, so I followed him. Still, this wouldn't help and what if we got in trouble for wandering off? The ground around the pond was mushy, most of the snow melted now. The air was wet, and I tasted that faint chemical smoke smell again.

"Don, what are you going to ask her?"

"'Why'd you give our grandmother a lobotomy'?"

"She didn't do that," I said. "It was Dr. Waller or whoever."

"Calm down," he said. "I just want to meet her."

Yeah right.

Ahead, there was paint on the Virgin Mary shrine. No, not paint. It was moss. Green fuzz covered half of her face, and small white caps—mushrooms—were growing around her chin.

"Somebody needs a shave." Don laughed as we passed the statue.

That moss and fungus wasn't there yesterday. I would have noticed it. They don't grow that fast. It wasn't possible. But I kept going, and as we crossed to the parking lot outside the stone buildings, I scanned for the chicken man's car. Not here. And no one was around. The chicken man wasn't about to jump out from behind something. *Calm down.* Being back here made my pulse quicken, like my body knew someone was watching, even if I couldn't see them.

The buildings were all connected in one lumpy stone and ivy facade. It reminded me of a person's head and shoulders in the center, with arms outstretched on either side. Like someone sitting in the booth at a restaurant. A sign said that this was Brescia Hall, and all visitors had to check in. So we did.

The lobby smelled like lemon cleaning products—too strong, maybe to soak up other old-people smells. The walls were chilly stone around a central desk and some waiting room chairs with cooking magazines arranged between them. A TV blared from one wall, so the front desk staff and anybody in here could watch. There was also a gruesome crucifix on the wall opposite the TV.

The woman at the front desk examined Don's folded note. "It's on the third floor, all the way back on the right."

We took the stairs. The third floor was quiet. Ferns and tropical plants were spaced out along the blank hall, and we passed more crucifixes. The doors were all closed, like a calmer, cleaner version of the nursing home in Chicago where we'd visited Grandma Elizabeth last summer.

Before the end of the hall, we passed a wide-open door, where an old woman was lying in bed, talking to a priest who stopped to watch us.

"Excuse me," the priest called. "Where are you boys headed?"

"We're here to see Sister Maria Theresa," Don said. "We have an appointment."

"She knows you're coming?" He came out, already gesturing back the way we'd just come. "Let's see if we can sort this out."

He touched Don's shoulder, then snapped his hand away, as if he'd been shocked, like with static electricity. The priest looked at his hand, at Don again. He crossed his arms, more serious.

"The exit is that way. Whatever *this* is ..." When the priest said 'this' he seemed to mean both of us, but I had the feeling he was talking about whatever just happened when he touched Don's shoulder. "... you need to take it somewhere else."

But we were almost to the room. This was 3G, which meant 3E was probably only a couple more doors down. It was just static electricity. That was all.

The door of the room across from us banged open, and a small woman in a nun's habit, called, "Quiet out there! Some of us are trying to get into heaven in here."

She came out, using a heavy-duty walker to move.

"Who are these boys, Father Thompson?"

"Sister Catherine, I'm trying to determine that myself."

"Are they visitors?"

When Don started to explain who we were, she cut him off, angry with Father Thompson.

"So take them. She'll be glad to see some young blood, I'm sure."

She didn't let him argue and shooed us down the hall.

Father Thompson grumbled about how we really shouldn't be here, but he showed us to 3E.

"Ah, so these are the boys who learned the word 'lobotomy.'"

Chapter Six

Sister Maria Theresa had bright green eyes and pudgy, chalk-white cheeks. She was in bed with a romance novel, the fingers of her left hand covered in cheap, multi-colored plastic rings, like what you'd get for a quarter out of a gumball machine. She wore all black and a dark shawl, so we couldn't see her hair.

Father Thompson backed out, leaving Don and me standing in the doorway.

Sister Maria Theresa blinked and smiled. Then, as she got a better look at us, the smile went away. She raised one hand, her rings splayed out. "Stay right there. The doctor says I shouldn't be too close to any germ factories. From a distance, if that's okay?"

Nobody had called me a 'germ factory' since my kindergarten teacher and then as a joke. But Sister Maria Theresa's expression was flat and serious.

"What did you bring me?" she asked. "It's customary to offer a gift when you're asking for something."

"We're not here to ask for anything," Don said. "We just want to know how you knew our grandmother."

"Information is *something*." She pointed to my backpack. "What have you got?"

I flipped it off my back and unzipped it: school books, a few notebooks and folders, a Snickers candy bar ...

"That," she said. "Place it on the wardrobe, there."

She meant put the candy bar on the wooden dresser to my right. It had drawers where she probably kept her clothes. Her room was sparse, with just that dresser and a waist-high half bookshelf—packed with creased paperbacks—below a window that looked out on the front lawn and pond. She had a little mirrored closet, a wall crucifix, and a bathroom, but that was it.

I set the Snickers bar down, and Sister Maria Theresa dog-eared the page of her romance novel, carefully closed it on her lap, and looked at us, waiting.

"So," she said, "they told me your last name is Morris. And your grandmother is Elizabeth, is that right? Did you read what the doctors wrote about her?" How did she know I found the report—only the librarian and Don knew. "What kind of candy bar is that? Does it have nuts in it? I like nuts, even if it's bad for my teeth. I'd rather choke on a candy bar than live with Jell-O. To paraphrase Milton."

I looked at Don for a reaction.

He frowned. "How did you know our grandmother?"

"That's simple. She's my kid sister." She waved her book at the Snickers and told me to slide it closer, then picked it up and opened it, watching the wrapper—not us—as she spoke. "You don't believe me? We grew up in Dudweiler, before the war. And then, when it started, my uncle took his two sons and me to America. My parents and Elizabeth refused to go. She already knew your grandfather then and didn't want to leave him. He was a rising star, who she thought would make a fortune."

She gave me a knowing look, as if we both understood how naïve that was. She didn't acknowledge Don, even though he'd asked the question. What did any of this have to do with the lobotomy? *This woman is lonely. That's all. She might be making all this up.*

"My sister hoped Karl would get an estate in the east after the war ended," she said. "I used to tease her. 'Baroness,' I called her. She really believed for awhile, and your grandfather believed even after it was all over and they were living in this country."

Don crossed his arms, still in the doorway behind me.

"Believed what?" he asked.

Back to her candy bar wrapper, she continued tearing it open, and I smelled the chocolate, even a few steps away.

"Do you know your history? In the new world they were creating. I stopped speaking to Elizabeth for years after they moved here. Your grandfather drank and complained about how he had been betrayed and how the war could have been won. Ask her to show you his picture. I bet she still has it. In his uniform. 'Bright, promising young man' they used to call him." She laughed, took a bite, and spoke with a mouthful, "Married into the wrong family."

Our grandfather fought for the Germans in World War II? Is that what she meant? The report said that, too, didn't it? What about the lobotomy? And 'Sister Maria Theresa,' that name was nothing like 'Morris.'

"Why is your name different?" I asked.

"Good question." She swallowed, then kept unwrapping, all the way down to the bottom. "As a nun, as part of this sisterhood, we take on a new name and life in Christ. I chose 'Maria Theresa' for a number of reasons I won't bore you with right now. But I also chose the name to prevent *this* ..." She gestured at Don with her book. "... from ever happening. It worked for a while. But then your father told me that Chicago or wherever you were living wasn't safe anymore. So I shouldn't be surprised you're here, I guess."

Dad told her we were moving here? We weren't safe in Illinois? What was going on?

Don shook his head, bouncing a little, like he did when he wanted to pace. "That doesn't make sense. Why would our dad tell you that and not us?"

She kept eating and answered me, like Don wasn't there. "Maybe he wanted you boys to look me up. Who knows?"

Don stepped in, still looking like he wanted to pace. She held up her hand with the rings again.

"No, please stay in the doorway over there. Thank you. I apologize. I can't let you in here right now. My immune system isn't up for it."

She was lying. I don't know why I thought that, but all of this—her story, the way she avoided Don—felt like she wanted to tell us something without saying it. Talking around the real purpose. *The library report.*

"Did you convince our grandmother to have surgery?" I asked. "In her brain?"

"Yes, I did. The icepick lobotomy, I remember. I was there. It was right here." She finished the candy bar and carefully folded the wrapper, then sighed. "You boys have already read the report, so you know. It was terrible. Even at her worst, I still loved her. She was my sister, but she married the wrong man. When I say he *believed,* you understand what I mean?"

Again, she stared at me, and now there were tears in her eyes.

"He was a Nazi, a real one. Not a cartoon or someone who had no choice. He was right there from the start. It was part of his debt, I think. I believe he chose it *because* of the debt."

Our grandfather was a Nazi? What did that have to do with the surgery in the 1950s? *Stop asking. Turn around and leave.*

"What debt?" Don asked.

Sister Maria Theresa wiped her eyes with both hands and sniffed, looking away from us.

"After her two sons were born, your grandmother believed that one of them would be taken, and that it was your grandfather's fault. Truthfully, she had what they would call nowadays 'postpartum depression,' but back then it was 'hysteria.' She had it bad, especially after your father was born. She came to see me ..." Sister Maria Theresa hesitated, turned to me. "Boys, this is not simple. Do you understand? People are not just sick or well, sane or insane. Sometimes, if everyone else hears music, when there's only silence, you pretend, too."

Like the chicken man's song. I heard that in our house, when I was dying. But then he played it again in the parking lot. My palms were clammy, but I was going to stay calm. *What about the report?*

"Why did Grandma Elizabeth come to see you?" I asked.

Sister Maria Theresa closed her eyes and carefully turned one of the rings on her left hand. Then she turned the next one, and a third one. What was she doing—praying? Using the rings like rosary beads?

Eyes still closed, she said, "Your mother believed something was coming for her first child, that he had been *marked*, the way an animal marks its territory. She wanted to keep the animal away." She opened her eyes and looked directly at Don. "Her husband's family did things a long time ago, so that now there was a debt that had to be collected. And when I told her it was hysteria, and there was no animal demon,

Elizabeth said she planned to kill all of them: her boys, her husband, and then herself."

Don made a skeptical, throat-clearing noise, and Sister Maria Theresa looked him up and down, as if she were disappointed.

"Better to give both her sons eternal life than let one be tormented in Hell. That's what she said."

Don held the doorframe the way Dad had when the chicken man came, like he needed it to steady himself. "But why did you do that?"

"It was routine back then," she said. "Thousands of women did the procedure for things nowhere near as bad as what Elizabeth was telling me."

She finally turned away, settling on the bed, like she was exhausted.

"What was the other son's name?" Don asked. "Her first boy?"

Oh shit, I hadn't told him that. He didn't know.

"Donald."

Don nodded, as if he wasn't surprised. "What happened to him?"

Sister Maria Theresa shrugged.

"They lost him, kidnapped. I really don't know how it happened. Elizabeth changed after the surgery, and Karl refused to speak to me. I didn't see him again until he was on his deathbed. They never should have stayed in Dudweiler during the war." She pointed her romance novel at me. "You *don't* know your history. Look it up. I wasn't there. I was in Ohio."

Why should we look it up, when Sister Maria Theresa was right here? What wasn't she telling us? Why go through all this and hide part of the story?

"But Grandma Elizabeth's son *was* taken," I said.

"That's enough." She opened her romance novel again. "I'm tired, and I'm sure you boys have some place to be. And all of this ... ancient history."

I turned to go, but Don didn't move.

"Why won't you let us in your room?" he asked.

With one finger, she found her place in the book, not even looking at us. "When someone gets old, their immune system doesn't work so well. You came from a playground or school, I'm sure. It would be like Columbus and the Indians all over again."

Was that supposed to be a joke? In preschool, I remembered performing a play about cooperation between the European colonists and American Indians, on the anniversary of 1492. Later, on the drive to a restaurant for dinner, Don had told me it was all lies. The Indians and Spanish didn't work together to create America. Columbus landed in the Bahamas and Cuba and killed everyone he could or made them slaves. And besides, how could you 'discover' a place where other people were already living? I remember Mom rolled her eyes in the front passenger seat, and Dad said something about borderlands and how even if suffering and death came with 'first contact,' eventually *someone* was going to land in Cuba. The world just *was*, Dad told us, then said, "Unless it isn't," and laughed.

Somehow Sister Maria Theresa's joke that wasn't a joke reminded me of that.

"You know my name but don't want me in here? Would Mark be okay?" Don stepped closer. "Tell us what is really ..."

She sat up, arms stiff on either side, like she wanted to be ready to vault away if he came nearer. "*You.* You're bringing it here. I don't want it in my room. It's a disease. And I've lived too long to deal with it now. Step away."

"Why?"

"You are *marked.*"

Don stumbled back, as if he'd just been slapped. He shook his head, and I kept waiting for him to answer back—*What do you mean? No,*

I'm not!—but instead, he walked into the hall. Wasn't that what she said about Dad's older brother, Grandma Elizabeth's first son, who was kidnapped? Just like Abby. I felt weak, hollowed out.

Sister Maria Theresa nodded to me. "Do you want my advice? Stop digging. Stop asking questions. Just let it lie. A child disappears in this country every forty seconds. I saw that on the news."

Was she trying to scare me? She was just a nun.

"You aren't alone, Mark."

I should follow Don—where was he going? Maybe all the way back to school, without me.

No, what if I never got to see her again? This might be my only chance. She knew about the report and my grandparents. When I was out of my body, I had felt someone touch my cheek, say '—un.' I thought it was 'run,' but it wasn't, was it? What if it was *nun*?

"My grandfather—"

"Your grandfather loved his family. But he was a complicated man. If there were any way he could protect you boys, I know he would."

I felt my stomach curling even before I said it—but I had to push. She *knew*. Of course she did.

"Who is the chicken man?"

Sister Maria Theresa dropped her book, and it bounced across the floor to hit my shoe.

"No! Don't touch it. You ..." She blinked away emotion and smiled, her whole body somehow relaxing *snap-snap*, just like that. "Please leave me in peace. *Chicken man*, honestly."

Like I was making it up. I backed away and found Don pacing in the hall. No telling what time it was. We were probably beyond late. Before I could speak, he bolted down the hall toward the stairs, and I followed him through the lobby, then outside and across the parking lot. My side was burning, but it felt better than the tightness in my gut.

Back at the carpool pickup, no Mom. No cars at all. Mom should have been here by now. But Don seemed relieved.

"What do we know?" He panted from the sprint back. "Sister Maria Theresa is Grandma's sister, that makes her our great-aunt, right? She *does* believe in magic or demons or whatever you want to call it. She said I was cursed."

"*Marked.*" I was sweaty and winded from the run. "She called it 'marked.'"

"Whatever. Mom and Dad know about all of this, too, and they sent us to school here anyway." He started scribbling notes, like we needed to document this or it wouldn't be real. "They owe money to somebody back in Illinois, and that's why we moved here, not for Dad's job."

While he ranted and jotted notes, I sat on the cold steps. They would get the bottom of my pants wet, but I didn't care. Don wasn't just anxious, he was angry. And it probably wasn't because of all this, but because of his friends, too. He only had time to investigate with me, because he didn't have any friends here yet. I hadn't really seen him hanging out with anybody after school, almost like he didn't want to get too attached. Maybe Don just wanted something to do.

Let it lie.

Finally, he put his notebook away and tossed rocks across the street to see if he could hit the pond. He made it on the third try. When Don's rock broke the surface, I felt a sharp chill that made me hug my knees on the school steps. What if something came out of that water? *Stop it.* Ridiculous, but it was hard to look away. I made myself open my backpack and start on my math homework.

After Don's eighth throw, Mom's car rolled up. She looked disheveled. We didn't ask why she was late. Don was afraid she might have stopped by earlier and then gone off searching for us. But she hadn't.

We drove home, with the radio news playing. I should ask about Sister Maria Theresa, but how? If I did, we would have to talk about the library again and how Don lied to figure out where Sister Maria Theresa lived. *Stop digging.* The same thing Mom used to yell at Calvin at our old house. All of this would be easier if I had my dog back.

At home, there was no light on in the front window.

We shouldn't get out of the car. We should leave.

The whiskey lamp must have gone out, maybe the bulb needed to be changed. When we got to the porch, Don picked something up from the welcome mat, a small blue box of matches. They had been placed between the two potted plants, so we wouldn't miss them. They were for some kind of bar. Don put them away before I could see.

Mom opened the front door. "Give that here, Don."

"Why? I found them."

"They're trash. We don't need more matches in the house. Give them ..." And then she stopped.

When the door opened, we all froze. The smell hit us in a wave: natural gas.

"Shit," Mom said. "Don, Mark, get back in the car. Now."

Don started to argue, and Mom shoved him off the porch. He stumbled into me, almost knocked me over. She'd never pushed us or really touched either of us like that before.

"Car," she said, "*now.*"

And then she ran inside the house. I got in the backseat, and Don slowly climbed in beside me.

"She's being so dramatic," he said. "It's nothing."

"What are the matches? Can I see?"

He showed me, and I flipped over the pack.

Cadillac Club
115 Water Street

There were no pictures or anything, just the name and address. This had to be connected to the gas. Whatever was happening to Mom and Dad, now somebody was trying to scare them. But a gas leak was serious. Houses exploded because of that.

Mom came back out and opened my door to stand over us.

"It's okay," she said. "I must have left the stove on after I made tea this morning. I opened the windows. It should clear out in a few minutes. Do you have a lot of homework?"

And just like that, we were talking normally again. Mom forgot about the matchbook. She joked about how startled she'd been by the gas smell and apologized for pushing Don off the porch.

"A mother's instinct, I guess," she said.

Don slouched back in his seat. *We never should have come here.* I wanted to stop Mom from talking about school and dinner, ask her why they were lying to us. What was really going on? But instead, we went inside. There was still a faint, slightly sweet smell of natural gas, but mostly it had cleared.

"No lighting any candles today," Mom said.

I sat in the living room to play video games, and Don went to his room.

"What the hell?" he shouted from the hall.

"Don, watch it," Mom yelled. "Don't use that language, understand?"

She crossed in front of me to go see what he was so worked up about.

"I don't understand," she said.

I got up to see. Both of them stood in the hall, staring at Don's room. He had his hand out to touch his bedroom door ... except there was no door. There was no room. The hall across from my bedroom was a solid wall, painted beige, as if Don's room had never been there.

CHAPTER SEVEN

Mom was stumped, a hand to her face, and Don kept patting the wall, as if hoping maybe this were an optical illusion. It was impossible. Period. Not real.

"Did you check outside?" I asked.

"Good idea," Don said.

We banged out the front door, across the wet lawn to the side of the house, where his bedroom window should be. It wasn't there. The wall was solid red brick, no window. It matched the rest of the house, like it had always been there. No sign that the bricks were newer or discolored, nothing.

"This is great," Don said. "This is fucking great."

Mom came onto the front steps. "It's gone out here too? I'll call your father. Maybe there was a mix up."

She went in to use the phone. *A mix up?* Don picked up one of the potted plants on the front porch, then whipped it down fast. The pot exploded in a cloud of gray ceramic shards and dirt.

"What's wrong?" Mom called from inside. "Did something happen?"

Don kicked the debris off the porch. "Yeah, my Goddamn room disappeared."

I'd never seen him break things like this.

On the phone in the kitchen, Mom said, "Right, I know. But I wasn't out of the house for more than an hour and a half, two hours. Okay. You go to your meeting. We'll see you tonight."

She hung up, and Don and I sat on the living room couch, but we didn't turn on the TV.

"Your father thinks there must have been a mistake with another house in the neighborhood. That may have been why the gas got left on too, if workers were in here during the day." She sounded like she was trying to convince herself, not us. "We'll sort this out. Don't worry, Don."

He smirked. "Oh will we? Everything is just going to magically turn out okay? Our dog is going to come back, and there's a totally normal explanation for my room disappearing? What is it, Mom?"

"I told you," she said, "a construction crew in the neighborhood."

"That makes no sense." He got up. "You know what? I don't care."

He walked out the front door. It was chilly and gray out there, everything still, like the trees and houses were holding their breath. *They want to watch where he goes. No, stop it.* None of it made sense, but there was still an explanation. Mom was right.

"Don," Mom called, "you have homework."

He left without answering. Mom didn't go after him. Instead, she asked if I was hungry and made me a tuna sandwich.

A few hours later, I was playing James Bond, and Don banged back in the front door, red-faced. I started to say something, and he stomped past me into the kitchen.

That night, Dad tried to make a joke out of it.

"The disappearing room," he said. "Some people would pay good money to see that, or *not* see that, as the case may be."

They set up a bed for Don on the living room couch, with the whiskey lamp lit again in the window. I brushed my teeth, said good-night to him, but Don ignored me, curled in a ball under dark covers on the couch.

What do you want from us? What is all of this about? Just before I went into my bedroom, I stared at the wall where Don's door should have been, right across the hall.

"Give us a break," I whispered, "please. Put his room back."

And there it was. The door was right there, where it had always been, partially open so I could see Don's floor cluttered with boxes and clothes, leaving a path back to his bed.

"Don! Quick, come here!" When he didn't get up, I went into the living room, glancing back to make sure the room didn't vanish again. "Your room is back."

"What are you talking about?" But he came to see, and then froze in the hall. "What did you do, Mark?"

"Nothing. I was going to bed, and it came back."

Mom and Dad joined us.

Dad grinned and clapped. "The incredible *re-appearing* room."

But Mom didn't go near it.

"This is insane," she said. "It wasn't here."

Don opened his door all the way.

"Wait," she said. "I don't think you should go in there."

He stepped inside anyway. "There's nothing strange in here."

"If it can disappear once, it can do it again," Mom said.

"Now *that's* insane." Dad went in after Don to check it out. "It's your room all right. I'd know that smell anywhere."

"Dad ..."

"Is that a moldy Tupperware? You know, if you bring food into your room, you have to clean it up."

Mom stood beside me. "We didn't see it earlier. We must have been too distracted. Or it could have been the gas. Gas leaks can cause problems with vision. We should have waited longer to come into the house after I turned off the stove."

Did she believe that? No way. It *wasn't* there. It really wasn't.

After awhile, Mom and Dad kissed us goodnight, and Don got into his normal bed across the hall. I said goodnight from the doorway, didn't go in. In the dark, all those piles of boxes almost looked like people or hunched animals.

"You did something, didn't you?" he asked.

"I asked him to put it back."

"You asked *him*? What do you mean? You stood there and asked, and the room came back?" He threw a pillow at me that bumped off the doorframe. "Well, at least he likes you. You should ask for other things."

No. I went into my room and shut the door. Cigarettes. My sheets and pillows smelled like cigarette smoke. Carefully, I stripped them off and found clean ones at the bottom of a pile in my closet. It took awhile, but I got the new ones on. Then I climbed in. Good. It smelled normal. But I was shivering, had to grip the mattress to keep my hands still. It was fine. Don's room was back.

"Thank you," I whispered, then realized I was staring at the empty space around my legs. What about Calvin? What if he had Cavin, too? If Don's room could reappear like that, maybe Calvin could come back? Don had been joking, saying I should ask for more. Maybe I could. And then what?

This didn't make sense, even Mom and Dad couldn't believe it. We were like ants crawling on a computer screen. What if this was bigger and more complicated than we knew? The chicken man warned me. He warned Don first. And Sister Maria Theresa, too. Maybe we should listen to her. Just stop asking questions. Asking the wrong question or for the wrong kind of help might make things worse. Maybe Mom was right, and it was the gas leak. Don's room had been there all along.

There was a debt, and it was up to Mom and Dad to handle it. Trust them. If they weren't telling us everything, it was for a reason.

That Friday, after school, Mom said that Dad was getting off work early and we would all go out to dinner at a Mexican restaurant called *Chico's* that someone had recommended.

The phone rang. Don and I were playing video games. Mom answered in the kitchen, and her voice immediately got low, then spiked and became urgent.

"Please don't do this now," she said. "Let's talk about it tonight. It'll be dangerous no matter what time it is. No, we're not eating without you … We'll go to a hotel tonight, if you think … It doesn't change anything. What can I say?"

Mom sounded frantic, helpless. Like someone sinking in a pool, reaching for a hand, a branch, anything to stop her from drowning.

Beside me, Don sat very still. We paused the video game to listen.

"I love you too," Mom said. "Just come home. Or we'll come there. Just … no. I won't hang up."

For a long moment, the house was silent. I heard my heartbeat. My chest was tight, and I swallowed deep, even breaths to calm down, but it wasn't working.

The kitchen phone clicked into its receiver. Then the backdoor opened and shut again. What were we supposed to do?

"Where is Dad?" I asked.

Don shook his head and got up. I followed him through the kitchen and into the backyard. Mom sat on the steps, hunched over and hugging her knees. The yard was foggy and damp, a film of mist hovering over the lumpy roots and dips in the ground

She gave us a weak smile when we came out. "You overheard, I guess?"

"Is Dad going to be okay?" Don asked.

"Who knows? You know your father." She sighed. "Of course he's going to be okay. Your father is always okay. Back in college, at U of C, you wouldn't believe the dumb things he did when I first met him. He once jumped out a fourth-story window. I thought he would break his legs, but nope. He just danced out into the middle of the quad and gave me a thumbs-up. Another time, he threw himself out of a moving car in the middle of traffic. I think we must have been going 35 miles an hour."

Why was she telling us this? Mom never talked about her and Dad before they got married. I sat beside her on the back steps.

"Really?" I asked. "Why?"

"Our dog jumped out the window of the car, and there was no place to pull over. That was Sadie, the beagle. Again, totally fine—not a scratch on either of them. You don't need to worry about your father."

She was worried about him, though, but I didn't say that.

Don stood in front of us. "Can we help him?"

"He wouldn't want us to do anything," Mom said. "He really will be okay."

"But where is he? Can you at least tell us what's going on?"

She sagged a little and held her knees tighter. "I wish I knew."

"We know about Sister Maria Theresa," Don said. "We met her this week."

Mom nodded. "I know. She called. She gave your father an earful. She said you boys disturbed her prayers and were dangerous to the other nuns with all of your germs. *Germ factories*, I think she said."

Stop it, Don. He wouldn't meet my eyes. *Don't ...*

Don said, "You knew, but you didn't ..."

He was balling and releasing and balling his fists again, shifting his weight like he wanted to pounce. And his fingers looked extra jointy, matching his neck and cheeks. He was getting so thin, and I kept forgetting to say something. I was just getting used to it. Why didn't Mom notice how thin Don was?

"What is going on, Mom?" Don asked. "Why did we even move here? And who is the Goddamn chicken man?"

She let go of her knees and straightened, her whole body tense. Don froze. What could I say to stop this?

"Watch it," Mom told Don. "Your father is being stubborn and a little stupid. A *lot* stupid if he ..." She caught herself. "I know you think you can handle this. You believe you're grown up enough to know all about this ... where your father is, the whiskey lamp. You're not."

Don started pacing, his cheeks flushed. "Yes, I am. Tell me. If Mark is too young, he can—"

"It's not about that." She stared at him, unblinking, like she was daring him to look away. "You know the lamp inside, that homemade thing we have on the windowsill? What do you think that's made out of? What do you think is covering the wood that holds up the bottle? Do you think that's leather, like cow leather?"

The tension in my chest got worse again. Why were they doing this? Mom never talked this way. The edge in her voice was new, unpredictable. What if she yelled or pushed him again? Why was this happening?

"Don," she said slowly, "do you want to know what it is?"

He had paled but was still holding both fists, like he wanted to fight. He nodded. "What is it?"

"It's from a *person*. That's human skin in there. Your grandfather made it during the Second World War. There. How does that feel? It's from a little boy or a girl or an old man. I don't know who, but it's from someone just like you. He cut off their skin and used it to make a lamp."

The skinny lamp.

I felt an icy charge up my legs, back, and arms that made me huddle closer to Mom. But she didn't touch me. She should have rubbed my shoulder to warm me up, but she didn't, just kept staring at Don. I had to get away from them. We weren't supposed to be talking about this.

"Does that make you feel better, Don?" Mom asked.

"Why is it in our house?"

"Oh, you don't like it now that you know? It's in our house, because your father says so. You *can't* handle this," she said. "That's it, understand?"

Finally, Don looked away, opened his hands, shaking his arms loose. "Whatever. When is Dad coming home?"

"Tonight." Mom's shoulders slackened, and she sank down beside me, like a slow-deflating balloon. "He'll be back, probably late, but we can still try that new restaurant without him, if you want."

I said that sounded good to keep them focused on something else, not our grandparents or the whiskey lamp. It was behind me right now. If I turned, I would see straight through the kitchen into the glow in the front window. And my chest still clenched, I was breathing too fast. Mom said it was nice it wasn't snowing. She'd heard there was a foot of snow or more up in Chicago, and we talked about school and dinner, but my mind kept snapping back to the idea of that leather—that skin—being cut off someone's arm or back, blood streaking around the wound. And I had touched it. I'd inspected it closely the other night and never even known. Don was right. What was it doing in our house?

A few hours later, when it was getting dark, we went to dinner. For a while in the restaurant, with bouncy, brassy music playing, surrounded by brightly-colored furniture and walls decorated with sombreros, skull tapestries, and photos of old churches and mountains in Mexico, for that little bit, it was okay. The tacos were good, and even Don lightened up, but he still wasn't eating. Back in Illinois, we used to argue about who got more chips at Mexican restaurants, competing to grab the most salsa and cheese dip. Now, I had it all to myself. And Mom didn't notice, but I saw how he cut up his chimichanga and stirred it around, only taking a few bites. She was in full-on normal mode, *over-normal*, acting like we did this all the time, just the three of us out to let off some steam.

Back at home, though, nothing had changed. The whiskey lamp was still lit in the front window, and no sign of Dad. Mom asked if we wanted to watch a movie, and Don said no, he was tired. So she made a big show of kissing his forehead and hugging him, looking Don in the eye to say, "I love you, and I always will. You're more important to me than anything … except your younger brother." And then Mom grinned at me. "You're both tied for the best son ever. But there will be an award this weekend for cleanest room ever. If you get everything unpacked, that could tip one of you over the top."

Don pulled away. "'Night, Mom."

He locked himself in his room.

Mom and I watched some TV, and when it got too late, she switched it off and asked me, "Is your brother going to be all right?"

How am I supposed to know? Don was smarter and braver than me. Of course he was going to be okay, but ever since we'd gotten here, he'd been changing.

"Yes," I said, "he's just upset with Dad being gone."

"You're a lot stronger than he is. I know I'm not supposed to say that, but it's true. You always have been." She smiled, tousled my hair, like she did when I was little. Her hand was a little heavier than it should have been, probably because she'd been drinking. "Even when you were a baby, your father and I used to joke that you were ready to run for Congress, that we would both be working for you someday."

She hadn't stopped drinking red wine since we got home, and I could hear it in the slurs at the end of some sentences. But she sounded like she meant it. It wasn't true, though. Did she know that?

"I love you, Mark. Thank you for being so strong through all this. I really need it, and I appreciate it."

I wasn't being strong. I wanted to make this disappear. I didn't want to look at the whiskey lamp—*skinny lamp*, whatever—ever again. Where was Dad? What if he were hurt or never came back at all? This had to do with the chicken man and whatever debt Mom and Dad had. Everything they wouldn't talk about. But I wasn't being strong. I just didn't know what else to do.

"Tomorrow's Saturday," she said, "so you can sleep in."

Normally, at the old house, I never got to sleep in, because I always had to get up and let Calvin out in the backyard to pee, usually by 8:00 a.m. at the latest. I still couldn't sleep past then anyway. Like my body didn't believe Calvin was missing and insisted on waking up, as if he were about to start scratching my bedroom door. Thinking about my dog brought another rush of emotion that I tried to clamp down and ignore. I was tired. That was all.

"If Dad doesn't …" I stopped myself. "When will he be home?"

"Soon."

Except he wasn't.

CHAPTER EIGHT

D ad didn't come home that night, and the next morning all normal-ness was gone. It was as if there were invisible strings stretching through our house from the hall to the living room and into the kitchen, where I smelled Mom making pancakes. Usually those invisible strings were dangling and loose. Now, though, they pulled super-taut, so the air was tense and claustrophobic. In the kitchen, Mom barely raised her eyes from the stove, where smoke from the cooling pancakes was twisting in the air. Her robe was sweat stained down the back and in the armpits. I asked about Dad. Where was he—out. When would he be back—never know, he's busy. Work had come up.

When Don came in, Mom told us that Dad had to go out of town for a conference. All very last minute. She didn't look at us as she served pancakes, then fidgeted with her University of Chicago coffee mug.

She doesn't believe that. And she doesn't really expect us to either.

Mom scalded her mouth on coffee. She seemed shrunken, as if the lack of sleep and worry were sucking her skin to her bones. Don wasn't much better. He stared at his pancakes.

"Why aren't you hungry?" I asked.

He blinked at me, as if the thought had never occurred to him. Then, unspeaking, he scraped his food in the trash, put his dishes in the sink, and went to his room. He slammed the door. Mom cradled her coffee and took a slow sip that made her jaw relax.

"You and your brother should get some fresh air today. Get out of the house and stretch your legs. Go for a walk or something."

Maybe we could all do something together? I imagined Dad surprising us on an outing and Mom laughing, trying to be mad at him for scaring all of us. We would joke about it for days.

"Do you want to see a movie?" I asked. "Or we could play miniature golf or—"

"I have to be here," Mom said, "when your father comes home. I have to make sure someone's here to let him in, in case he lost his keys."

Why would he have lost his keys? I nodded and finished breakfast, as if that made perfect sense. Then I went and rapped on Don's door.

"Mom says we need to go outside," I said.

He opened up, looking serious and distracted. "Why?"

"For fresh air, so we can—"

"Fine." Don grabbed a coat off a box pile and led the way.

That wasn't what I'd expected. He should have argued or complained that there was no reason for us to wander around the neighborhood, that we had better things to do, but he didn't. He opened the front door, and I barely had time to throw on a coat and hat to follow him out. The air was dry and cold, still with a sharp morning bite, the sky shimmery pink from the sunrise through the trees.

On the sidewalk, when we were three houses down, Don asked, "What do we know? We know Dad is missing, and he probably went to see the chicken man."

Was he saying this so I wouldn't ask about him not eating again? Whatever we talked about, this was good, because we could discuss it in peace, with no chance of Mom overhearing. A guy jogged across the street, and a minivan passed slowly over the speed bumps, but the street was still quiet, as if the day hadn't started yet.

"He left last night after telling Mom what he was going to do, and he hasn't come back. On the phone, it sounded like Mom said Dad saw the chicken man, and there was something about the timing of it that made Dad want to go find him now."

"We don't know it's him," I said. "Mom didn't mention him by name."

"That's a good point. So it might not be him, but it's probably connected. Mom is scared, and everyone seems to want us to stay totally away from this. Okay, that's part one. Part two is Mom either made up all that about Dad's whiskey lamp to scare us, which is messed up, or we have some kind of zombie lamp in our living room."

We reached the end of the block, deeper into the neighborhood, away from the main streets with strip malls and gas stations. Here, there were more houses, and the roads were darker, even more crowded with trees. Barren branches hung over everything with arching trunks that split and segmented into skinnier, multi-faceted tendrils. The pink-yellow sunrise shined through like flesh or glowing skin.

"She said Grandpa made it," I said. "That's like what Sister Maria Theresa said too."

"Right. It fits. She said he was fucked up, a Nazi or something. They didn't come to the U.S. until *after* World War II, and during the war, he was fighting for the bad guys."

"Do you think she was telling the truth?"

"Why would she lie about that?" He rubbed his hands together and bounced a little. "I think it was true, or she thinks it was, and it matches up with what Mom said about the whiskey lamp. I can't believe she turned it on last night, after what she told us."

He breathed out hard in a white cloud. It was still getting colder, not warming up.

"And what do we know from the medical report? Something about a debt and a debt collector, about firstborn children and a dragon."

Now that we were picking through the details, I tried to remember the report. All those German words were probably nonsense. But what if they were like pieces in a puzzle or word scramble, like my social studies teacher gave me for homework? Even if they didn't make sense to us right away, the foreign terms fit for Grandma Elizabeth, which meant there *were* connections. Maybe?

"And a coal mine," I said. "And wasn't there something in German about an empty part of the world?"

"Right, some kind of poetry. Very dramatic. So Grandma believed ... maybe she thought her firstborn son was going to be taken, just like the nun said, and she blamed a debt collector when he *did* get kidnapped or whatever. Maybe all this goes back to that. Whatever it is, Dad is gone now, so it's real. We need to figure out what to do."

"Mom said—"

"Mom is going to do jackshit," he said, voice rising. "She's practically brain-dead, you saw her. She might as well have been the one who got lobotomized."

I imagined the chicken man tapping on Mom's face and my pulse pounded in both ears. I tried to shake away the sudden tension by shifting my weight from one foot to the other, the way Don did. Didn't work.

"Don't talk like that," I said.

"Why? She kicked us out of the house so she could drink. You didn't see her pour Jameson into her coffee? You can smell it from here."

We walked to a park at a four-way intersection. It wasn't much, just a semi-circle of concrete columns, with a green fence and some well-kept bushes and a bench. I sat, Don paced.

I'm not afraid of this. Not with Don working it out. If we cut it all up into recognizable pieces, we could make a plan, solve this. Don knew what to do.

"That surgery really happened," I said. "To Grandma, I mean. She really had ... I don't think we should joke about it."

"Whatever, fine. So what are our options? One: we do nothing. We putter along and wait for Mom to sober up or Dad to come home. We hope everything gets magically better." He made a noise like a negative buzzer on a game show. "Wrong answer. I'm not doing that. So what else? Two: we try to find Dad. We call his work, and we go through his stuff. Maybe we even call the police, if Mom hasn't already."

He watched me for a reaction. What was I supposed to say? That was like something from a movie or book, where the kids solve crimes, because the adults are all too busy. I never liked those stories, always seemed phony. That was all this was, too, right? *A story.* Don knew the two of us wouldn't find Dad, didn't he? He had to. We could help Mom, but we wouldn't fix it all ourselves. Or maybe he already had something else in mind?

"Is there a third option?"

"Yes. We don't look for Dad, because we won't find him. Instead, we look for the chicken man." He watched me closely, like he was waiting for me to agree, then tapped his right thumb to the fingers on his left hand. "Think about it. Dad's missing, Mom's losing it, and you and me are completely in the dark. The only reason we know *anything* is because we found it ourselves."

We're just talking. We're not going to do anything. We're just kids.

"So you want option three," I said.

He shrugged. "Maybe. Why? You don't think we should go looking for him?"

I watched the rustling empty branches overhead. Don was saying this to make himself feel better, less powerless. Maybe I could climb up one of these trees and wait until Dad came back.

"No," I said.

"Are you scared? He's just a person, Mark. And this is the real world. He can't hurt us. He's all talk. The only thing he's done is talk."

Don hadn't seen him at school or heard the song. Don was trying to convince himself, but anytime I thought about it, my stomach felt wrong, like he was a sickness. Still, though. Don should know better.

"What about what he showed you in his bag?"

A shadow passed across Don's face, but he waved it away and kept pacing. "Bullshit. I think he's a con artist trying to rattle us."

Was Don looking for an excuse to find the chicken man? What was wrong with him? Strange things *had* happened. Things we shouldn't even be talking about.

"What about the gas in the house?" I asked. "Or your room?"

Don opened his mouth, his cheeks flushed, like he was about to argue, then stopped himself.

"You're not wrong," he said at last. "I don't know what that was. So fine, we'll try to find Dad. I need you to distract Mom, get her out of the house. We need to look through their room. Maybe there's something on Dad's computer."

"How?"

"Get her to drive you somewhere." Don frowned, arms crossed, then he poked me in the shoulder and smiled. "What about your new girlfriend? What's her name, Rachel? Didn't she ask you to hang out with her today anyway? Get Mom to take you there, but don't stay too long, just a couple hours. That way, Mom will run errands while you're there, instead of coming home."

We shouldn't be out here talking about this. We should be back inside, waiting for Dad. The stillness in the trees and early morning light felt unnatural, like someone was holding everything steady to listen to us. No, absurd.

"You've planned this out," I said.

Don's hands jittered in the air. He tapped his fingers again to make his points but more frantic than before. "*We're* planning it right now. I need to look through Dad's stuff. And I need time to put everything back the way it was, understand?"

"What if he's really hurt?"

Don waved that away with one hand, as if it were a silly question. "Then we'll call the police. This isn't a movie. We're going to be careful. Are you okay with this?"

If I told him "no," would he stop? Would he go back to option one?

He would. He really would. If I weren't in this with him, Don wouldn't do it. He didn't want to have to manage alone. We were here in Kentucky together. We shouldn't be, but we were. Maybe we were stronger together, too, with Don at the lead.

"Mom isn't going to get better," I said.

"No."

"And if Dad comes back?"

"Then great, we can try to find out what's going on, and where he was. What do you think?"

"I don't think we have a choice."

That wasn't true, but I said it anyway. I wanted Don to feel like we were tacking down a slope. Climbing was more like what it felt like, though.

"Don," I said, "why aren't you eating?"

He turned away fast, hustling onto the sidewalk back. "Come on. Let's go so you can call Rachel."

We went home and followed the plan. I called Rachel, who was excited to have me come over. I did it while Mom was in her bedroom, so I could ask permission after. Mom wasn't thrilled about having to drive me but decided it was good for me to socialize with a new friend. Don could stay home in case Dad got back, and I would only be there a couple hours, so we'd all have dinner together as usual.

Near school and set back on a front lawn with massive trees and a long drive, Rachel's house was a big, old stone not-quite-mansion, with a circular driveway with an empty cherub fountain in the middle.

Before I got out, Mom said, "I'll be back at 4:00. Is there anything you want from the grocery store?"

Don was right. She wasn't going back home until after I was done. He had the house to himself.

I walked up the front walk past a strange stone block, about two feet tall.

"It's a mounting block, from when there were horses," Rachel called.

She was waiting at the open front door in a blue dress, her gray-haired dad behind her. He shook my hand and said he was making popcorn. Did I like butter on it? I told him either way was fine.

Rachel took me up to her room, past empty hallways and tables set with decorative stones and fake plants, as if the whole place were a pretend house full of props but no one living inside. Even her room was like that. It looked temporary, nothing out of place and few posters or anything on the walls, almost like a hotel.

"I'm usually at my mom's," Rachel said. "My dad is always traveling, and he got engaged to a woman in California, so that's why this is barely my room."

What should I do? Sit or stand? She kept the door open and perched on her bed.

"What do you think of Kentucky?" Rachel asked. "It's probably a lot more boring that Chicago, right? And we never get any snow here that doesn't melt."

I sat beside her, but at the edge of the mattress and folded my hands—*casually, try to do it casually.* I'd never been to a girl's house like this before.

"It melts because of the imaginary fire underground?" I asked.

"It's real. People pretend it isn't, but I heard there was a whole town in Pennsylvania that had to move, because of an underground fire like this one." She went to a bare desk on the opposite wall and rooted through the drawers. "There's a book about it, a children's book, we all had to read. If you grew up here, you'd know it, too. It's this story about a runaway slave who hid in a mine so he wouldn't get caught. I thought I had it here somewhere, maybe it's at my mom's house."

A slave? Like from the 1800s? In third grade, at my old school, I learned a little about U.S. history, and I remembered a page in the textbook with an old black-and-white photo of people standing in a cotton field, staring straight ahead, dead-eyed. A woman with a basket on her head and muscular men, without shirts, along with kids who were blurry, probably because they had moved when the picture was taken.

"What happened to him?" I asked.

"Who, the slave in the story?" She came back over and sat beside me, close enough that our shoulders were touching. "Oh, when the dogs and all the other men found him, the slave set the whole place on fire. Sounds sad, right? But in the book, there was also like a Civil War battle, here in Kentucky, and it was symbolic and happy at the end, because the slave turned into a bird or something to fly away. You think I'm making this up, don't you?" She laughed and bumped into me. "Swear to God, it's a real book. That's what they taught us about how the fire started."

"Knock, knock." Rachel's dad was smiling in the doorway, a metal bowl of steaming popcorn in his hand.

"Mark, do you like movies?" he asked.

Downstairs, I sat with Rachel on their big cushiony couch. Her dad kicked back in a recliner by the wall. He put on a teen comedy that I hadn't seen, something Rachel told me I would *love*, and then we ate popcorn and watched. The movie was dumb, with actors who all looked way too old to be in high school. Plus, Rachel's dad kept pausing it and switching the channel to check the score on the University of Louisville basketball game. Every time, U of L was winning, but by fewer and fewer points. Rachel insisted we finish the movie, though.

She touched my hand—a sharp pain, and I jerked away. Rachel started to apologize, and I said, "It's okay, just a cut ..."

Screwed that up. No, the broken glass did, not my fault. My hand was still swollen. She must have touched it too hard. But we didn't really talk again until Mom got there.

I thanked Rachel and her dad, and Mom drove home, the trunk and part of the backseat full of groceries and other shopping bags.

At the house, Don was in the living room, playing video games, and he helped us bring in and put away groceries. He didn't say anything or even give me a secretive look. It stayed that way until after Mom went to bed. Then, just as I was falling asleep, he knocked and came into my room. He sat on the floor in the dark beside me.

"I don't know where Dad is," he whispered. "I couldn't get into his computer. But I called his office, and Mom *was* lying about the conference."

So that was it. But it wasn't. Don was still sitting here.

"What did you find?" I asked.

"In Mom and Dad's closet, on the top shelf, behind everything, there's a black case. It wasn't locked." He hesitated. "There's a gun in it."

"What? No there isn't."

"There is. Mom and Dad have a gun in their room. It's loaded and everything."

This was a dream. A gun was something on TV or a video game or maybe in a policeman's belt holster, not in our house. *But so what. Guns are just tools, right?* And this was Kentucky, lots of people probably had them. It was like a knife or a saw. If Mom and Dad kept it in their bedroom, out of the way, what was the big deal? Except Mom hated guns. No way she would allow one in the house. Unless she didn't know.

"It would be crazy for Mom not to know," Don said, as if I'd said that out loud, and I hadn't. "It's right there in the closet. Dad left on Friday, which means the police probably won't help us. People leave all the time."

Don had time to work all this out today, didn't he? Running it over and over again in his head, until the explanation was worn into his brain, like an after-image burned into a TV screen.

"But maybe they can find his car or ..."

He leaned closer to me, and I could smell toothpaste but no sloppy joes from dinner. He hadn't eaten anything.

"Mark, we have to do something, and that something isn't calling the police."

"I don't think we can," I said.

He sat back, away from me. His face was a gray outline in the dark, a forehead, the ridge of his nose and cheekbones. Deep shadows where his eyes and mouth should have been—no, *were*. Where they were.

"Okay," he said at last.

"Dad will come back."

"Okay."

The short way he said it probably meant he'd made a decision, a new plan, and I wasn't part of it.

"Don't do anything," I said.

"I'm not crazy," Don said. "Don't worry."

"Seriously."

"*Seriously*," he said. "It'll be fine."

And then he slipped away from me and left. Should I warn Mom? Should I tell her we knew about the gun, that Don had tried to learn more about Dad but hadn't, and now was going to try something else? He would go for the chicken man. He would use the address on the book of matches—*Cadillac Club*—and start there. At least, that was what I'd do.

This was a natural force. This was gravity. Mom could stop him, but she wouldn't. If I told her, she would get angry and hide the gun, maybe try to ground him, but that would only make Don more determined. He was too stubborn. The only way she could stop him would be to include him in all of it, let him know the police were involved, that she was taking this seriously, maybe even investigate the *Cadillac Club*, whatever it was, herself. And none of that would happen.

I was alone. Don had said we were in it together here. So why did he walk out like that? Why was I by myself? There should be a way to prevent whatever was about to happen. Maybe I would think of something tomorrow, a new option to convince Don we had more time, unless he was already gone.

He wasn't. The next day, Don wouldn't discuss anything and was in a better mood. He still wasn't eating much, but he helped out more with the dishes and cooking, and even unpacked most of the boxes in his room without Mom asking. That didn't really help her, though. She was still in a fog, back and forth from the kitchen to the bedroom, and she was drinking. There was whiskey in her morning coffee and in her tea at lunch, and then a bottle of wine at dinner and into the evening.

The day dragged, but tomorrow was Monday. I was looking forward to school. Except for my tedious library class, it would be good to be somewhere else, out of the sweat and alcohol stink of our house.

As I was brushing my teeth for bed, Mom called from the living room, "You're both in luck. School's cancelled tomorrow."

I went to see. She was watching the TV news, and it was a weather report. Ice and snow were predicted.

"Six to eight inches," Mom said. "Has it started snowing yet?"

I went to look out the front window, careful not to stare at the illuminated whiskey lamp. The lawn and street were dark out there. No snow.

"I don't understand how they can *pre-emptively* cancel school like this," she said. "But tell your brother."

I told Don about the snow. He nodded and said goodnight quickly, like he didn't want to get dragged into any discussion.

After I got in bed, Mom lingered in the hall near my bedroom door. At first, I thought she wanted to talk about Dad, maybe hear about how I was doing, but then she started singing, *"Don't worry, about a thing ..."*

I settled back in bed and tried not to think about Dad or what Don was probably planning in his room across the hall.

Mom sang a little louder, then said, "Good night, Mark."

The next morning, there was a blizzard. Mom sat in the kitchen, drinking coffee that reeked of Jameson, and watched a heavy snowstorm in the backyard through the window. "It's really something. The city is totally buried. Is your brother up? Ask him what he wants for breakfast."

I knocked on Don's door. No answer, so I knocked again, then opened it. His bed was empty. His coat was gone. Maybe he was in another part of the house or outside for some reason. If I didn't tell Mom, it wasn't real.

I went into Mom and Dad's bedroom. Quickly, carefully, I opened their closet. There it was, a black case on the top right, in the back, just like Don said. I pulled it out. It was heavy. I almost dropped it. But I didn't, and when I had it on the floor in front of me, I popped it open. Empty.

Mom stood in the doorway. "What are you doing? You can't be in here ..."

She saw the case, no gun, started to say something, and I looked up at her.

"Don is gone."

Chapter Nine

Mom sat me down in the kitchen, coffee-alcohol mug firm in her hands between us, and looked directly into my eyes. "I need you to tell me where he is."

"I don't know." That was sort of true. *Don't remind her about the matches until you figure out what to do.*

She placed the empty gun box in a chair beside us. "How did you know about this case?"

"Don told me. He said he was searching for information about Dad. It was an accident. He didn't mean to find it."

"Did he tell you what was in it?"

Odd question. Wasn't that the point? She was trying to avoid saying the word out loud: *gun.*

I nodded.

Mom picked up the kitchen phone and called the police. I sat at the table, as she talked through all of it: her husband was gone, her fourteen-year-old son was missing and might have a firearm.

I watched the snowfall in the backyard and tried to cut up the problem. Dad. The gun. Don.

Mom slammed down the phone. "They'll *see what they can do.*"

The police weren't worried. She said that they sounded more concerned about Don getting caught out in the snow than anything else. Out the back door, the snow looked wet and deep enough that it would take at least two shovelfuls to clear it all the way to the ground. I knew from experience, shoveling out our old driveway in Illinois. And it was still coming down, the wind gusting to shake the trees bare over high crescent snowbanks.

"Come on," Mom said. We went to a front closet crammed with unopened boxes that needed to go up in the attic, along with a spare car battery and snow shovels. I found my boots, gloves, coat, and hat, and then we shoved open the front door into the snow and wind. The car was buried like a marshmallow, and nothing had been plowed yet. We hiked out to the edge of the driveway.

"No tracks," Mom called over the wind.

She meant from Don. If he had left after the snow started, there might still be some trace of it. Or not. They could have been blown away or covered up fast.

We cleaned off the car, then went back in. Even if Dad and Don were gone, we had accomplished *something*. Mom made hot chocolate and insisted we watch a movie and keep an eye on the storm. It was supposed to continue into tomorrow. She wouldn't let me out of her sight.

Don had been gone since the middle of the night, and he had a gun. Dad had been missing since Friday. How far away was the *Cadillac Club*?

A little later, when the car was buried again, snow still coming down, Mom went out to clear it off. She told me I didn't have to help this time, if I wanted to get cleaned up. This was my chance.

As soon as she was outside, I went for Mom's purse in her bedroom. She was always getting lost, and every year, Dad bought her a different map as a joke birthday present. I had to be fast. If she caught me in here again, what would she do? Yell? Maybe just grab a wine bottle and lock herself in.

There: a small, laminated map of Louisville, all folded up. I checked her wallet. It was a complicated fold-out thing, stuffed with credit cards, receipts, and plenty of cash. So Don probably didn't take any.

I left the money, put everything back how it was, and took the map and phonebook into the bathroom, locking the door. The 'Cadillac Club' address on the matchbook had been 115 Water Street. On the back of the map, there was an index of streets. I found Water Street, then flipped it over to the A4 section, like playing Battleship. There it was, a curling street near downtown Louisville, not far from the river and a few blocks from the library. How far away was that? Using the legend, I tried to measure it out. Every inch was an eighth of a mile, so that was probably two miles or a little more away.

Last year, I had to run a mile in gym at my old school, and I did it in nine minutes, around the soccer fields four times. If I walked it, even if it took twice as long in the snow, I could still get there in less than an hour, right? That was nothing.

And then what?

I stared at the map. *Tell me what to do.* Don might not even be there. What if he were hunkered down at the Mexican restaurant or Radio Shack or the library, waiting for the storm to quit? No, wherever he was, he knew by now Mom would be upset. If he were okay, he would have called. The only reason for silence was if something bad. *Stop it.*

I showered and tried to clear my head. After, I hid the map in a towel and went to get dressed. Okay. I could do this. Just find Don and get him back. If he wasn't at the *Cadillac Club*, then I would check the library. It was just a little farther. And if he wasn't at either place, at least I would have tried. And it couldn't wait.

But Mom kept me with her the rest of the day, and two more times we went out to shovel. Still no sign of snowplows, but some of the neighbors were also out. They waved and groused about how unprepared the city was for all of this.

By night, the snow had slowed, but it was still coming down. There were probably two feet out there.

"It will be sorted out tomorrow," Mom said, as we ate homemade cheese pizza and salad.

We didn't talk much, and soon, she was tired. She took another bottle of wine into her bedroom and shut the door. *Their* bedroom, Mom and Dad's bedroom.

I went into my room and dumped all the schoolbooks out of my backpack. In their place, I put the phonebook, the map, a change of clothes, a flashlight, an extra pair of winter gloves, and then loaded up in the bathroom: a bottle of Tylenol, a box of bandages, and an ace bandage, still in its packaging.

In the kitchen, I found some candy bars, a few bananas, and then filled up two water bottles. Don might be hungry or dehydrated. I hesitated at the knife block on the counter. There were eight different blades in there: a big, butcher-like one, steak knives, and little sharp chopping knives. Should I have a weapon? I touched the handle of the biggest knife.

And do what with it?

Who knows, but what if I needed it and didn't have it?

I took out a steak knife. It was only about six inches long and slim, but sharp, serrated. If I stabbed somebody with it, it would probably do some damage.

What was I thinking? I was getting excited, my heartbeat faster. This was an adventure. I was actually doing this. March out into the dark and cold and find Don. I would bring him back. But not with a weapon.

I put the knife away.

My backpack was heavier with everything, but no different than with my schoolbooks. In the living room, I laced up my snow boots, prepped my coat and hat, and slipped on gloves. Then I opened the front door. Out of the corner of my eye, I saw the light of the whiskey lamp in the windowsill, like a lighthouse beacon.

I felt the strangest pull. *Grab the lamp.* I looked at it, really looked at it for the first time since Mom had talked about it. Nothing special. Just a whiskey bottle and that homemade base and stand.

No way I was touching that. I went out into the wind. Almost immediately, I regretted it. It was freezing, so cold that snot was already crusting on my upper lip when I got out to the road. Dragging my legs through the snowdrifts here was like dragging a chain of weights behind me. *I should go back and wait until morning.*

At the end of our road, the main street was plowed and salted, and cars passed, like this was the most normal night ever. The wind didn't stop, the snow kept up, but I could do this. And I did. All the way to the *Cadillac Club.*

The street up to the place was clear—perfectly plowed—and the parking lot was full of cars. Most everywhere on my walk had been closed or nearly empty, even the Kroger's grocery store parking lot. But not here. Everybody was here, apparently. My boots crunched in frozen salty mush at the edge of the lot. I should have had a plan, but

the biting snow and slippery sidewalks and roads had made it diffi-
cult to think on my hike. Whatever was inside, the black, single-story
building was windowless and lit by bright sodium lights at the four
corners of the parking lot and red neon above the entrance. The words
Cadillac Club were painted in red on the side. That was it.

A couple guys stood outside the front door, hugging their coats
against the snow, sputters of mist above their heads every time they
talked. My legs ached from the walk, and I had finished half a water
bottle, but my lips were still dry and chapped.

All right. Go in and ask about Don.

The two guys noticed me. One was a police officer, in uniform, but
with a bulky black overcoat on top. He was young and had short hair,
almost shaved. The second guy was bigger, with a gray-brown beard
and tattoos. Blue and black ink peeked up the bottom of his neck and
onto his wrists, under his wool coat, jeans, and biker boots.

They watched as I approached.

"You selling magazines?" the biker-guy asked and smiled.

"I'm looking for my brother," I said. "And my dad."

"How old is your brother? Because you can't come in here. Your
dad might be inside, but can't do anything about that."

The shaved head cop watched me, with raised eyebrows, as if he
expected me to back off. *No. Don came here.* Those matches were the
only evidence we had. He would have remembered that.

"My brother is fourteen. His name is Don. I think he's inside."

"Sorry," the biker guy said. "Not here."

They weren't going to let me through. No chance. The door was
right there, though, a simple black door. I tightened my backpack
straps, so it wouldn't slow me down if I ran in.

"What do you have in your bag?" the cop asked.

"Food and clothes."

"Can I take a look?"

He came over and I gave him my backpack. He unzipped the main compartment and poked around inside for a second, then zipped it up again and set it against the wall behind him.

"Go on," he said. "It's not for kids in there."

"Can I have my—"

"Are you stupid?" the cop asked. "What'd I just say?"

The biker guy grinned, as if this were a show and he wanted to see how it turned out. All my stuff was in that backpack. But what could I do? I felt numb from the cold, my legs too heavy. *Can't just leave.* I stepped away, so they wouldn't get more impatient. They started to talk again. *Do something.*

I dashed between them and threw open the door.

"Little shit!" the biker guy shouted.

I ran through a small, sparkly purple entry room to a second door, where an old guy looked up from behind a desk. There were signs and instructions on the wall behind him—*'Over 21'* and *'No Photography.'* I opened the second door, more shouting behind me, and was plunged into a cavernous room lit by blue-green blacklights and a flashing strobe. A wave of floral perfume and cigarette smoke made my eyes water. Music pounded over everything. Women were on two stages—one to my immediate left, another at the back—dancing naked, their bodies glittery and shadowed, with a few men below on chairs. I hurried past honeycomb black booths and little side passages, where more women lounged, half-dressed. The flashing lights and stench made the room swim.

A woman wearing a black bra and lacy panties and nylons stopped me, in front of a mirrored bar on the right wall, where more half-dressed women chatted with a trio of college-age guys.

"Hey, little man, you can't be in here." The woman had weary eyes and solid black hair.

I'd never seen women like this, real women.

"Are you lost?" she asked. "What's your name?"

"Mark."

Back by the entrance, the biker guy spotted me and walked fast.

Another young girl in a tiny red dress, her arm around a guy in a polo shirt, yelled, "... that kid doing here?"

"Mark, why are you here, honey?" The tired-eyed woman knelt in front of me, touched my shoulder.

"My brother and dad are gone."

The biker guy caught my arm from behind and yanked me back to the door. I spun, my legs banging into a table and knocking over a beer bottle, as the biker lifted me.

"Jesus!" the tired-eye woman called. "Break his arm, why don't you!"

But now I was in the entry room again. The biker guy tossed me into the wall, and I went down. I was trembling. My arm hurt from where he'd grabbed it, and my back ached from hitting the wall. I felt myself starting to cry. *Stop it. Get up.* This was just a strip club, no place Dad would be. And if they were throwing me out, Don wasn't here either.

The old guy watched from his desk, and the cop leaned against the other door, blocking the exit. I could still hear the music pounding through the inner wall.

"Take off your coat," the biker guy said. "And those boots."

"No."

He kicked me hard in the stomach, and I doubled over onto my side. I tasted tears, couldn't stop them. Dad wasn't here. Nobody but me.

"My boy is your size, and he can use a new coat and boots. Those look like nice ones. Take them off." He wrestled my arm out of one sleeve.

"Stop."

I couldn't fight him. He was too strong.

The cop laughed. The biker guy got one of my arms free, then twisted me around to yank off my coat, breathing a moldy cigarette smell on my cheek. He shook out the coat, grinning.

"I have to find the chicken man," I said.

The biker guy froze, his smile gone. "The fuck did you say?"

I wiped my face. I was still shaking, and my side throbbed where he'd kicked me every time I took a breath. *Don't think about it. Keep going.* "The chicken man, I think my dad came to see him."

"You're on your own." The cop shook his head and went back outside.

The old guy behind the counter made eye contact with the biker guy, and the biker guy wavered. He glanced from me to the front entrance, like he wished the cop had taken me out. Did I say the password?

"Who told you to say that?" the biker guy asked. "You can leave. I'll let you."

"Nobody. My dad has a debt or something. I think he came here. I need to see him." I struggled to my feet, but I didn't go to the door. I held my gut where he'd kicked me, tender but not too hurt. "I need to see him."

Whatever this was, the biker guy was afraid of the chicken man or at least shocked that I knew the name. God, my side hurt, and my left arm seemed to be sprained. I couldn't move it without a lancing pain. *Go. He's right. You can go right now.*

The old guy hit a buzzer on the wall behind him. "He's coming up."

The biker guy muttered something and went back outside.

If I left, maybe this wouldn't be real. This felt like I had flipped over a rock—an ordinary, unblemished rock—and found worms and beetles scrambling in the mud. Would my body hurt in the morning or would it all fade away, if I walked out now, put the rock back down?

The inner door opened, and the chicken man stepped in, still wearing the same gray suit. He started to say something, then saw me.

"Mark," he said, "I thought we weren't going to do this again."

"My brother and my dad, are they here?"

"You think they came in this weather?" the chicken man asked. "It's another storm of the century outside. How did you get here without a coat?"

I told him about the policeman and biker guy. The chicken man rolled his eyes and went out the front door. He was back a moment later with my bag and coat.

"Come on." He led me back into the strip club.

Walking fast, the chicken man went to a small, black door just past the mirrored bar. The women watched us, careful to get out of our way. And when the chicken man opened the door and held it for me, the tired-eyed woman from before made the sign of the cross: a hand to her forehead, chest, and then each shoulder, and I went in.

Down stone stairs, the chicken man walked me to a landing with a red door. Yellow lights cast uneven shadows across the rough-cut rock walls.

"They're both here?" I asked.

"They're both here," the chicken man said. "But I'm not sure why you're here. We weren't supposed to see each other again, Mark. Remember our talk at your school? I thought I explained things clearly."

The air got warmer and had a stingy, sharp taste that I could feel in my throat, tingling my nose. At the red door, the chicken man paused. Tiny black writing was painted around the frame, small and too jumbled together to read.

The chicken man watched me. "What do you think is about to happen? Do you think you're going to bust in here and rescue your brother and father? Do you think you know what's down here?"

My whole body ached. I was exhausted, but I wasn't shaking anymore. "I don't know."

"You don't have a plan, do you? You just hope things will work out. Is that pretty much it? Your brother had a plan at least. He tried to shoot me. Did you know that? I mean, I'm not the bad guy in this scenario. I don't know how many times I have to tell you that. I just work here. I'm trying to get through the day, like everybody else."

He opened the door.

Chapter Ten

I sat on the hard front steps outside the *Cadillac Club*, looking at the empty parking lot in the snow. Don was beside me, dressed in my spare change of clothes. They didn't fit him, and he looked smaller with his head against my arm. Five big plastic buckets were arranged around me.

What just happened?

The sun was coming up, smearing the sky faint gray over the blocky rooftops across the street. A siren blared as the red and blue flashing lights of a police car approach on the road, slowly turning into the parking lot. My arms and legs were heavy. I couldn't stand. And I ached, in my shoulder, my side, and in throbbing pain in my left hand, which was all bandaged up with a smiley face drawn on top in a permanent marker. Something inside—in-between opening the red door and ... Why couldn't I remember? Concentrating on that moment at the bottom of the stone steps made my heart speed up. Pain spiked in my left hand again. I had started to close my fingers into a fist. *Remember. Why can't I remember?*

Behind me, the front door was boarded up, no way into the *Cadillac Club*, and the sign wasn't there anymore. The red words on the side of the building had been painted over in black or scrubbed away.

I should stand. Figure out what happened.

"Don? Do you ..." I reached for Don, and he jerked away, panting and making groany noises shivering in the cold.

The police car pulled up, and a female cop got out, followed by a young, sleepy guy, with a Dunkin' Donuts travel mug. The woman started asking questions as she approached, then she shouted to the sleepy guy to call for an ambulance.

What's wrong with Don? And the buckets? The policewoman asked me about them, trying to get the lid off one. My mouth wasn't working, but I could feel my teeth and tongue. I was okay. She jerked the lid off, the bucket tipped over a little, and brown-black lumpy liquid spilled over the top. It stank like dead fish. The woman spun away and retched, vomiting in the snow. My guts clenched at the smell. I turned away, covering my nose. *Don't look. Don't think. It will be okay.*

After that, an ambulance arrived, then another police car, and even a fire truck. They put Don and me on stretchers, covered us in blankets and hooked up IVs in the back of the ambulance. I tried to tell them to check Don, not me. I wasn't hurt.

"...we can call?" a paramedic asked me. "What's your name?"

I coughed and heard my voice. It scratched, like I'd been screaming, but I told them our home phone number. The ambulance was loud from the siren and rattle of plastic and metal cases on the walls. I reached across to hold Don's hand. He looked at me—fast and frightened, then it must have registered that it was me. But the panic didn't leave his eyes completely. *We're out. Whatever happened, it's over.*

Wait. Touching his hand, I registered a thick plastic bandage over the top of his palm on his thumb—no, where his thumb *should* be.

Oh God. I pulled my hand back, started to sit up, and the IVs jostled. A paramedic caught my shoulder to hold me down, said we were almost there. Watching me, Don shifted. He had the same tight wrapping on his other hand, too.

"Don ... tell me what happened." I stared at his hands. I wasn't seeing right. This wasn't real. "Say something!"

Don't face split into a horrible grimace, and the paramedics saw it too: a bloody stump in the back of his mouth. *Where his tongue should be. Where his tongue ...*

I slumped back to my stretcher, one arm covering my face. Don moaned, but I didn't look, felt my chest shaking. I gasped, tried to swallow, then took another quick bite of air. *Is this happening?*

At the hospital, Don and I shared a room, and a nurse told me they had sedated him and were keeping a close eye. We were very lucky, she said. The hospital smelled like detergent and cleaning chemicals, and our window looked out on the snowy roof of a concrete parking garage. The storm had stopped.

A little while later, Mom burst in, rushing between us in tears. She squeezed me and kissed my forehead, and then fell to her knees at Don's bedside. He was too doped up to really respond, but he blinked weakly and tried to smile. Without his tongue, though, Don's jaw was off, hanging down and sideways in the wrong way, making his smile an ugly jack-o-lantern gash. Mom covered her face and cried.

"What were you doing there?" she asked me, still at Don's bed. "What happened, Mark?"

"I don't remember."

"Your brother is ... someone did this to him. The police are going to be here any minute. You need to tell them what you know." She pulled herself up, swiping at her eyes. "I know you left to find your father. I'm not angry, okay? I just want to know what happened to you both."

"Where's Dad?"

"They won't tell me. The police will have new information when they get here."

They did, but it wasn't new. Soon, a policeman knocked and took Mom into the hall. Through the mottled glass of the door window, I saw the hazy shape of them going to the nurse's station. Mom stopped, shaking her head, and then she shoved away a clipboard, refused to touch it.

"That's not him! Stop it!" She stomped back into our room.

The policeman came after her. "Mrs. Morris, the hospital has someone on staff who can explain this better than I can."

"I don't care," she said. "Find my husband. Do you know how crazy you sound?"

The policeman backed out. "The hospital will send someone in."

Mom sat in a chair by the window on my side of the room. "Why were you at that place? Don't lie to me, Mark."

"The matches," I said. "I remembered the matches from when there was the gas leak."

"That was some kind of club years ago, back in the '70s, I think. I remember when it shut down. It made the news all over the country. There was a big fire, lots of people died. They had to change building codes after that."

"It was open tonight."

"No," she said. "It hasn't been open in years. What was it, the *Cadillac Bar*?"

Close enough. Mom must be confused, mixed up after everything. What happened, though? How did I get out? Why couldn't I remember?

A knock at the door, and a calm woman in a purple dress and seashell jewelry came in. She left with Mom. I watched Don sleep, his breathing falling into too-deep dips and pauses, probably from the drugs. I went into the Cadillac Club, the chicken man took me through to another red door, and then ..? And then. Why were those buckets outside?

Mom came back in an hour later, her eyes and nose red from crying. She told us they weren't sure, but there was a chance—*just a chance*—Dad might have 'passed away.' I said we would get through whatever happened. We loved each other, and we were still a family. I said it like Dad would have before we moved and they started fighting again. A doctor came to talk about reconstructive surgery for Don. He reassured Mom that something would work. Then he examined my left hand again. I had a narrow, red-flesh cut straight through the back of my hand and out the palm. Something stabbed all the way, but I could move my fingers. "And," the doctor said, "it's a good, clean cut," as if my mystery wound were lucky. Not like Don.

After that, the days stacked up in a new, surreal routine. I didn't go back to school, and Don stayed in the hospital for days, while Mom and her family and a friend from Chicago made preparations for the funeral. Relatives I didn't really know kept asking me to do things with them. They wouldn't leave me alone in my room or to play video games, and when Don finally came back, he walked with a limp. But he wasn't completely broken.

That first night, Mom ordered Chinese food, and Don wolfed down his Kung Pao chicken so fast Mom laughed and said she should have gotten two. Even without a tongue, Don had an appetite again. *That's good.* We were healing, weren't we? Trying to start.

After lights out, I woke drenched in sweat with after-images of the white buckets that only faded when I kept my eyes open. Awake in bed, my pulse slowed again, and the memory of sitting with Don, surrounded by the buckets became plastic-fake. Something I saw on

TV that happened to someone else. It wasn't possible. No one said how Dad died or where he was. But of course I knew. I had smelled him when the policewoman opened the lid. A wrenching, rotten stink. *I smelled him.*

The next weekend, Dad's funeral was in a church near Holy Cross. Seeing his coffin made me cry, and I couldn't stop. Then so did Mom and Don, and plenty of other people, too. It wasn't a huge funeral, but the church was peaceful, all fancy white stone and stained glass, with a huge, crucified Jesus behind the altar, almost life sized.

When the ceremony was about half over, I noticed Grandma Elizabeth watching me from the back. I hadn't noticed her arrive. Dressed in a black dress, she had high bony cheeks and dyed black hair pulled back too tight, her lips neon red from lipstick. A nurse helped her stand, leaning on a cane.

Grandma Elizabeth mouthed something to me across the room. I couldn't hear. Then she smiled, lipstick on her teeth, her eyes a little too wide.

I looked away, back at the closed coffin at the front of the church. I hadn't seen Grandma Elizabeth since all of this started. Someone stuck an icepick through her eyes. She left that transcript with all the German nonsense. She had dementia, but she was connected to this, wasn't she?

"Did you know Grandma Elizabeth was here?" I whispered to Mom.

Don sat on the other side of her. He heard me too and closed his eyes, as if he wanted to pretend he hadn't. He couldn't talk, couldn't write. But he was healing, that was what was important.

Mom shushed me. "Yes. Of course she's here."

The priest said, "We'll now ask for people who knew the deceased to come forward."

Behind us, Grandma Elizabeth called out, "I knew him."

The priest tried to keep going. "We ask ..."

"I know that he's not in that box, not the heart or brain or penis or liver," Grandma Elizabeth shouted. "The dragon kept the most important parts."

We were all looking back as the nurse tried to coax Grandma Elizabeth out of the church, but she held onto the pew. Who was she talking to? Why was she doing this?

She yelled something in German, then said, "Do you think the dragon cares about God?"

The nurse pulled her away.

Grandma Elizabeth spat at the ground. More German, and then she gestured at me. "That boy knows!"

Mom stood to shield me, and the nurse took Grandma Elizabeth outside. *No. I don't know anything.* None of that was real, and even if it was, I couldn't remember.

We didn't talk on the drive to the cemetery for the burial. And when we stood by chairs around the open grave, more people I didn't know said how sorry they were. By the end, it was just Don, Mom, the priest, a few other relatives, and me. Dad's coffin hadn't been lowered in. It sat there, attached to metal and wood poles over the hole. And there was no tombstone yet either. That was still being prepared. Just a hole in the ground. That was all. *Not for Dad.* His name wasn't on it, and no one had opened the coffin. I hadn't seen his body. Neither had Don.

"This doesn't feel real." Mom hugged her arms, like she had at home in the backyard, when we talked about the whiskey lamp. As if she was cold but not from the air, like her bones were freezing from the inside.

"Time will help," the priest said.

More people would visit at the house, bringing over food and helping to clean up. But I didn't want to go back there. The Tyler Lane House wasn't our home, should never have been. *If we hadn't fucking moved here, none of this would have happened.* Dad shouldn't be buried in Kentucky, with a coal fire underneath him. Why was I alive? Don was broken, and Dad was in a coffin, ready to go into the ground. They'd had to bring in a heavy-duty digger, like from a construction site, to clear off the snow and open up the dirt. I'd seen it, still parked down the road in the cemetery.

"You're not a good listener," a woman said from behind me.

I turned. Sister Maria Theresa was dressed in her full-on nun outfit, with the habit and everything. Mom was still talking to the priest, and Don sat in a chair a little ways away. They hadn't seen her yet. She was still very white, and I saw those same plastic rings on the fingers of one hand. *What does she want?*

"Yes, I am," I said.

"You didn't listen to me," she said, "when I told you to let it go. To stop digging."

Did she say that on purpose, with the grave right there?

"My dad is dead," I said.

Everyone else was being extra nice, not pushing me. Telling me how brave I was and how nice I looked.

"Yes, and I'm sorry for your loss. But why did you come see me, if you weren't going to listen?"

"I didn't have a choice," I said. "Don went there. And Dad was already gone."

"That's exactly right. Your father was already gone." She squinted at me. "You had nothing to do with that, Mark."

"I know."

"My sister told me you're the reason he's even here at all, *any* part of him."

Stop talking about this. Leave me alone.

Another car pulled up, and a nurse walked around to help Grandma Elizabeth get out.

"Can you leave it be?" Sister Maria Theresa asked me. "After all this?"

I hadn't worked through most of it yet. What came next? The *Cadillac Club* was gone, never really there. Since the hospital, I had tried to look it up, but there was no listing in the phonebook. When I called the library, I learned what Mom already knew. It shut down in 1977, after a fire killed 35 people. All of them were trapped inside somehow. There was no *Cadillac Club* anymore, which meant maybe there was no chicken man. There was no any of this. Dad got involved in something bad, and so did Don. I got hurt, but we were lucky, and Don and I were alive. So what if I couldn't remember? It was like Don's disappearing room, maybe a gas leak or a dream. Now, even that felt like a false memory. Like tonight, Mom and Don would both tell me—and I would *know*—that his room never vanished. What was I thinking? Of course not. Something had happened, but not ... *that.*

"I'll leave it," I said.

Sister Maria Theresa smiled. "Smart boy. You can visit me again sometime, if you want. I'm all out of Snickers bars. But don't listen to my sister."

As Grandma Elizabeth came closer, walking with her cane and holding onto the nurse's arm, Sister Maria Theresa stepped away to go hug Mom.

"Donald, what lies was my sister saying just now?" Grandma Elizabeth asked me.

"I'm Mark, Grandma." We weren't supposed to correct her, but I couldn't make myself go along with it right now.

"I was telling the truth," she said. "He isn't in there. All of my son isn't in that box."

The nurse told her to calm down, so she wouldn't get agitated and have to go back to the car. But Grandma Elizabeth shook her away. Mom noticed us.

"Why isn't there any music?" Grandma Elizabeth asked. "Did he play music for you? He played 'Barbara Allen' for me."

Everything lurched, but I caught my balance. I was lightheaded. That was all. *Don't think about anything else.*

"Okay," the nurse said. "Let's say hello to your daughter, and then we'll head back."

Grandma Elizabeth muttered something in German and tapped hard on my shoulder. "*You* can kill him. You wouldn't be here otherwise. Don't tell anyone. Don't let him know that *you* know."

Somehow, she knew what happened, didn't she? She was making sense, even if I didn't understand. She was trying to warn me.

"Promise me something, please, Donald."

"What?"

"Promise you will be there with me, when I die." She snatched my left hand.

A flash of pain made me cry out.

"No! His hand is hurt," Mom shouted as she ran toward us." Stop it, Elizabeth!"

But Grandma Elizabeth didn't let go. "And when you see him again, kill him for me."

PART TWO

Eighteen years later.

Chapter Eleven

I was running late to meet Caitlyn because of delays on the L train again from Brooklyn into the city. When I got to the restaurant at 38th and Park, she was waiting in the rain outside Al Forno under a blue-jay-blue umbrella. That was what she called it, "blue jay blue," because she brought it down from Toronto. She looked perfect.

She was tall, almost 5'10", with brown-blonde hair. They called it "dirty blonde," but I didn't like that. It didn't fit her. She always wore a slim dress or black pencil skirt and starched white button-down shirt, like today, so she could show off the shadow of her purple bra underneath. She teased with flashes of skin out the sides of the buttons when she turned, because the top was always a little too tight. A month ago, when we were drunk on rum and lying together in bed, she'd said, "I do that for you on purpose, you know. To keep you on your toes."

When she saw me approaching on the sidewalk, Caitlyn brightened. I had changed out of a stained Radiohead t-shirt and dirt-streaked jeans into a black suit, 'fresh steamed' from the subway ride over. At the new build I was wiring in Bed-Stuy, I'd told Susan to run interference if the client stopped by. Leaning into an exposed rut of drywall, she had grinned and adjusted a length of pipe with a wrench. 'Anniversary, huh? Did you buy Caitlyn a ring already?'

'Not tonight,' I'd said and stuffed spare wires into my bag. And before she could argue, I called, 'Soon, though.'

'Caitlyn is out of your …'

'Out of my *motherfucking* league,' I'd finished Susan's usual sentence for her, smiling, and we knocked our fists together.

'Always covering for you,' she'd faux grumbled.

The self-described 'hardest working plumber in Brooklyn,' Susan had been my lifeline ever since she stopped in to fix a busted sink pipe at my first shitty walk-up on Flatbush eight years ago. Ducking out from under the sink, she wiped sweat from her trademark purple bandana and sized me up fast. 'Your landlord is a cheap SOB,' she'd told me. 'Should really replace the whole fixture, not just patch it up.'

Shifting awkwardly in that damp studio apartment, cluttered with boxes and Mom's hand-me-down suitcase, I had nodded and made an inane comment—'You're telling me'—as if I knew pipes the way I'd learned electricals. Susan's work shirt was sleeveless, exposing tanned, muscley arm covered in animal tattoos. An eagle and bear wrestled on her right shoulder and bicep; horses ran down her left. I tried not to stare.

'Still,' Susan said, with a half-smile. Yeah, I had been staring. The tats were intense. 'Somebody did a decent job on the washer install.'

'That was me.' And when she raised her eyebrows, I'd explained in what sounded like an apology that the landlord agreed to knock fifty bucks off the security deposit if I wired the new front-loading laundry machine myself. 'I finished an apprenticeship last year in Kentucky.'

'You're legal to work in the city? Shit, I have jobs for you. If you actually did the electricals in there.'

I had, and she did. We'd been working together, sharing a mix of new build and refurb contracts, and the occasional corporate project. She ran the pipes; I zapped the lights. And usually, I was the one covering for Susan, so she could get home to her wife or pick up her daughter from preschool. But not today. Today was important.

"Happy anniversary," Caitlyn said.

We kissed.

Maybe not a wedding anniversary, but today, November 1st, was the two-year anniversary of the day we met. She had just moved to New York, and Adriana had left me a month earlier. I was out drinking with Susan and my brother, Don, who was visiting for a long weekend. After a big settlement for a client, all the junior staff at Caitlyn's law firm were already hammered at 4:00 on a Friday afternoon. Caitlyn had been the new, hot girl, just arrived from Yale Law School, who still spoke with a cute Canadian accent. Don bumped into her, and I'd apologized for him. Later, she ditched her coworkers. Susan begged off to get home, and I put Don in a cab to the airport so I could sit with Caitlyn until 3:00 AM.

Now, the table at *Al Forno* wasn't ready, so we went in to get drinks at the bar. It was packed and loud, standing room only, with a buzzy liquor and warm bread smell.

"Work was good?" I asked, when I had my bourbon, and she had a Chardonnay. No telling what they were going to charge me for the drinks, but I handed over a credit card and tried to put it out of my head.

Caitlyn rolled her eyes. "Today was a shitshow. Fire drill, fire drill, fire drill. I was afraid I might have to fake a broken limb to get out of there for dinner tonight. How about you? You look tired."

"Thank you."

She grinned and nudged me playfully. Even brush of her arm could still almost make me hard. She was so beautiful. People were watching, guys especially, probably wondering who the hell I was. What was I doing with her? I was too skinny and, at 29, my hairline was already receding. Plus, I hadn't shaved since Sunday and still carried my work bag over one shoulder. No time to stop by home first.

"All of the pasta here is homemade," Caitlyn said. "And everything is local, as local as it can be in the city. I like your tired eyes, by the way. Super sexy."

Susan was right, of course. Caitlyn was of out of my league, but somehow she was oblivious. And after two years, I still wasn't used to it. That was something I was supposed to work on, Dr. Laymon said, self-love and acknowledging that I was worthy of other people. Or something. But he'd never met her. If my therapist saw Caitlyn, I had the feeling he'd sit back in his big, brown chair and throw up his hands to surrender. 'You know what, Mark, a Canadian-born Yale lawyer—and you're, what, an electrician from Kentucky working only intermittently? I give up. I renounce psychiatry. No more pills and sessions for you. You clearly lucked out.'

When our table was ready, we carried our drinks over from the bar, and the waiter brought sparkling water. It was a good spot, a white tablecloth booth of cushiony black with a view of the whole restaurant and all the wall art of semi-abstract horse paintings and black-and-white Italian landscape photo. Windows looked out on the taxis and Park Avenue traffic.

Caitlyn talked about the menu, told me we should split the calamari appetizer and maybe a salad too—they were supposed to be huge—and then said, "Oh, something weird happened this afternoon. I almost forgot. I got a phone call from an unknown number and—"

And the waiter interrupted to take our order. I felt my pulse quicken. This was nothing. It was going to be a funny story about a telemarketer or a prank call, a strange wrong number.

When the waiter left, Caitlyn raised her glass to toast. "Thank you for taking me out tonight."

I clinked my bourbon rocks glass to hers. "Of course. It comes but once a year."

"You can come more than that tonight, if you want," she said, more quietly, her cheeks suddenly flushed. "I got you a present that I'm hoping might help. But that's all I'll say right now. My lips are sealed until later."

I couldn't focus. "I'm a complicated man."

"*So* complicated."

"The phone call, you were saying you got—"

"Oh right. Some woman called who claimed to be your sister."

All the air went out of the room. I hadn't told Caitlyn about Abby. I was planning to, but I hadn't yet. I hadn't talked about her in years. Mom and Don, Grandma Elizabeth, and Sister Maria Theresa were the only people who knew. But even on the anniversary, Mom didn't call anymore. I guess early on, I told Dr. Laymon too, but he hadn't really pushed me to talk about it. As for the rest of it, he knew bits and pieces that he chalked up to childhood trauma associated with my father's death. Very normal to imagine things, even things that were completely and utterly abnormal, like Don's disappearing room. Of course there was. That was what I had repeated to myself for eighteen years. Because it was true.

"That *is* odd," I said.

"Because you don't have a sister. But she knew your name, and she said some kind of bird man was keeping tabs on you."

I felt a quick wave of nausea, my stomach gurgling.

This was a joke. "Did Don put you up to this?"

"What? Your brother? I just thought it was strange. It was just a bizarre call. That's all I was going to say. Are you okay?"

I drank more whiskey, almost finished the glass, forced myself to put it back down. "What else did she say?"

"I shouldn't have brought it up."

"It's okay. No big deal. Just tell me what she said."

"Let me think. She told me that she was your sister, something about a bird man, and she said something about how she was *out*. I don't know what that means, but she said she was calling from a place with a name like 'Dunder Mifflin,' like from The Office."

My gut clenched up. I felt like I was holding my breath through the muscles of my stomach and arms. *Breathe. Stop it.*

"It wasn't a long call," Caitlyn said. "I was in the middle of a lot of other things, and the reception was really bad too. It was staticky, with snaps and crackles on the line, like she was making popcorn or something. Anyway, she said she was there, at Dunder Mifflin or wherever, and she wanted you to come find her. It was weird the way she said it, like 'he has to come soon, because he's Mark.'"

Come soon *because he's Mark*? That didn't make sense. "She wanted me to find her?"

"That's right, and she said she didn't have a lot of time. I think if I hadn't hung up, she probably would have asked for our bank account numbers to help a Nigerian prince flee the country or something."

I made myself relax. First, my breathing, then I concentrated on my stomach—*loosen, you bastard*—and I opened my fingers on the table to expose the scar on the back. That was on the other side, too, a permanent lump across my palm. There were a thousand explanations for the call. Except the voice in my head, the same one I'd heard all my life, pointed out that it didn't matter what I believed, what I convinced myself of. The only thing that mattered was what was real, what was waiting out there in the world. Everything else was the fake part, *pretending.*

"I'm sorry I freaked out," I said. "I haven't told you this, and I was going to, but you know I always try to not be the guy with a deep, dark past."

She stroked my hand, right along the white scar. "Okay ..?"

"I did have a sister, when I was a kid. She died when I was four. I don't really remember her, so it's not like a major childhood trauma or anything. It's just...that's what it is."

She got serious and a little sad. "I shouldn't have brought it up. Some asshole probably figured that out. I'm really sorry."

That's right. That's all it was.

The waiter brought the appetizer and salad, and I downed the last of my whiskey. He asked if I wanted another one.

Caitlyn watched me. "It's okay. Maybe you should."

So I did, and we talked about other things: Thanksgiving plans with my mother and Don in Louisville. The food, when it came, was everything it was supposed to be. Hearty, filling pasta and spicy local-ish vegetables with sauces just rich enough to let you know they might have eggs in them, but not so over the top that you needed to down a bottle of red wine to eat them—at least that was what Caitlyn told me.

I couldn't taste any of it. The pasta was dry thread, the sauce, bland paste. The vegetables might as well have been balls of paper. At first, I was sure I had gotten a bad batch and this was some kind of mistake. But that wasn't it. When she tried my food, Caitlyn closed her eyes, made quiet purring sounds, and said how jealous she was she hadn't ordered mine. But I could still taste the bourbon. Something was wrong with my mouth. Maybe I burned my tongue on the first bite or something and didn't realize it? I didn't eat much, but I drank. So did she.

When we were leaving, Caitlyn put her arms around me on the sidewalk outside, and I pulled her close, breathing in her perfume, shampoo, wine, and body scent. It was so specific. All of this wrapped together was her. I slipped my hands under her coat and inside the back of her shirt to feel the smooth, tight skin of her lower back. She jumped a little and kissed my chin.

"Your hands are cold," she said. "Let's take a cab."

I hailed a taxi. It was a $30 ride that wasn't much faster than the subway to our place in Bushwick, but that wasn't important right now. In the car, we made out like it was our first time, her fumbling and gasping as I touched her thighs under her skirt, and she pawed at my chest and down my stomach. Somehow, I was already too drunk to get hard. That was strange. Maybe because we had sex that morning before work—and a scare, when the condom broke. Almost forgot about that. Sure signs of being almost 30 years old, random limp dick and memory lapses.

At one point, I gave the driver directions to avoid traffic.

Caitlyn was just drunk enough to think that was funny. "*Dunder Mifflin.* Make sure you skip Dunder Mifflin."

Dunder Mifflin. No, not Dunder Mifflin. Avoided it before, but I knew. The woman on the phone didn't say Dunder Mifflin.

Dudweiler.

Chapter Twelve

"Why do you think this person would call your girlfriend?" Dr. Laymon asked. "Instead of reaching out to you?"

Out his office window, it was a dreary gray Saturday on the Upper West Side. I promised Caitlyn I would stop by Zabars at 79th and Broadway on my way back to bring home black-and-white cookies, smoked whitefish, and a couple other things for brunch tomorrow with our neighbors. I didn't want to forget, but I hadn't stopped there first because I knew Maxine, Dr. Laymon's black cat that was now rubbing back and forth on my right leg, would target all the food. I was allergic but not too bad. If I didn't press the cat to my open eyeballs, I would probably be fine. I was half-sprawled on Dr. Laymon's spongy red couch, and he sat across from me in his beige chair, hands folded on a notebook. He hadn't started writing yet, sometimes didn't at all. His office was on the ground floor of an apartment building, with an entry hall crammed with bookshelves and cat scratchy posts. Maxine had her pick.

"I don't know why she called," I said. "Obviously, it wasn't Abby."

"But you hadn't told Caitlyn about your sister?"

"No."

He found his pen but still didn't open the notebook.

"Why is that?"

"I didn't want to freak her out," I said. "My background is already sketchy enough without extra dead kids in the mix."

"Your sister wasn't *extra*," he said. "Is it possible *you* didn't want to talk about it? Since that dinner, you haven't enjoyed eating food or making love ...”

Not exactly right but close enough. I still couldn't taste anything except booze, and every time Caitlyn and I tried to have sex, my dick didn't work. I was suddenly broken somehow. It had only been three days, but Caitlyn was worried. She had read things on the Internet about how I might be malnourished, or my nervous system might be busted or a brain tumor. 'That's why the internet was invented,' I'd said, trying to smile. 'To make you think everything is cancer. Fatigue? Cancer. Trouble sleeping? Cancer. No symptoms? Guess what that is?'

'Mark, it's not a joke.' But her expression had loosened a little. 'This isn't normal.'

'Ah, what *is* normal?' I'd said, throwing out a bad French accent and then held up both hands to surrender. 'Okay, okay. Let's see if it gets better in the next day or two.'

'If not, you go into the doctor.'

'I don't feel sick,' I said. 'But do you know what that's a symptom of? I just read on the internet ...'

'Mark ...'

Now, at my usual Saturday afternoon session with Dr. Laymon, I knew he didn't believe anything was ever *just* one thing. So what were my tongue and dick repressing?

Maxine was really going to town today, purring and slamming her whole body and tail against my leg, back and forth, back and forth. She looked up at me, and for a second I saw the strangest flash in her green cat eyes. Something base and vulgar. I started to laugh, but the cat wouldn't stop.

"What I think is potentially important isn't the phone call," Dr. Laymon said, "but how you *feel* about the call, and how you react."

I tried to push Maxine away, and she snapped her front claws, then came at me again.

"I guess," I said. "It doesn't really matter, though, does it? My sister died a long time ago."

Now he uncapped his pen and opened the notebook. That must have been a psychological signal flare, huh? Shrugging off my sister's death, because of a silly little thing like time.

"All of these things happened years and years ago," Dr. Laymon said. "But I think what we're seeing now is another opportunity to face them and move on. Trauma doesn't just happen once. It's a process. We've talked about this before."

We had, many times.

"We can understand all the fantasies and walls you have created to moderate this trauma," he said, "and make peace with it. What I'm saying is: think back to some of our first conversations, a year and a half ago or so. You told me stories that you *knew* weren't true, about an evil bird man ..."

The chicken man. Why couldn't anybody remember that?

"... and an adult nightclub, the one that had burned down years earlier, and all other manner of things. A disappearing door, an out of body experience—do you remember all that? When we first met, you told me you knew it never happened. You knew how it sounded, but you also had no trouble talking about it, *because* it wasn't true. You did have trouble talking about your sister and your father. Those are real sources of trauma, those are the real scars—as real as the cut on your hand. And now you can discuss your sister and maybe even your dad, *without* bringing up the bird man."

"Chicken man," I said.

He frowned. "I'm sorry?"

I sighed. *Get it right, Dr. Laymon. Take better notes, man.*

"He's called 'the chicken man,' not the bird man. I think I understand. Normally, if someone had called pretending to be Abby, you're saying I would have preferred to talk about the imaginary things, rather than telling Caitlyn about my dead sister."

He brightened, like I was a student who had found the answer. He'd given me that look before, when I said what he wanted.

"But you didn't," he said.

"But I didn't. So that's progress?"

"I think so," he said. "Don't you? But the trauma is still there, and it's a real wound. Your body may be acting out. Losing your taste for everything except alcohol is nothing I've heard of before. It sounds like a *nudge*."

A nudge back to the bottle, he meant. My body was trying to get me to fuck up my liver again, was that it? By shutting off everything else, so I would only care about whiskey.

Maxine finally settled down and curled up on my right foot, wrapping her body around it, eyes closed, as if I had moved in and were now her new permanent pillow.

"It's dangerous," Dr. Laymon was saying. Alcohol and so forth—he launched into a familiar lecture about how I needed to watch out for old patterns of behavior. Self medication with alcohol was a short-term solution with long-term, potentially catastrophic consequences—*that* lecture. But *someone* called Caitlyn claiming to be my sister, who knew about the chicken man. Even if he wasn't real, someone knew the story. What if my dead sister were alive? I knew she wasn't. But *what if?*

Wasn't that what Don had said years ago? We never talked about that night, about any of it. Once, I'd tried to bring it up: *what happened with the chicken man.* Except it never happened. And as soon as I started talking, he went out the front door. "Harass someone else," he'd said. Don could talk. He stammered and slurred words sometimes, but the tongue they had transplanted in 2005 mostly worked. Except to talk about that. Nobody discussed it. Not Don or Mom, not even crazy Grandma Elizabeth or Sister Maria Theresa on the two times I had visited her since. *Let it lie,* she had told me. So eventually I did. The chicken man hadn't shown Don anything to do with Abby. How did I know? Because the chicken man wasn't real. Neither were the buckets. Simple as that.

But the Dudweiler thing bothered me. Dr. Laymon was telling me to exercise more, and I nodded, said that my moods had improved—they *had,* until this week—but really I was thinking about the Dunder Mifflin-place, Dudweiler. Of course, I had some idea what it was. In high school, I became an amateur scholar on the city and region. Turns out, Dudweiler was sort of a suburb of a town called Saarbrüken, both in a part of Europe called Saar, wedged in-between France and Germany. It was a borderland that had gone back and forth between the two countries for centuries—since before they *were* countries.

Dudweiler was north of Saarbrüken, and here's what really caught my attention: since 1668, there had been a coal fire burning underground there, like in Kentucky. At the same time that everyone in the region was leaving or dying, something caught fire underground and wouldn't go out. Supposedly, it was still burning today, and tourists wandered off into the woods to find vents of steam and gas rising from the rocks.

Later, the whole area went back to Germany in 1935. It was one of the first big Nazi coups. Apparently, they took a vote and overwhelmingly chose to do that at the same time my grandparents got married. Very soon after, things got ugly. Like most of Germany, people in these towns turned on the Jews and anybody else targeted by the Nazis. They were brutalized, killed, or worse. But there was something else, too. In the books, I found a story from Dudweiler in the late 1930s about families that were rounded up by the SS and marched so they could be mocked by the townspeople. They were taken to the center of town and forced to dig their own graves, and then—then the story ended. Somehow every historian seemed to get distracted at this point, returning to the larger war and atrocities. They dug their graves, Several hundred people, and there was a new church on that site now. But no one ever said how they died.

It always bothered me, though, like that damn scar on my left hand. Maybe because of the whiskey lamp. It was connected. The 'skinny lamp' was a sacrilegious, hateful name for it. And senior year of high school, I had stormed into the living room after an argument with Mom—I'd been skipping school, and the assistant principal warned that I might not graduate—and I had gone to grab the lamp. I had wanted to smash it or burn it, I don't know what. It wasn't there.

The windowsill was empty. Mom didn't know where it had gone, and Don was already living in Old Louisville, near downtown. No one else could have taken it. At the time, I was sure Mom was lying. But she swore not to know where it went. Just *poof*, gone. A fixture of our lives, vanished. Dad's Goddamn Nazi talisman, just as well. At least we weren't lighting the way for a Gestapo Paul Revere every night. Good. I never wanted to see it again.

"I know none of that was real," I said. "I know Abby is gone, and so is my dad, and the trauma of seeing my older brother injured caused me to block it out and create ... *other explanations*. But how did she know about Dudweiler?"

His pen was poised, but he still hadn't written anything down. I guessed this was a boring session, no note-worthy breakthroughs. We'd gone over Dudweiler before.

Dr. Laymon hesitated. "Let's remember your girlfriend only said the name reminded her of a 'D' name in a TV show. So, isn't it also possible that *you* believe the caller said Dudweiler?"

Right.

"And if that's the case," he said, "the real issue is *why* do you want it to be from Dudweiler."

I stiffened at the word 'want.' *That's the last Goddamn thing I want, Herr Doctor.*

"Is it possible some part of you still believes in the fantasy, because it is connected to a place where real atrocities took place? Because you've never been there."

Way off. Dudweiler and my Nazi grandfather weren't a fantastical mystery I wanted to unravel. They were baggage, a part of me I wish I'd never discovered, like a hereditary disease.

"I don't want to go to Germany."

"I'm not saying you should," he said. "What I'm suggesting is to think about whether this place is acting as some kind of weight that's preventing you from letting go of the fantasy."

So I was hung up on Dudweiler as a way to *not* let go of the chicken man? And because some random person had said 'Dunder Mifflin' on the phone to Caitlyn, my lizard brain was trying to lump that in with all the things I knew now weren't real? It definitely made a kind of sense.

He started to say more, and I heard music from a passing car out-side, turned way too loud. A woman's high voice, and a guitar:

"I toasted all the ladies there,
"And gave my love to Barbara Allen!"

Panic spiked up my back in a wave of adrenaline that made me hunch forward, sweating. My stomach spasmed, started to rise—I covered my mouth. *Get out of here.* Maxine was still asleep, and when I moved my foot to stand, she rolled onto her side like a lump, eyes closed.

"I'm sorry. I have to go," I said. "Forgot something."

I was going to vomit, felt my belly clenching again, sweat on my scalp and armpits.

"Mark, are you all right?"

The song faded outside, but when I went to the door, my hand quivered on the doorknob. *Just get out. Go home.*

"Maxine, your best friend is leaving," Dr. Laymon said to the cat. "Do you want to get up and say goodbye?"

I looked back. The cat still wasn't moving. When Dr. Laymon knelt to shake her a little, she stayed that way, like a stuffed animal.

I squeezed the doorknob. *Go.*

I asked, "Is everything all right?"

He sat on the floor next to her.

"This is the damnedest thing." He pressed on the cat's chest and neck again. "I'll see you next week, Mark."

I stepped out. The cat was dead, wasn't she? Maxine had died on my shoe in the middle of our conversation about Dudweiler and how I needed to be more disciplined about separating what was real from the imaginary. How fucked was that?

I got out of there and caught my breath on the sidewalk outside. *Jesus Christ, calm down. Get it the fuck together.* This block was all big stone and brick apartment buildings, with health food stores and restaurants at the corner, over on Broadway. Tourists took videos with their phones and a pair of nannies pushed strollers passed me. Okay, I was fine. But standing here surrounded by people and the steady swell and noise of yellow taxis, cars, and loud delivery trucks didn't help.

"Hey, you okay?" Slowly, the voice registered: a well-dressed guy walking a yellow lab had stopped and looked genuinely concerned. He was Black, shaved head, maybe in his forties, with grayish stubble. His suit jacket, loose tie, and jeans reminded me of Dr. Laymon's practiced professional-casual act.

"Yeah, I'm ..." *I'm fine.* But the words caught, my chest seizing up, and I slipped, scraping my elbow on the wall, as I slumped to sit on the pavement.

"You're not," the man said. He came closer, already had his phone out. His dog sniffed my shoe, where Maxine had just died. No, not died. The cat was fine, stop it. "Who can I call?" he asked. "Hey? Buddy, look at me." I did, and he gestured to his phone. "Want the police or an ambulance?"

I shook my head. "Just need a second."

He noticed the building I'd just exited. "Guess this is a one-star review?" When I frowned, he smiled, nodding to the door. "Are you a patient at the psychiatrist office in there? No judgment, I'm just trying to disarm you with a joke, while we wait for the paramedics."

"Did you call ..?"

"No." Still smiling, he offered me a hand. I took it, let him pull me back up. Legs numb, but I could stand, and the curl in my chest loosened. This was helping. It was easier to breathe. "Don't worry," he said. "I used to get them about once a month."

"Get what?"

"Panic attacks. That's why I stopped. All part of living in this damn city, right? You want to walk for a minute, watch me clean up dog shit?"

No. Who was this guy? I'd never been helped by a stranger here. But for some reason, I followed him to the end of the block, closer to Central Park, and soon we tracked the stone wall toward a main entrance. Birds clacked and thrummed overhead. I was fine.

"I'm Robert, by the way." He said it without offering a hand, maybe because hauling me up off the sidewalk already checked that box.

"Mark," I said.

"Not a psycho, just a concerned citizen," he said. "What triggered you?"

I slowed but didn't stop. "I don't know." *That fucking song.*

"With me, it was money. Always money. I'd feel it start when I got to my mail slot or even when I opened my email. Final notice. Credit warning. You name it, all of it set me off. That's the past, though."

"It was a song."

We neared the park entrance. Children squealed and shouted on an elaborate playground just inside. The entry path ran back, splitting through a wide network of trees, low hills, and exposed rock.

"A *song?*" he said, as if he didn't know what the word meant.

This guy, Robert, this stranger, wanted to know. And I could tell him—in the way Dr. Laymon wouldn't tolerate, because Robert was blind to the whole thing.

"I heard it as a kid," I said. "I didn't grow up in New York ..."

"Me neither." Robert paused at the park entrance, gave his dog a look. "Bowie, what are we thinking?" Then, to me, "You got someplace to be? I'm trying to avoid grading papers and looking at carpet samples. That's why I'm out here."

The sharp edge of tension had dulled under my ribs and in the loops of my guts, waiting to snap back, if I started off on my own. No, I was fine. This helped.

"I'm good," I said. "So I imagined a bunch of things when I was growing up in Kentucky," I told him. We entered the park, letting Bowie guide us by the playground, into a long row of benches with street musicians on drums at the far end.

"Does that set you off?" he asked, pointing at the drums.

"No, it's a specific song called Barbary or Barbara Allen. Old folk song. It's not important."

"Sounds like it might be, but I've never heard of it. My focus is all long before that. You know people say something is 'ancient history'? That's me." Robert explained in stops and starts, as if embarrassed by the title, that yes, he was a tenured professor of Ancient Rome at Columbia. "And we don't know what *anybody* sounded like singing *anything* 2,000 years ago. Or much of anything, really. Anybody who tells you different is a liar. Why that song, though? If I can ask." He laughed, shaking is head, as if he'd just surprised himself. "Shit, I just did anyway, didn't I? Ask."

"When I was a kid, my sister and my dad—they both died. And I made up a bunch of things, fake memories—coping mechanisms—to deal with that. One was this guy ..." *Don't talk about him. Don't tell a stranger. What are you doing?* But this conversation made it easier to breathe. We clicked like old buddies, as if this were routine. "Anyway." I stopped, and Robert gave his dog, Bowie, more leash, so he could wander off to sniff a nearby tree. "Thanks for stopping. I don't know what happened to me back there ..."

"I do. Panic attack. An abrupt surge of intense fear or discomfort. Technically, I think they use 'panic disorder' to describe the underlying clinical state. What's your deal, Mark? You all right?"

Nevermind the repressed buzzing in my skull or shakiness in my arms and legs. The call from Dudweiler, the song, and the dead cat—it felt like the air spotting as the pressure dropped. Temperature shifting. Something had changed, something right in front of my face that I should recognize. In just the last 48 hours. What?

"Thanks, I'm okay," I said. "Got to get back."

"You don't know a reliable window guy, do you? Strange to ask, I know. But I'm desperate, man. Asking everybody I see. My wife bought—I should say *we*, but really it was all her, she works on Wall Street—a place in Harlem that's a total money pit. Needs new floors, kitchen, bathroom, you name it ..."

I nodded, as he went on, laughing and open, totally trusting of this loopy mental patient he'd stumbled across. That was *why* he opened up, wasn't it? Clearly, I needed too much help to be a threat. Or he really was a psycho. This city had trained me not to meet people, but here I was, meeting someone new.

"... and it's all about the *energy savings*," Robert said, laughing. Bowie came back to watch us, tail wagging. "Okay, good boy. Yeah, yeah, we're moving."

If I let him go, I would never see Robert again. But I didn't have many friends, just Susan—and Caitlyn and Don, but counting my girlfriend and brother felt like cheating, right? Since moving to the city, I had been a little isolated, hadn't I? Or just too busy, with site job after job, and keeping up with plans with Caitlyn's friends.

"You know," I told Robert, "when I'm not collapsing in the street, I'm actually a halfway decent electrician."

He brightened and clapped his hands. "I knew it! Excellent, man. We don't have anybody looking at the fuse box yet, and you know people for the other systems?"

Maybe I didn't have many friends, but yes, I knew people. After swapping contacts on our phones, Robert made me promise to stop by early next week—"Counting on you, Mark!"—and I finally looped back out of the park, then a couple more blocks to *Zabars* and the train toward Penn Station.

Barbary Allen *was* just a song. Sitting on the rattling train with plastic bags of groceries, the memory of hearing it felt softer. Because what if I *hadn't* heard it outside Dr. Laymon's office? What if I just latched onto another tune that was vaguely similar. Had to be. I'd looked it up back in high school, of course. 'Barbara Allen': a song so old nobody knew who wrote it or where it came from. People from Scotland and England brought it with them to Virginia in the 1600s, and eventually, it became popular in lots of places, like Kentucky. Really, though, it was just a mean old foreign ballad about a dying boy and the girl who watches him waste away. Period. Maybe there was more to it, but I stopped studying it one night, when the singer on an old recording playing on my desktop computer crooned too high, almost like an animal yelp. Since then, I'd decided it wasn't a song that could be understood. It was like birdsong, not human, as if people had learned it in the wild and never quite got it right. Of course that was nuts, but I never listened to it again. I paid more attention to birds, though.

That night, it rained, so we ordered Chinese food and watched a movie—*tried* to watch. My right leg was jittering again. My pulse was still on edge, not fast, just *poised*, as if my heart wanted to be ready for a starter gun to go off at any minute. Talking with Robert had helped, but it hadn't smudged out the anxiety, only dialed it down to a background hum. I couldn't make myself eat. Food had no taste, and my stomach still ached from earlier.

"Talk to me," Caitlyn said. "What happened today?"

So I told her: about the cat, how I had been thinking 'Dunder Mifflin' meant Dudweiler, Dr. Laymon's theory on that, and then—then I almost told her about the song but stopped myself. Of everything, that was the least worrisome part, right? That was just an old folk song, probably recorded by a hundred different musicians. No need to bring it up, because there was nothing there. Except even thinking about it set off my pulse, like the fucking music was plugged into my spine. *So don't.*

"I met a guy who might have a job up in Harlem," I said. "Randomly on the street."

"That's great," Caitlyn said, but she still looked worried. "But what aren't you telling me?"

"I have this stupid feeling," I said. "It's probably the weather. Did you ever have tornadoes in Canada?"

She was sprawled on the couch beside me, both of us under a blanket with a tapestry tiger decorating it. "You mean like in the Wizard of Oz? Sometimes, not so much in Toronto. There were some bad ones in Manitoba."

"They happened in Kentucky all the time. We used to have to do tornado drills at school. And one time, I actually saw a funnel cloud forming. I was at home on the front porch, waiting for my brother's bus to drop him off—this was after he switched to the special needs school, because of his thing." *His missing tongue and thumbs 'thing.' That 'thing.'* "My mom wasn't home yet either, and the sky wasn't even that dark, sort of gray. But then I remember watching it change. The clouds went from gray to a puke green to purple." *Like bruised skin. Or a scar.* "And not that far away, I saw a little upside-down pyramid of clouds forming above the houses and the trees on our street."

Caitlyn shifted closer to me under the covers.

"Creepy," she said.

"Every bone in my body told me to get inside. Total instinct, like a jolt in my blood from the clouds. I don't know how to describe it."

Just like the chicken man. Except tornadoes are real. He isn't.

"We're okay now," Caitlyn said. "It's just a little storm."

"Yeah." Except it wasn't the rain. The air was still changing. Not a funnel cloud, though, something else. My palms were slick and trembling, when I wasn't holding my water glass or squeezing my fingers into fists. I looked across the main room of our one-bedroom apartment: from the living room area into the kitchen, where a big bottle of Bulleit bourbon was collecting dust way back on top of the stainless-steel refrigerator. It was almost full. The apartment walls were packed with bookshelves—mostly Caitlyn's law books and skinny DVDs and Blu-Ray cases—and framed posters. A Yale drama poster cluttered with signatures from her senior class, a black-and-white photo of Muhammed Ali standing over Sonny Liston with the words 'Get Up' in big white script overhead, and a few pieces of knock-off Ikea art. I'd had the Ali poster since high school. It was supposed to be motivational, but now I barely noticed it. The rest was Caitlyn's.

"Maybe you need to take your mind off it? We're here now, Mark." She shifted closer to me. "Should we keep watching the movie or ..."

The power went out. In a sudden electronic snap, the lights and TV, everything went off, and we were sitting in darkness with the sound of the rain. My heartbeat was loud in both ears. *It's nothing. Calm the fuck down.*

"The decision has been made." She climbed on top of me.

We kissed. I held her waist as she slid under the covers, her legs straddling my waist in pajama pants, chest pressed firm against me through her T-shirt. Her body started to rock a little as our tongues touched, and I felt up her side and breasts and then down to her lower back. She pulled back and took off her shirt, her bare breasts indistinct and blurry in the darkness. But the tightness in my chest and belly didn't go away.

"Touch me," she whispered and took my hand, moving it to her stomach and down, under her pajama pants, through a patch of hair and to soft, open flesh that was already eager and wet. Caitlyn kissed me again, harder, as I slid my fingers inside.

I didn't feel anything. I should have, always did. Until this week. Now, my cock was shriveled and limp. This wasn't because we'd had sex too recently or been drinking. My body just didn't react. In another moment, I knew she would want it. She already did, as I touched and kissed her.

Jesus, what's wrong with me? Why is this happening?

From the other side of the room, someone said, "Because you taste dirt."

In one motion, I flipped Caitlyn off me and was up, standing between her and whoever was in here. "Who's there?"

"What the fuck, Mark?" Caitlyn asked.

All the tension in my body focused in my fists and legs. Someone was there.

"I heard someone. *Who's there?*" We had candles in the bathroom, at least one flashlight in the kitchen, maybe two, but I couldn't leave Caitlyn. Someone was in our apartment. Where?

"You *heard* someone?" she asked.

Slowly, I backed across the room into the kitchen and around the island counter to a drawer near the stove. Feeling around in the blackness I found it: a heavy plastic tube.

"Mark, you're scaring me."

I clicked on the flashlight, and the sudden white-light glow made Caitlyn flinch, covering herself with the blanket on the couch. Nothing out of place.

"What are you doing?" she asked.

"I'm sorry," I said. "Look, I heard something. Someone in here."

I went back over to her, shining the light around the corners of the room, then checked the bedroom, our closet, and back through the kitchen to the bathroom. Nothing. Not a Goddamn thing.

"You probably heard someone in another apartment or outside," she said.

She was right. I came back over and stood beside the couch, but I didn't sit. I was losing it.

No, I heard someone. Not from another apartment, from in here.

In the flashlight beam, Caitlyn's bare shoulders looked bleached, like pale stone. Her eyes pinched into squints. She was still beautiful, though. *Sort this out somehow.* If I sat, tried to relax, all the nervous momentum would slink back into me. As long as I stayed focused, I could do this. But my fucking hands were shaking again.

"Do you want a drink?" I asked.

"What?"

"I'm going to get a drink." I glanced back at the bourbon bottle. "Do you want something?"

"Mark, don't use it to self-medicate ..." Caitlyn stopped herself. "It's okay. I'm going to take a bath."

"Sorry," I said. "I don't know why I'm so wound up."

Yes, you do. Of course you do.

Caitlyn patted the couch beside her. "Sit down, Mark."

I did.

"You were jumpy before, and I thought I might be able to help." She took my hand and eased the flashlight out of it. "Just turn this off for a second."

She clicked it, and the room was black again, darker even.

Someone stood in the room. By the window, a slender shadow with a bony outline and long hair, motionless.

My whole body clenched up, and Caitlyn held onto me, her face against my chest. The shadow walked closer, ten feet from the couch, five feet, then stopped. It was still too dark. No sound. I heard my breathing and the dripping of the rain. *I just looked over there with the flashlight, and the room was empty.*

"Jesus, your heart," Caitlyn said. "Are you okay? Mark?"

"Look," I said.

Caitlyn sat up and turned to see.

"Do you believe in Hell and Paradise?" the shadow asked.

It was a woman.

This was real. Someone broke into our apartment. *Wait. I know that voice. Who is it?*

"Whatever we tell ourselves, our *bones* know what they believe, don't they?" the shadow woman said. "Our bodies believe."

Caitlyn was gone. I was alone on the couch, the shadow woman in the same place. The room was spinning a little. Even in the dark, I could feel the tug at the edges of my vision when I turned my head. My arms were heavy, my hands totally still, and I felt a hot, reassuring burning in my stomach. Whiskey. I smelled sharp whiskey on my breath.

"When we die, the blood stops flowing to our brain," the shadow woman said, "but our brain cells try to stay alive as long as they can. Our brains: *us.* You and me. We try to stay alive as long as we can."

She stepped closer, and as she reached toward me, the voice registered: *Grandma Elizabeth*. She sounded different—more contemplative, as if she were in a dream or high, but it was her. The alcohol buzz kept me calm. She touched my cheek with fingers that were cold and damp, a little rough. I heard dripping, not from outside—here, on the hardwood, where she stood.

"As we get older, time goes by faster," she said. "And then, when we die."

I took her hand, but it wasn't skin. Her fingers were stalks of sticky flesh. But I didn't let go, and she pulled my hand to her face. I touched raw exposed muscle, and she pressed sunken teeth to kiss my hand.

"When we die," she said, "our brain makes what our bones believe real to keep us from disappearing. The experience of brain death can last an eternity."

She said something in German, then lowered my hand again. It brushed past her exposed ribcage and the wet tissue of her stomach and side. A body without skin, that was what she was. Where was the rest of her?

"Hell is real, and he is coming. You taste dirt, because you are marked. The only way ..." More German, then: "...light the lamp for the sunken lady." She let go of my hand and shuddered. "I'm frightened. You told me you would be here with me, but you aren't. I don't want to go with them. Don't let me go."

She reached for me, and I got up, bumping into a side table and something fell, smashing on the floor.

"Mark?"

Grandma Elizabeth was gone.

Caitlyn stood in our bedroom doorway, a lit tea candle in one hand. "Are you still up?"

She came over. There was a broken glass and liquid all over the floor.

"What happened?"

My vision was still swimming, paddling around me. *Like duck paddling.* I smiled, remembered taking our dog Calvin to Fox Lake in Illinois, when we'd gone hiking the year before the Kentucky move. He had chased the ducks, swimming in circles after them, and Don and I laughed, because the birds were so much faster than him. Anytime he got too close, they flew and settled again a little farther away on the lake, with Calvin steaming after them, grinning, as if it were a game invented just for him. *Duck paddling,* we called it. I felt emotion I'd told myself was done years ago, a twinge of tingly pain like a phantom limb. *Stop thinking about that.*

I'm drunk. How?

"Don't know what happened," I said.

I tasted dirt because I was—what did Caitlyn say about the phone call? I had to find my sister, 'because I was Mark.' That was what she told me, but that wasn't what the person pretending to be Abby said, was it?

"What happened is I took a bath," she said, "and then we went to bed. But you ... got up, apparently? Mark, do you really not remember coming out here? How much did you drink?"

Because I was *marked.* Like Don was. Except that made no sense. Why? What did I do?

The bourbon bottle was open on the kitchen counter, and she was right. I stank of whiskey. I went to put it away and find a towel to clean up the glass. My left hand pinched a little when I lifted the bottle. I must have cut it. Again.

"There was a person here," I said. "My grandmother, except it wasn't her. Maybe I was dreaming, I don't ..."

Caitlyn held up a hand to cut me off.

"Not now," she said. "It's the middle of the night. I don't want to hear about a drunken dream about your grandmother right now."

She wanted me to come back to the bedroom with her, but the room wouldn't hold still. It kept lurching from side to side. My stomach had an unsettled, full feeling. Good old-fashioned alcohol poisoning. Fifty percent chance I would have to run to the bathroom any second or risk vomiting all over the floor. How did this happen?

"I can't go to bed yet," I said. "Need to drink some water. But I don't know if it was a dream."

Caitlyn's cheeks flushed. "I'm sorry, Mark. I'm trying to be patient. You're saying you *don't know* if dreaming about your grandmother, who lives in a nursing home in Chicago, was real or not?"

"She was here," I said. "It's why I dropped the glass."

"Or, you dropped the glass, because you're drunk. We have brunch with Sal and Patty tomorrow, in just a few hours from now."

"You're right." Even those two words slopped together into a single noise. "I'm sorry. The stress ... I must have ..."

"Please, just let's go to sleep." She went to get two pillows and a spare, musty blanket from the closet, tossed it all on the couch. "Goodnight, Mark."

I went to sit on the closed toilet in the bathroom to wait out the nausea. What did Grandma Elizabeth say? The memory was foggy and would probably only rupture into muddier fragments as time passed. Even if it was dream nonsense, what did she say? I was marked, I had to light the lamp, our brains stretched out our experience of death to make it last forever and that was what the afterlife was.

Hell is real, and he is coming.

Cheery thoughts like that. This followed what happened with Dr. Laymon's cat, Maxine, and hearing the song outside. Of course it did.

I was inventing things again, like a child seeing patterns and animals in the sky. Regressing.

After a long Time, I went to toss on the couch and was woken by a hand shaking my shoulder. Caitlyn was still in her rumpled sleeping t-shirt and shorts. She pursed her lips, with wide, frightened eyes. She didn't look like she'd been crying but was pale, as if she were about to say something she knew I didn't want to hear. Last night wasn't going away. No easy fix. She held her dark phone in one hand.

"Shit," I said.

And she threw herself onto me, her arms around me tight, her head against my shoulder.

"Mark, I'm so sorry," she said.

"What ..?"

"Your grandmother," she said, "she just died."

CHAPTER THIRTEEN

That week, things got worse—my relationship with Caitlyn set to a slow boil. It took three, 18-hour shifts to finish a new Prospect Park job with Susan, but what choice did I have, with the funeral on Saturday? "You've got to take care of yourself," Susan told me, as we passed midweek. The site apartment still needed paint, but all the guts were working behind the fresh-plastered walls. An electrical nervous system and circulatory plumbing. "You look bad, Mark. I say that with nothing but love. You two want to do dinner tomorrow night, before you fly out?"

"Can't," I told Susan. "I've got a new job I'm going to try to rope you into, up in Harlem."

She made her usual grumbly noise, still arranging wrenches and towels in a wheelie bag in the middle of the floor. My gear was mostly packed. "Harlem is *far*, man. Is it worth it?"

"I'll let you know."

"Take care of Caitlyn. I'm serious."

"I will." But I didn't—couldn't. By the time I got home, Caitlyn was asleep. That week, we'd traded bleary-eyed words that meant nothing, before my commute on Friday across the city to meet Robert.

"And there he is!" This time, he shook my hand on the front steps of a brownstone that would have looked stupid expensive, except for the boarded-up, glass-less windows and posted warning signs. "Like I said, Mark: a work in progress."

Inside, he showed me a print-out of his wife's master plan, as we walked through open walls and half-finished floors. Susan called these 'movie sets.' Houses that weren't functional except as the 'idea of a house.'

"So what do you think?" Robert asked at last, when we returned to the entry hall.

"It's a nice place. It ..."

He burst into laughter, clapped me on the back. "You are the worst fucking liar, man. I love it. It's a wash. Money-money-*money* pit. But we're going to make it work. Can you help me out?"

I could, and after we talked through the details, I got to work, testing old wires and outlets. That night, Robert insisted I share a pizza with him on the bare floor of the kitchen.

"Do you think I'm crazy?" he asked. "No—don't answer that. But I am over-compensating at least?"

"For what?" Tasteless pepperoni and cheese turned my tongue, too hot. I drank a mouthful of Coke that felt like fizzy water. Nothing. I hadn't gone to the doctor. I needed to, but the funeral and work—everything was scrambled now, moving faster.

A mechanical *pop* shook the floorboards, and Robert sprang up, leading me back to the basement stairs. "Shit," he said. "What did you break, Mark?"

Before I could point out that I hadn't worked on the fuses yet, barely touched the basement, we clomped midway down the stairs. A chemical smell locked my legs. My fist closed on the railing.

The red door opened to a pair of blue eyes. A woman with a shaved head, duct tape over her mouth, was chained by the neck to the opposite wall. Scabs along her scalp and neck, and below that, her pale, bruised skin shivered, flexing against bulging ribs and a distended stomach. Naked. A naked chest, small breasts, and groin ... but her limbs.

Eyes closed, stomach acid frothed up the back of my throat. I heaved, kept it down with one hand. That bitter, antiseptic smell was the same: a blended bite of bleach and natural gas.

Inside the red door, the woman's arms and legs were cut off into black-bandaged stumps, tied with plastic tourniquets. Her eyes went wide when she saw me, and she thrashed against the chain. I heard scraping. Chains clinked overhead.

"Mark?"

One hand to my mouth, I forced a slow breath of air in, too shallow. Another one, and I opened my eyes, swatted away tears. Those blue, desperate eyes were still there when I blinked.

Robert looked up at me from the bottom of the stairs in his ordinary, unfinished basement. No red door. No one mutilated and chained to the wall, just an empty space for the washer-dryer hookup and an old boxy boiler near the water heater by the antique fuse box.

"It was the heater," he said. "Guy who came to clean it out yesterday didn't tighten the filter all the way." He said it automatically, staring at me. "Should be set now."

The smell dissipated, almost gone, when I took a deliberate, slow breath. "Okay. No problem."

"What's up?"

I shook my head, blinking fast. I knew my bullshit smile probably looked like a wound. A dog pretending not to be hurt. "Nothing."

"You had another one? Just now?" He didn't move.

If I was going to collapse into a sweaty ball every time the boiler burped, could he trust me on this job? The money was important. With travel and the holidays coming up, I could last maybe an extra week without a job, but Susan didn't have anything until mid-December. If Robert kicked me out, it would be cutting it close for my half of next month's rent. Pushing Caitlyn on our finances was the worst idea right now. Plus, I liked Robert. *Don't fuck this up.*

"Do you really want me to ..?" I said, and he waited, arms crossed. "A panic attack or whatever it is, my psycho drama bullshit ..."

"You like that word, huh?" He grinned. "It's not 'bullshit,' man. Don't hide behind that, especially not when you almost puked on your first day on the job." And before I could apologize, "I'm fucking joking. Come on now, let's hear it. What actually happened just now?"

"There was a smell."

"Yeah, my lame-ass boiler." He sighed. "Scent is wired right into memory, you know. It's not conscious. So I'm guessing you had an association with it?"

"I think so." *Don't talk about it. Walk out. Leave this place, the job isn't that important.* Hand tight on the rail again, I felt my pulse quicken, sweat along my hairline, but I kept going. I'd only told Dr. Laymon, and he'd heard the whole story as a stack of symbols to be un-riddled, not as something that actually happened when I was twelve years old. *You don't know Robert at all. Don't tell him.* But I said, "When I was a kid in Kentucky, my dad was murdered—no, let me finish. And the same time it happened, someone hurt my older brother. I was there, when it happened. This place, a strip club, I think, in Louisville. The thing is, I remember going in. I remember people yelling at me, hurting me, even, but a guy took me inside. To a red door in the basement ...”

Robert glanced around, no longer smiling. The water heater tocked and clicked.

“But that’s it,” I said. *Blue eyes. Chains. Her arms and legs gone below the elbows and knees.* “I don’t remember anything after that.”

“After the red door,” he said.

“The next thing, I was outside again, with my brother ...” *And five plastic buckets. Five full plastic buckets that a policewoman tried to open.*

Robert let out an uneasy breath, gestured back upstairs, and we returned to the kitchen pizza box. My stomach still knotted, acid stinging my throat. I smelled repressed vomit in my nostrils. *Get out of here. Never speak or think about this again.*

“That’s shit to carry,” Robert said, sitting against the unfinished cabinets again. “Your therapist never figured it out?”

“No.” Dr. Laymon listened but didn’t believe it. We talked through it—all the events back then—like literary scholars, decoding a hand-me-down fable. ‘The Tale of the Cadillac Club.’

And the chicken man.

“And just now?” Robert asked.

“A smell reminded me of that red door.”

“But not what you saw inside?”

Yes. I shook my head.

“What about the song the other day?” he asked. “It was playing in the strip club?” I stiffened, hadn’t touched the pizza again, and he held up a half-eaten slice in apology. “Don’t mean to keep pushing you, Mark. We don’t have to get into it any more.”

So we didn't. Gradually, our conversation settled into a rhythm about each other: how I'd trained to be an electrician because I liked learning how things worked—the circuitry behind the magic—and maybe, possibly, because I couldn't atop arguing with my professors at the University of Kentucky that first semester. Until I finally said, 'Fuck it.'

"Braver man than me," Robert said, laughing and told me how he'd dreamed of a 'life of the mind' and still felt a spark when ides clicked for students. "Even if I've given that lecture fifty times, it's new to them. Sometimes they see things I don't. That fresh perspective keeps me going."

"Do you think it's real?" I asked, before I'd realized I was forming the words. Like my mouth rushed the question, before my mind could clamp down. "What I told you, about the strip club and blank memory—that place."

"Why wouldn't it be?"

"After ..." *What am I doing? Opening up to him?* I'd dodged this, even with Caitlyn, for years. Just so I could share over a fucking pepperoni pizza? "They told me it wasn't," I said. "Because the club burned down. It went up in a famous fire in the 1970s."

He squinted at me, as if waiting for the catch. "So?" Robert said at last.

"So of course I couldn't have gone inside. The wall was black, the entrance didn't open. None of it was there."

He shrugged. "Okay, but so what? I don't know what you believe. We only just met, right? But you seem like somebody who doesn't want to trust things he can't prove—like with your circuits. Mark, let me tell you something about studying the ancient past: it's all faith. Sure, we have a few things, books and artifacts, that survived, but that's maybe one percent of what existed back then at any given time. I was raised with Jesus, and believe me, when I told my mother I was going to study Rome—the people who crucified him—she had a few things to say. But knowing there's a reality behind it doesn't mean there isn't room for a miracle or two at the same time. Do you understand what I'm saying?"

How was it possible to trust wires and electrical signals—and magic? It wasn't.

"It is, though," Robert said. "Miracles happen everyday, Mark. Whether we like it or not." He finished his slice and wiped grease from his fingers onto a paper towel. "But that also means—as I was raised—you've got to leave room for the other side, too."

"The other side," I repeated.

"Well, yeah. You're really not going for another slice?" He knocked back the pizza lid to cradle a slice dripping with cheese. "If there's a home team playing, there's probably a visiting team in the field to root against, isn't there?"

"You don't really believe in angels and demons and things, do you?"

Again, he smiled, blowing on his pizza. "Depends what you mean by that, I guess. Two thousand years ago, everybody *knew* gods and supernatural beings were alive, like you and me—more so, really—and active in the world. They knew it. Not faith, this was knowledge, Mark. They saw it around them, created what we would think of as contracts with deities, even. Gods lived and breathed in the world. I don't think I'm smarter than they were, and every other day, somebody in the Physics or Astronomy department confides in me that 'Oh God, I hope they don't find out what a massive fraud our science is.' We don't have a unified theory. Grad students in lab coats are proving the world doesn't work the way we think it does. Maybe doesn't exist at all. So maybe the red door in a ghost building really does and doesn't open, based on what you believe."

'Hell is real,' Grandma Elizabeth said. She stood in my living room moments after she died hundreds of miles away. And now I needed to bury her.

Chapter Fourteen

That week with Caitlyn, things didn't get better. When she pressed me to talk, I deflected and drank. Not like with Robert. Our conversation in Harlem helped me sleep, but it felt disconnected from all the time and importance I'd placed on 'real life.' Telling Caitlyn would make it real, prove that I was losing my mind—*had* lost my mind as a child and was still a wounded kid adulting. I didn't want her to pity me, which meant avoiding her.

Maybe stupid, but somehow my mind logicked the sequence into place: first, get through the week. Then, bury your grandmother. After that—only after that—level with Caitlyn. In my mind, it made sense, but by the time we landed at O'Hare airport and took a cab to the Schaumburg hotel for the funeral service, Caitlyn felt more like an uncomfortable old friend, rather than the woman I had loved for two years. We still hadn't had sex since before the anniversary dinner, and I didn't push it. My body still wasn't working. It was mid-November, and Thanksgiving in Kentucky was close. What if we didn't make it that long?

After checking into our hotel, I went down to the lobby, while she 'cleaned up.' It wasn't quite noon, and I found a coffee dispenser and pressed on the top to fill a Styrofoam cup. It was a suburban chain hotel, with faux everything: faux brick out front, faux marble floors and palm trees inside, probably faux coffee, too.

"You trying. To kill the planet?"

I turned, already smiling: Don. My older brother wore a black suit and gray tie that, together with the weight he'd put on and the white-gray in his beard, reminded me of Dad, even though Dad never had a beard after I was born. Maybe it was just the suit. Dad didn't wear suits to work, and when he did slip them on—for events or church—he always looked stiff, just like this.

"Is that your Dad costume?" I asked.

He gave me a hug. "Asshole. It's. Good you came in."

He still spoke with a halting catch, as if he were still trying to get control of the foreign body in his mouth. Like Don's tongue couldn't keep up with his thoughts. Whoever had it before him maybe had a drawl.

"Of course I'm here," I said. "Where's Mom?"

"Already at. The funeral parlor. Where's. Caitlyn?"

"Upstairs changing. It's not ... she's going to be here in a second, so I'll just say it—we're not doing well."

He got a cup and nudged me out of the way to fill it with coffee.

"What did you. Do?"

"Oh come on." I sipped and scalded my tongue. Shit, well at least my nerves still worked. Whatever was wrong with my tongue, it wasn't that. I led him over to sit on soft chairs stamped with the hotel logo near the front windows, facing the parking lot. It was grim and dark out there, with a fine mist of sleet coming down, creating discolored puddles on the concrete and muddy lawn. "Did you drive up?"

"Yes. You can both. Ride with me. But what happened? What's the deal with. Caitlyn?"

I had to bring it up, because he would notice in two seconds when he saw us together, and now that he asked, I realized I was desperate to talk about it. Except for Dr. Laymon, I hadn't told anyone. Usually, I opened up with Susan over the hours we spent together at a jobsite, but not about this. Because I couldn't imagine a version of that limp-dick, bland-taste-bud conversation that didn't roll into an awkward, pitying silence.

"Just a lot of little things coming to a head," I said. "I don't know what's going to happen."

"Is it because she's prettier than you?"

No trouble saying that. Maybe the whole speech-impediment thing was an act, a character he played to underscore his missing thumbs. Most people didn't notice Don's hands right away. He had gotten so good at hiding the stumps and over-compensating with his index and middle fingers. Years ago, they had tried transplants. Supposedly, it was much simpler than a tongue, but the thumbs hadn't worked and had to be removed again. In the late '90s, a tongue transplant had never even been done, and Don went seven years without speaking, all through high school and trade school, where I think it may have actually helped him to win over his mentors and coworkers.

As a kid, Don said what he thought, could be pushy or come off as arrogant, but when he'd had to learn to survive on gestures and impaired sign language, people looked out for him. By the time his new tongue finally arrived, eleven years ago, in 2005, he was already second-in-command at a car mechanic-body shop downtown, with clients across Kentucky, southern Indiana, and Ohio. People knew and trusted him with their vehicles, and when he suddenly could talk again, it was if Don had a superpower. It shocked people who hadn't known him before, in a good way.

"You should try not. To fuck this up," he said. "She's good for you."

"Yeah, I know that. Thanks. How's Mary Ann?"

Her name was actually Ann Marie, and he told me she was gone. Don was seeing someone else now, a U of L grad student who was starting a nonprofit about sustainable housing. Nice, except he was 32 and looked almost 42. Something was grinding him down, making him age. *Kentucky,* a part of me said, *living so close to what happened.* How did he do it? Every time I visited for the holidays, there was no dodging the Tyler Lane House—Mom still lived there—but I never drove past Holy Cross or the lot downtown where the Cadillac Club used to be or the library. Don lived right there.

"Do you remember what she did at Dad's funeral?" I asked. "When Grandma Elizabeth—"

"I remember." He got up and checked his watch. "We should. Go. Can you call her?"

The elevator dinged, and Caitlyn stepped out, looking sexy as hell in a dark gray dress, black coat, and silver-pearl necklace and earrings. She hugged Don, kissed him on the cheek, then took my right hand without looking at me, and we all went under umbrellas to Don's car. At the funeral home, I greeted relatives I didn't know and staff from Grandma Elizabeth's nursing home, then sat with Mom in front of the open casket. The funeral home smelled of flowers from a perimeter of arrangements around the walls, and cinnamon air freshener that Mom said Grandma Elizabeth would have loved. Mom didn't seem upset and had only talked to me about logistics since it happened. Soon, she told me, we were heading over to the church, then the cemetery. Grandma Elizabeth looked small and fake, like a papier-mâché version that hadn't been made quite big enough.

"They told me it was really peaceful," Mom said, "in her sleep. And she left some things for you. I can show you after the service. They gave me a box. It's in the car."

Mom's dark dress was wrinkled around the sides, like she'd forgotten to iron. That wasn't like her. The room was about half-full, mostly old people I'd never seen before, some with caretakers in green uniforms, probably visiting from Grandma Elizabeth's care facility. Don was somewhere at the back of the room visiting with other people. No sign of Caitlyn.

"I saw her," I said.

Mom frowned at the body. Mom's hair had gone solid white a few years ago, but she still dyed it brown. Now, though, it looked like it had been awhile. I could see bright gray roots coming in along her scalp.

"I don't understand," she said.

"I'm sure it was a dream or something, but she was in my living room. She spoke to me the same day she died."

"Mark, I love you." Mom patted my hand. Her fingers were dry, felt weak. "But I don't want to hear about that right now. Your grandmother needs out prayers, That's all."

Then she got up and left me alone.

Since when was Mom religious? But she was: at the church, Mom knelt and closed her eyes during the service, her head bowed, murmuring right along with the priest. The church was small and clean, with brass candles, and a big stylized wooden crucifix behind the altar that made Jesus look blocky and afraid. At one point during the sermon, I even saw tears in Mom's eyes. *Not for Grandma Elizabeth. She feels another kind of connection.* This was brand new. Mom believed. I tried to say something to Don, but Caitlyn shushed me. And after the burial, at the cemetery, as people went back to their cars, she told me that she had just gotten a call from her office, and they needed her back in New York. Caitlyn's law firm had a Chicago office, I knew. When people traveled, it wasn't unusual to drop in to use a spare desk.

"You should be here for your family," she said.

I'll fix this when I get back. Not now. Away from the cemetery, back in our apartment, I'll make this right. But I just nodded, said I understood.

Mom insisted on driving her to the airport.

After they and everyone else were gone, Don waited for me in his car to head back to the hotel. But I stood alone by the grave. The cemetery was sprawling, with hills of monuments blocking out the nearby neighborhoods. I sniffed in the cold, wet air and knelt beside Grandma Elizabeth's headstone. Her coffin was already at the bottom of the hole, a green plastic mat draped around the edges, like a rug so nobody would slip on the dirt. Water was beading and sluicing around her coffin lid. She had a simple stone right beside my grandfather:

Elizabeth Morris
1922—2016

And:

Karl Morris
1919—1980

Not many people came to the burial. Probably because the people she knew had to get back to their care facilities. And where was Sister Maria Theresa? She was old, too, maybe too frail to visit? I would have to ask about that. What if I couldn't solve my relationship with Caitlyn? What if she asked me to sit at our bare kitchen table, so she could ask if I was happy and say that we both knew this wasn't working, didn't we? It would sound sensible, calm. The end of our relationship, like an animal being put down. That was coming next. As long as I stood here in the freezing drizzle and muddy grass, her leaving me wasn't real yet. Maybe I could just stand over Grandma Elizabeth's open grave forever. Maybe something different would happen.

And something did. A small, webbed hand grasped the edge of the grave and pulled itself up. A fish head came over the top, a blue-green fish, with vacant, dumb eyes and jointy frog arms on a man's torso above a naked pelvis, shriveled cock, and human legs. Carefully, it climbed out of Grandma Elizabeth's grave and raised a stick with a fabric square that caught in the wind: a black flag with red horns and other foreign markings on it.

Impossible. But my mind went limp, not questioning or objecting.

Ignoring me, the fish man walked down the hill away from the main road behind me, where Don waited in his car. Now muscley human hands grabbed the edge of the dirt hole. A corpse—a skinless man with red, bleeding flesh—pulled himself out. Then two small insect-things, about the size of mice, wearing masks that looked like the heads of flies and carrying silver trumpets exited the grave. A fat, faceless man with stumps where his hands should be, with chains fixed to the stumps heaved up a vehicle out of the hole that tore the green mat off the edge of the grave with stone wheels. The gigantic, naked torso of a child—the top-half of a boy the size of a car, with pale yellow eyes and no arms—begged in another language. As he passed, I saw that he had been hollowed out. Looking into the hole where the flat edge of his waist should have been, I saw shadows moving around, glints of knives, and heard someone gasping for air. And then another fish man, larger than the first one, came out of the hole, carrying a flute made of bones and then—Grandma Elizabeth.

She stumbled over the top of her grave, skinless, bleeding and shaking. But it was her. They formed some kind of parade, all of them in a line. More black flags went up, protruding from a pole in the faceless man's back, fixed to the giant child-thing, and the second fish man began to play its flute. It was high pitched and dancy, like a medieval minstrel song. Drums beat from inside the child's body.

Grandma Elizabeth saw me, her eyes gaping and wild. She tried to say something, but they were already moving over the hill. Other instruments joined in, and now I heard singing in a screechy, lilting wail, another language that ended in English words at the end of each verse:

"... and she will always be with me."

Pound-pound of the drums.

I couldn't think. My body wouldn't move. Grandma Elizabeth looked back at me.

"...and how happy we will be."

"The sunken lady," she shouted. And more in German.

Pound-pound.

More came out of the grave behind her.

A hunched creature with rusty red arms, draped in a moss green robe that dragged in the dirt was next. The skull of a horse was under its hood, and it held a bowed harp made of painted bone with a small black, featherless bird perched on top. The horse-skull thing rode a pair of giant yoked worms—one yellowish and fleshy, the other oily and brown—both with open, gaping, sucking mouth holes lined with tiny teeth, rimmed with gray whiskers. Behind this thing came a man's head with a tight black wrap around his hair, walking on legs without a torso or arms, just the head on top.

And then a hairless, mole-looking man in red robes, almost a mockery of a priest's robes stopped when he saw me. There was a tear in the side of his robe, and in the gaping hole, I could see the exposed ribs and red-black flesh of his insides—and faces. Small, white faces moved inside him, huddling in the darkness around his organs, away from the light.

The song: *"...like a maiden running free."*

Pound-pound.

"You don't go with her," the mole-thing said, and I heard tiny screaming from the hole in his side. "You have no contract."

The rest of the parade was disappearing out of my view. They were almost over the hill, and Grandma Elizabeth tried to stop, but she couldn't, her exposed muscles bleeding across the lawn. The black bird from the horse-skull creature's harp darted over to peck at her shoulder, and a wedge of flesh peeled back. Grandma Elizabeth screamed.

Still, the song: *"...and the world will be for me."*

Grandma Elizabeth's wide-open eyes locked with mine. The bird landed to dig its beak into her shoulder. She said, "Dudweiler."

And then she was over the hill and out of my view. All of them but the mole-thing were almost gone. He still stood here, watching me with small black eyes.

"Make a contract with me?" He wheezed a little, and someone started laughing in a small voice from inside him, then went quiet. "Fix your love with Caitlyn? Give you a flower growing from a meteor, make her love you forever, and you will belong to me, yes?"

Don't listen to it. Don't answer.

"Give you a phone with the numbers of all the cities in the world, even dead ones? So you can hear your sister and father again? And you will belong to me?"

Now this mole-thing in its red robes seemed to notice the rest were gone. The grass curled away from the dirt around his feet—not animal feet. They were bare human feet, swollen red at the toenails.

"Give you a knife made from the bone of the first man, unbreakable. So you can slay the collector? And then you belong to me?" When I didn't answer, he adjusted his robe and made a snorty noise. "Your light goes out anyway. Burn and sad, death in the branches."

He left, and the ground died around him in a neat path, all the way over the hill.

Jesus Christ.

I sat in the dirt. The song was gone, but the grass was still dead, and there were brown smears where Grandma Elizabeth had walked and bled. What the hell was that? I was insane. This was full-on schizophrenia, a waking nightmare. Things that couldn't be and weren't there in broad daylight—or in gray, rainy daylight, same difference. My legs weren't working, and I felt numb. *Not real. Fuck.*

Finally, I dragged a foot back and got up, went down to Don's car. He sat there, with the engine idling, listening to the news. Tell him about it? No, impossible. I couldn't tell him or anyone about this.

Because it didn't happen. I sat next to him, warm and dry, and he shifted gears, drove us out into the cemetery road. Except the grass, the edge of the grave. It was torn up. They were there, all of them. I saw that.

Don was talking politics and this crazy year of 2016. Like maybe this was the year when we all slipped into an alternate dimension without noticing. The Chicago Cubs winning the World Series—of everything, didn't that seem the most improbable? He probably wanted me to smile and agree, say something inane about how unpredictable and bizarre life could be. But I didn't. I watched the cemetery, spotted another crowd of people in dark clothing with umbrellas at the top of a hill. The car smelled of strong artificial pine, from the green tree air freshener on his rearview.

"Everything all right?" he asked.

Yeah. Fucking fantastic. Wasn't real.

"No," I said. "Caitlyn went back to New York."

"I saw. She. Got into Mom's car. To go to the airport."

And I just saw a fucking demon parade. And they had Grandma Elizabeth. They took her out of her grave and away. They were singing and playing music. The world didn't care what I believed. It just *was*. A rock in a void, with monsters waiting. *Enough*.

"What did the chicken man show you?"

The car jerked to a stop.

"What?" he asked. "Are you fucking. Are you serious?"

I would stay calm through this. We were in the car together. He couldn't leave this time. I had him trapped. Eighteen Goddamn years ago. Right now, I needed to find some sense in this. Because, yes I might be nuts, but he saw the chicken man, too. Don was at the *Cadillac Club*. Maybe it was imaginary and had been smattered together from trauma somehow in my mind, but Don was there. *Tell me. What happened?*

"Please Don," I said, "what did he show you? What was in his bag that freaked you out? Why did you talk about Abby?"

"Fuck you," he said. "Don't take your. Relationship bullshit out on me."

We were stopped, with a straight shot down to the gated entrance of the cemetery that opened up to splashing cars and squat houses in the residential neighborhood on the other side. If we left, maybe he'd never talk. No, I had to know now.

"Tell me what it was. Tell me it was nothing, and everything from when we were kids wasn't real. Tell me the truth. Whatever you say, I'll believe you. I want to know. I just saw—things are happening that I don't understand, and he showed you something."

"He showed me." Don closed his eyes, both hands tight on the steering wheel. "He had her head. Shrunken like a doll. But it was her head. The size of a softball, maybe. It was alive. Mark, she had duct tape on her. Mouth. And she was older, beaten up. But it was her. She saw me."

The chained woman inside the red door—my neurological record skipped so that I glimpsed that in Robert's basement. The first thing I saw as a kid when the chicken man opened the red door. My heart was going too fast, could hear it in my ears. I was having a hard time sitting still. I wanted to jump out and run. I was holding the door handle. *No.*

"That couldn't have been real," I said quietly. "How could that be real?"

"You asked me. I told you," he said. "Can we go now?"

He started driving again, and we were quiet for a long time, watching the windshield wipers. My pulse wasn't slowing down, but I was still. How was he driving the car, steering out into the street? I probably would have sideswiped a telephone pole or crossed directly into oncoming traffic. How the hell could he be so calm?

"Do you believe all that shit happened when we were kids?" I asked.

"Why do you. Want to talk about this now?"

What kind of question was that?

"The other day, Caitlyn got a phone call from a woman who said she was Abby." And before he could cut in, I said, "Yes, I know—of course it wasn't. But how did we get out of the Cadillac Club?"

"Stop it, Mark. You know I don't. Remember."

"I do," I said.

As we stopped at a red light, he turned to me. "What? Is this. A joke? It's not. Fucking funny."

"There was a smell," I said. "Something that triggered it for me earlier this week ..." He cleared his throat to stop me again. "No," I said, "let me finished. It was a woman. He took me through a red door, and a woman was cut up, chained there. No arms or legs ..."

"Stop it." We jerked forward with the green light, and Don shook his head, glaring at the wipers. "What's. Wrong with you?"

"What's wrong with me that I want to know what happened?"

"Yes! It was. Eighteen years ago! Fuck off. With your questions. Please."

Our dad in buckets, my brother mutilated almost beyond recognition, a scar straight through my left hand—but yes, let's just leave it. The statute of limitations on repressed demon nightmares had passed.

"I'm not saying," Don said. "It doesn't. Matter."

As if I'd said that out loud. He still knew me, didn't he?

"She's gone," he said.

What if she wasn't?

"I saw Grandma Elizabeth," I said. "Not in the coffin, I saw her ..."

Shit.

We were already approaching the hotel, and Mom stood by herself in the middle of the rainy parking lot outside. The whole drive up, she didn't move, just stood there, watching us like a statue. Why wasn't she under the overhang by the front doors? What was she doing?

We pulled up slowly, and Don rolled down his window. "Mom?"

She smiled. "Hi, Don."

"Mom, what are you. Doing?"

"I drove Caitlyn to the airport, and I was getting out of my car, and there was ..." She seemed to suddenly realize where she was and how cold and drenched she was getting. "Wow, it's late, isn't it? Let's go inside and figure out what to do for dinner, okay? Oh, and Mark, I have Grandma Elizabeth's box for you. And the lamp."

Chapter Fifteen

After we took Mom out to dinner for burgers and beers in a loud chain restaurant with too many license plates and street signs on the walls, I sat alone in my hotel room and stared at the whiskey lamp. The skinny lamp. I wasn't drunk, but I hadn't stopped drinking either. After the beers at dinner, I had opened up the minibar in my room: six more Heinekens in there. I was down to two. At dinner, all three of us chatted about the food, sports, politics, anything but Grandma Elizabeth or what came next. Now, the lamp wasn't plugged in. I had set it on a little dresser at the foot of the bed, the plug cord dangling off the edge like a tail over Grandma Elizabeth's box that had *For M* written in black marker on the side. I hadn't gone through it yet.

I texted Caitlyn:

> *Are u up?*

It was after 11:00 on the East Coast, but it was also Saturday night. I imagined her out at a bar with friends from work. Imagined guys cozying up alongside her, all smiles. Or maybe she was still at the office or asleep. She wasn't answering. No way of knowing, but I could trust her. *Stop and breathe.*

I sat on the floor and opened Grandma Elizabeth's box. Something to do. A tray full of silver utensils, a bulky black photo album, some old fat Western novels, and a cassette recorder were inside. There were folded up yellow papers, like from a legal pad, in one of the books, covered in illegible German scrawl in blue ink.

My phone buzzed. Caitlyn texted back:

> *Yes but going to sleep soon. How r u?*

Me:

> *Ok. I love you.*

Caitlyn:

> *U too. Night.*

She never said 'I love you,' she always let me say it first, then answered like that: 'you too.' Why hadn't I thought about that before?

I set the books and utensils aside and opened the photo album: pictures from a riverboat cruise in Germany. The photos were sepia-tone shots of boxy, fairytale-looking houses and castles. There was Grandma Elizabeth, on the third page, her hair bright brown, almost red, wearing big sunglasses, on a bridge over a waterfall. The shot was blurry, but she'd been shockingly pretty, with a sly, intelligent smile, as if she were in on a private joke. That expression was new. Something they took out with the icepick. I paged through, then stopped on the last page: a small square photo of a kid in a military uniform with two lightning bolts on his collar. He was glaring and had an eagle and swastika pin on the left side of his coat. My grandfather, not just a soldier, part of the SS, one of the fucking thugs who—*It's just a picture. Stop it.*

I put the album away, then lifted out the cassette recorder. It was an old-fashioned black block, with a red button for record, and an unmarked tape already inside. I pressed *Rewind*, and when it clicked all the way, tried playing it. With any luck, Grandma Elizabeth saved some music or something.

"All right," a voice said impatiently. It was crackly and distant, a recording without a good microphone of a man's voice, with a stocky German accent. "I'm talking now to my son. This is the story you need to know before your first child is born. Boy or girl, doesn't matter. He will take them. This is why ..."

What the hell? My grandfather left some kind of historical interview about kids being taken ... he *knew*. He wanted to explain? I kept my breathing steady, one hand poised to click it off. The old Nazi prick wanted Dad to have this.

"A long time ago, Hell opened under the hills near Dudweiler in Germany. Back then, it was a time of war. There were no countries or laws, just marauders looking for food, warmth, and people that they could use. A new apocalypse was near. And the trees were full of bodies with warning signs nailed on them: '*Let the dead hang, or you will join them*'."

In the hotel room, my phone buzzed with a text message, but I didn't read it. *This* was the story my grandfather wanted to preserve for my father? Nothing about the war or his life in America. Instead, it was some kind of fucked up fairy tale? The strangeness of it bothered me. I should've turned it off. But I didn't.

"One night, a woman named Jana heard her dead baby crying in the woods and ran out to find it. Her husband lost her in the hills. The next morning, he found her clothing, torn, by the entrance of a small cave. So he started digging."

There was a pause, and the tape made a low *notch-notching* sound as it played. The hotel room was still, and I realized I'd stopped drinking, hadn't even noticed. How long ago was this supposed to have happened? Online write ups traced the mine fire near Dudweiler back to the 1600s. Was this a fable about that?

"He dug deep underground and discovered a chamber with walls marked by handprints and charcoal drawings of giant horses and extinct animals with horns, all glowing in an unnatural white-hot light. There, he found his wife, Jana, dead, and a dragon. The man swore to avenge her.

"'No,' the dragon said, 'you cannot kill me. But I can help you. I can punish your enemies and protect you. You will collect sacrifices for me, and in return, I will save all your faces in the stone.'

"The village of Dudweiler agreed to the dragon's terms, and for a long time, they were safe. Until, eventually, the hills brightened. Bodies were cut down from the trees. Old warning signs were burned. Memories of war and Armageddon became scary legends elders told. Still, the chicken man collected, because the villagers paid their tribute in cheap fowl. Then, one day, they stopped paying. A new age of reason had begun, they said. The dragon wasn't real."

In the hotel room, my phone buzzed again. Another text. Probably Don. Alone in my room, this story felt like a waking dream, like maybe I was imagining the whole thing and this cassette tape wouldn't exist in the morning. My grandfather's voice, preserved with his photo.

"The chicken man delivered their message to the dragon, and the next day, the mayor's oldest son went missing. For days, more children disappeared, until finally, the villagers apologized, desperate to set things right again. This time, when the chicken man went into the cave, a quiet farmer followed him. In that first, oldest chamber, where the dragon still waited, the farmer saw a hole into Hell itself. He attacked the dragon, but it smashed his weapon and broke his body. Yet, it didn't kill him. Instead, the farmer would live the rest of his life with a debt. From that day on, his family would be marked. Every generation, the dragon would take the first-born child of all his descendants. The villagers never saw their stolen children again, and most never knew about the farmer or his debt. *Our* debt. That's the story, not all, but most of it. And when the war started, I decided to put a stop to it ... But I don't want to talk about that."

The tape clicked. That was the end. I took it out, flipped over the cassette and tried the other side—nothing on there. He had only recorded one side. No hint of confusion in his story, and he had died in 1980, so this tape must be almost 40 years old, more. What did all of that mean? The chicken man, the debt, and my grandfather did something to try to fix it—*and failed*. I was wide awake now. Screw the time. Nothing was going to get my mind off this.

My phone buzzed. Another text. I checked: three texts, all from Caitlyn. They said:

> *R u there, I need to talk?*

> *I am stressing and it's important*

> *Mark I'm sorry please call me*

It was after midnight in New York, but I pressed the button to call Caitlyn, and she picked up after the first ring.

I started to say, "I'm sorry I didn't see your texts until—"

"Mark, I just took a test, after I was late this week." She sounded frantic. "I have it here. I can take a picture if you want to see."

That didn't make sense. "You were late? For what?"

"My period," she said. "I'm pregnant."

Chapter Sixteen

We talked about it for over an hour like forensic scientists trying to piece together the scene of a crime. We always used a condom, but what about the morning of our anniversary, weeks ago, the day of the fake Abby call and everything else, when the condom broke? That was probably when it happened. When it started.

"Well," I said at last, "it's … how do you feel?"

"I don't know. What should we do?"

"What *can* we do?" I asked.

There was a long pause, and I heard her heavy breathing on the line.

"My job would be screwed. Everything would be screwed. Now is not the right time," she said. "Right?"

My taste buds disappeared the same fucking day. This was connected—no, not just linked, this was *why*.

"I'm not sure," I said. "We don't have to decide right this minute. We have plenty of time."

We didn't, though. Not because of the baby—if she wanted an abortion, that could happen weeks or even months from now—but because of *us*. We were on a timer counting down, almost to zero. And now this. Right after my grandfather's damn story about stolen children. *What do I do?* No way to tell Caitlyn about that, impossible. But the reality was here, now, as solid as someone standing in the corner of my vision. Not for me, for my child.

"You're right. We don't have to know now. I bought the test earlier this week, totally forgot about it until tonight." She let out an exasperated breath. "I wish you were here."

"Me too," I said. "I'll come back early tomorrow, as soon as I can."

"I'm scared."

I started to say that she didn't need to be, that there was nothing to worry about and it would all work out. But that wasn't true, was it? "I love you."

"You too."

"We'll go to the doctor this week. It might not even be right. Tests can be false positive. That's definitely possible."

But that wasn't an answer either, not even close. Chances were, she *was* pregnant. The condom broke. That was all. This baby was *us*, us before the bullshit with the fake Abby call and my broken taste buds and Grandma Elizabeth's death. Us in love and happy, and together, creating a relationship. I got up, my legs stiff from sitting on the floor, and went to stare out the window at the dark, rainy parking lot. *Leave the cassette tape.* This wasn't a crisis. This was hope.

Unless *he* came for it. That familiar quiver in my stomach, but I shoved the thought down. *Figure it out, we'll find a way. He isn't real.*

Caitlyn and I talked for a little longer, until she said she was too wiped out, and we finally said goodnight. Already the conversation was different. All the hostility and distance from earlier melted away by this new discovery, a shock, an opportunity. Maybe a family.

I called Don's cell. He didn't answer, so I tried him again.

"What's. Going on?" he asked. "It's late. And tomorrow—"

"Tomorrow, I have to go back to New York. I need you to come to my room right now." He was staying on the next floor down in a hotel room across from Mom's. "You have to hear something."

I wanted to bury the tape, melt it down maybe. But I couldn't yet, not until someone else knew. So I wasn't out of my mind and alone. He argued, but eventually agreed to come up. Don sat on the foot of my bed, and I waited by the window, as we listened to the tape.

He rubbed his face. "Jesus. He made that. For Dad."

Don stretched and stood. And there it was, the old pacing energy in his legs. He was fighting the urge to move around, to help me work this out, wasn't he?

"He called him the chicken man," I said.

"Just a story. An old folk tale. It did sound like. He said 'chicken man,' though. I heard it too."

But he shrugged it away, as a coincidence. *Bullshit.* Don was stiff, standing over the cassette player. No way he believed that.

It was too late, and I was too tired for this. The booze was wearing off. My hands were starting to shake again. "Really? After everything, it doesn't matter? Or—what, the 'chicken man' used that name because of an old, German fable?"

"I don't. Know." He looked down at the cassette recorder. "What do you want. Me to say?"

"I want you to tell me that I'm not insane. Is it real or isn't it? This scar in my hand—everything that happened, Don. There's a fucking demon taking apart our family."

Don backed away to the door. No pacing, no notes, he didn't even look at me.

"You do sound. Insane." He stopped. "But maybe there is. Yes."

"What are we going to do?"

We. Not me—us, together. I couldn't do this on my own.

He frowned "Where did she. Call from?"

"The call from Abby—Caitlyn said it sounded like ..."

"Dudweiler," he said.

"Right."

"So we have to." He hesitated. "We have to go there."

And then? I wanted to ask. But I knew. Then we had to find a way to kill him.

***

I got maybe five hours of sleep, then Mom drove me to the airport. My suitcase and Grandma Elizabeth's box were stowed in the trunk, with the whiskey lamp and the rest inside. There was an accident on the highway, so we were sitting in traffic, listening to the radio, talking about the funeral and my job at Bed Life, until Mom said, "I listened to the tape, you know."

Up ahead, two of the right lanes were blocked off in a sea of flashing lights, oranges cones, and police in neon green safety vests. The highway and concrete neighborhoods beyond were still damp from yesterday, but bright now in the clear, fall air.

"The one Grandma Elizabeth left in that box for you," Mom said, without looking away from the road. "I played it two days ago. You and your brother both heard it, too, didn't you? Mark, you should throw it all away or burn it."

Between last night and this morning, an ugly knot had formed in my belly, as I let the idea of the chicken man reform. Maybe it wasn't real, but the more I thought about my grandfather's story, the more solid my memories became: him in the Tyler Lane House, by the shrine at Holy Cross, and guiding me to the red door under the *Cadillac Club*.

"I worry about you," she said. "Facing this without faith."

Faith? In what?

"You didn't believe, Mom, until just now."

"That's not true," she said. "I was baptized, take communion—"

"You used to roll your eyes at church."

"As you get older, you start to appreciate these things," she said. "Rituals are important. Your father believed, too, but in the wrong ways. It's why it was so easy for him to see demons everywhere."

She'd never talked like this. Now Dad saw demons everywhere and was deeply religious? She was going to rewrite my childhood on the drive to O'Hare.

"Trust me," she said. "Why do you think we kept the whiskey lamp on all those years?"

This was like my conversation with Don. Grandma Elizabeth's death had churned up everyone's feelings, raised the stakes. As that older generation passed away, we were all still trying to understand them. What happened to my father eighteen years ago?

"You scared us with that lamp when we were kids," I said.

Ahead, the traffic was already clearing, the overlapping glass towers of the Chicago skyline distinct in the distance, almost like a painted backdrop. Another ten minutes, maybe less, to the airport. Just like with Don, I had to get this out, before Mom could shut it off. While we were alone together.

If I was going to get any answers, now was the time. "Tell me what it is."

"I told you already, Mark."

"No, you told us it was made from human skin." Years ago, I'd read about that, too. But not for long. When I'd started researching the

Holocaust, the black-and-white images of stacked bodies and ruined people, films and documentaries—all of it lodged in my skull, until I couldn't focus anymore. Several times, I'd tried to go back and look into what my grandfather might have done, but each time the stories and images were too much. Every time, I told myself that the genocide was so familiar in popular culture that I could deal with it, the same way I might study another long-ago atrocity. But it wasn't the same.

Because we had a fucking lamp. In high school, I read about a museum in Poland that displayed objects made from people. Men, women, and children who were turned into *things*. The last time I tried to study it—the first year I moved to New York—a documentary historian patiently explained that there were still everyday objects being used in Germany today with bits of people inside them. It's why the Nazis shaved everyone's heads, keeping mounds of human hair that could be used to produce blankets and socks. The scale and horror of it made me turn away every time. But not now. For just this moment—because she gave the whiskey lamp to me.

"What is it?" I asked.

Don't tell me. I don't want to know.

"It's …" She was driving faster, shifting into the far-left lane, cars flying past on my right. "It's like the opposite of a crucifix or a Jewish menorah, okay? It's something that was made to keep God *out* of a place, not bring Him in.

I watched the blocky green numbers on the dash amping up: *65 mph, 68 mph, 73 mph*. She was trying to end the conversation. Get me there, so it stopped.

"My grandfather made it?"

"That lamp is a sick joke," she said. "Yes, your grandfather made the first version during the war. He made it *from* people, do you understand? Your grandfather lost his mind, but it isn't a *lamp*, Mark.

I know we call it that, but it isn't. Your dad used to light it, just like your grandfather, because he believed it created a vacuum, a link to some kind of *thing* that could protect us. He called that thing the *sunken lady*."

Shit, we were driving fast, and signs for the airport approached overhead, with a list of airlines in each terminal.

"Like a guardian angel?" I asked.

"I wish. Do you really want to hear this? It's not real. You know that, right? I'm just telling you why we kept the whiskey lamp all those years. And all this nonsense is still a part of it. Your grandmother asked for it back, after your dad died." Mom clenched her hands on the wheel, and we hit *81 mph*, then slowed around a turn and up onto a ramp toward Terminal 2. "I lied to you about that. I'm sorry. When you were younger, I told you we lost it. But really, I gave it back to your grandmother."

But that wasn't the important part.

A taxi blocked our lane ahead, and Mom slammed the brakes. The drop-off area wasn't far away, past a dip in the road, under an overhang. Almost out of time. A plane roared overhead and cars honked on either side.

"My grandfather—Grandma Elizabeth's husband—made that thing in some kind of deal with a guardian angel?" I asked. "With the sunken lady? In exchange for turning it on every night, she—"

"Yes, that's more or less it." She honked at the taxi in front of us.

"Mom, tell me."

"Your dad lived his whole life, just like *his* father, believing that people weren't evil exactly, but indifferent, amoral. I know that's not true," she said. "But that lamp, that ugly lamp, is a symbol of that belief, at least to me. Because your grandfather made it in the worst hell on Earth, and then he invented some kind of blood pact nonsense to distract us from what it really was and what he did over there." Finally, the taxi drove on, and we followed, almost to the drop off. "It's a war crime is what it is. *That's all.*"

She said it like she expected me to argue with her.

"Why didn't you destroy it?" I asked.

"Your grandmother left it to you. And I am *not* about to cross that woman after she's dead. I don't want her haunting me." She shook her hands to relax them. "I'm sorry I snapped at you about that yesterday, by the way. It's very normal, you know, to see someone, after they pass."

Yes, it was all so normal. As normal as the demon parade at Grandma Elizabeth's grave and the cassette tape story about the chicken man in seventeenth-century Germany. And my grandfather's deal with a Nazi demon called the sunken lady. We slowed at the drop-off area to wait for a black town car to clear a space. The driver shook hands with a couple and helped with their bags.

Time's up.

"I really saw her, Mom." *And other things. Not just now, years ago.* "Not in a dream. In our apartment in New York. She was standing in the middle of the room."

The town car moved, and we pulled to the curb. Mom hugged me. "I love you, Mark. Caitlyn told me that she's worried about you."

"It sounds crazy," I said. "But I'm not making this up."

I opened my door. Real or not, no point arguing now. We were here, and Mom wouldn't believe me. *I* barely believed me.

Mom popped the trunk and got out to hug me on the curb. I grabbed my suitcase, slammed the trunk shut again.

"I love you. But you have a responsibility now," she said. "More than just for yourself."

"Caitlyn ..."

"Right. For Caitlyn, *and* ...?" She gave me a sideways look, almost a wink without winking, as she walked back around to her door. "There's something you're not telling me, isn't there?"

How the hell did she know?

"Neither of you said it," Mom said, "but I can tell. And I'm beyond excited to be a grandmother, Mark. Truly."

I held onto my suitcase handle and stared at her. *Unbelievable.*

"Seriously? I told her I wouldn't tell anyone."

"You didn't tell me." Mom pantomimed zipping her mouth shut and got back in, then rolled down the passenger window and called, "Pesky mother's intuition. It'll be fine. Don't let ... just take care of her."

"Caitlyn can take care of herself."

She smiled. "I don't mean Caitlyn."

***

Back in New York, I took Caitlyn to the doctor. Her primary care physician had a last-minute cancellation on Monday morning, so I told Robert I'd be late to get started rewiring the bathroom and second bedroom. *'No problem,'* he texted. *'Hope it's good news.'*

Me too.

At St. Luke's Roosevelt in midtown, we barely had to wait. I sat beside Caitlyn in the exam room while a nurse took her blood pressure and gave her a cup to pee in.

When Caitlyn left the room, the nurse asked me, "And are you here for anything else, sir?"

"No, it's my girlfriend's appointment. I just came with her."

The nurse gave me a skeptical look. "How much do you weigh?"

Bizarre question, but I actually knew exactly. I had weighed myself in the bathroom last week. "One-hundred and seventy-two pounds."

She nodded to the metal scale beside the examination table. "Only take a second."

The exam room was cramped and windowless, but I brushed past her onto the scale, and she adjusted the blocky weight-tracking pegs to 100 pounds, then 150 pounds ... and it balanced out at 155 pounds. It was broken. I didn't want to deal with this. Today was about Caitlyn, not me.

"I weigh 172 pounds. It must be the scale or maybe my clothes."

"The scale is new, and your clothes don't weigh 17 pounds," she said. "Have you been eating? Able to keep food down? Have you traveled outside the U.S.?"

Caitlyn came back in with her little plastic cup. "What's wrong?"

"I'm concerned about your boyfriend's weight loss. I'd like to recommend bloodwork on you both. He'll need to make another appointment."

"His *weight loss*?" Caitlyn asked.

But I agreed and told her about the scale.

When the nurse was back to pinch Caitlyn's arm and start filling test tubes with blood, Caitlyn said, "You do look thin. I'm sorry. I can't believe I didn't notice before."

"It's nothing."

But the baby was. Everything checked out, and the doctor, a gray-haired woman who laughed at the end of every sentence, as if childbirth were endlessly amusing, gave Caitlyn a long list of new routines to follow, promising that a check-in next month would give us a lot more information.

"Your only job now," the doctor told me, "is to keep this woman healthy and happy."

Back outside, the midtown street was wet and crowded with people out for lunch, tourists, and delivery workers. They all hurried under the sidewalk canopies, around massive piles of black garbage bags, and flat-bed carts full of potted plants, boxes, and furniture. Caitlyn said she had to get back to her office, so we walked east, across town. When we crossed the street, I positioned myself in front, watching for anyone who might bump into us. Last night had been good. I still felt off, couldn't make my body work, but for the first time since Abby's call, Caitlyn and I made out. I went down on her for a long time, until she squirmed and thrashed and cursed, grabbing the bedposts. And after she finished, Caitlyn wrapped herself around me, as if I were a life raft. We hadn't talked about much. I didn't want to risk anything that might start a fight and avoided bourbon. Then, this morning, I woke with a vivid dream of dancing women and strobe lights that faded when I made coffee.

At Columbus Circle, we crossed up through the southern walk of Central Park, past people lounging on benches, eating, chatting, or staring at their phones. This was a pro move, much less chaotic than the midtown sidewalks at this time of day, and Caitlyn held my hand. We passed a family playing Frisbee with a golden retriever on the lawn directly past a 'Keep Off the Grass, Absolutely No Dogs' sign. Two kids, a boy and a girl, were chasing the dog, trying to get back the Frisbee, while the dad coaxed the dog on, and the mom smiled from a quilt-blanket.

"We should get a dog," Caitlyn said. "After, I mean, to keep everybody safe ..."

She frowned at me, and I realized I was squeezing her fingers, tried to stop.

"Mark?"

"Sorry." I was breathing fast, watching the dog sprint. It had a stupid doggy grin, as the kids tackled it to wrestle away the Frisbee. I hadn't thought about Calvin. But now I felt an old flash of emotion, like I'd scratched open a shallow scab, not even a scar. "I don't want to get a dog."

"But didn't you have one growing up?"

I'd mentioned Calvin to her but tried not to talk about him. Never told her how it took me nights and nights—*years*, really—to sleep without imagining him lying in a ruined pile in a concrete alley somewhere. And I was over that. So why was my chest constricting? I coughed, tried to open it up.

"It's okay," she said. "Come on."

We kept going, and by the time we got to the sidewalk outside her office building on Madison Avenue, I was almost calm. We kissed, and she promised not to be too late.

Back in Harlem, I got to work rigging wires along the exposed wooden joints in the wall of Robert's second bedroom. Finally, when I'd nearly finished, he knocked on the doorframe to come in.

"Good to have you back," he said. "Your family okay?"

I started to tell him that sure, things were fine, no problem, but somehow the sentence skidded sideways into how my mother and older brother were dealing with trauma—and maybe the whole thing traced back to my Nazi grandfather in Germany 80 years ago.

Arms crossed, Robert wasn't smiling. *Shit.* I was going to lose this job. Why did I ...

"Sorry, I didn't mean to get into that. I can wrap up ..."

"He was really a Nazi?" My mouth went dry. Robert waited, with a blank, unreadable stare. "Mark?"

"Yeah, I think so. I never met him. He died before I was born." I said it almost like an apology.

"So how does the stuff in Kentucky link back to Germany?"

"Robert, I'm sorry. I'm just tired from traveling and ..."

"No, don't apologize." He rolled his eyes. "Please. I asked. If you don't want to talk about it, that's one thing. But if you do ..." He gestured, as if he were giving me the floor. "Mark, I like you. Whatever your grandad did, that's not you. Is your life living in the wake of that? Like a ship on the waves of boats ahead of it? Yeah, maybe. Where in Germany?"

"It's a little town called Dudweiler ..."

"That's near Saarbrüken?" Robert grinned, when I started to ask how he possibly knew the name. "Ancient historian, remember? You have any idea how many language I had to learn? Mark, I taught for two years in Germany on a postdoc and published a couple papers about the Roman frontier. You take any history in college? No? Well, you should." He laughed, so easy-going and infectious that I smiled, too. "The Romans were maybe the first to write reliably about the people living in Saar—in that region. Julius Caesar called them the 'Mediomatrici,' a tribe of Gauls that literally means something like 'Middle Mothers.'"

The rest of the apartment quieted, the only sound the thrum of my blood behind my ears.

"Why?" I asked.

"Why that name?" He shrugged. "Geography, maybe. Couple years ago, I heard a conference paper that argued there were pre-Mithraic vibes in the name. If 'Middle Mothers' meant that the people living there occupied a position between heaven and the underworld—literally, 'mothers of the middle world'—then maybe the name alluded to subterranean sites of worship."

He noticed my probably too-tight stance. But not because he'd veered into lecture mode. No. I didn't want to hear this, because the visions were a mash of stress and brain chemicals. I didn't want to think about 'subterranean sites of worship.' Like the kind that might be hidden behind a red door?

So back away. Run out of the brownstone, conjure up an excuse.

The whiskey lamp was in a box in our apartment—here, just a few miles away, in this same city, right now. It was physical and real.

So when Robert started to apologize for 'history nerding out,' I said, "No, it's okay. Are there underground religious sites in Dudweiler?"

"In that region of Germany?" He shrugged again. "Sure. But there are hundreds of Mithraic sites around Europe and what used to be the Roman Empire."

"What does 'Mithraic' mean?"

Something creaked down the hall, and he glanced around the empty room. "You really want to get into this?"

We did a brief back-and-forth: Robert, half-heartedly apologizing for keeping me from finishing my work, and me, waving that away and insisting that yes, I wanted to know.

"Your girlfriend isn't going to kill me for making you late? We'll have to do dinner at some point, the four of us. Maybe after Thanksgiving, before we hit holiday craziness?" He laughed, as if I were in on the joke of how willingly we succumbed to seasonal stress. I didn't want to think about visiting Kentucky, but Thanksgiving was only days away. Almost out of time.

Strange thought.

Why did it feel like a countdown? Not just because of the wobbling in my relationship with Caitlyn. No, it was more than that.

"Okay, so *briefly*," he said, "Mithras or 'the cult of Mithras' was a religion in the early Roman empire, first two centuries of the Common Era. At the time, it was actually a contemporary, rival religion to early Christianity. There's a decent chance it was originally picked up out east in Persia. And yes, I think there is at least one site in Saar."

"Near Dudweiler." I shifted awkwardly, waiting for the pieces of this ancient pagan cult to lock into position with everything else. My electrical tool bag suddenly looked surreal on the floor, like a prop. As if Robert's history were more relevant. "What was it?" I asked. "Mithras—what kind of religion was it?"

He frowned and started away, letting me grab my bag and fall into step behind him, without discussion.

"I'm not a specialist," he said. We wandered back to the main entry hall, then stepped out to sit on the front stoop. Loud, rumbling street noises of cars and trucks, and a group of teenagers shouted and laughed at the end of the block. The air tasted like exhaust and faint trash, but each breeze brought a fresh, cleaning rush. "But basically," he continued, "we think Mithras may have been a kind of Zoroastrian deity, connected to the sun. He was depicted as being born from either a rock, an egg, or a tree. Classic Mithraic iconography: you've got a shared banquet with Sol—that's your sun god—and ritual bull sacrifice."

My chest clamped, and I closed my eyes, one hand up to hide my face. Slow breathe in, easy back out. My lungs were too tight. *Stop panicking. You asked him to tell you.*

"Mark, you okay?"

I opened my eyes, focused a smile that probably looked weak, thin. "Yeah, I'm good. What else?"

Studying me, as if he wasn't sure he should go on, Robert said, "There isn't much. We don't have written texts, and plenty of the sites were damaged. By all accounts, it was a complex cult, with different levels of initiation, rituals, symbols. Fortunately, it was popular enough at the time with Roman soldiers that some temples do survive to help us make *some* sense of it. You sure you're okay? This almost looks like the start of another ..."

"It's not." Pacing my breathing helped, and my cheeks felt warm, which meant I was probably red-faced, starting to sweat. But no immobilizing attack.

"What I don't understand," Robert said at last, "is what this has to do with your Nazi granddad?"

"Me either."

I started to wave that way, say it didn't connect. I was just interested, but Robert cut in, "Don't bullshit me, Mark. You lit up like a fireball when I mentioned cave temples in Germany." He waited.

My chest twinged again, and I pulled myself up.

"Hey," he said. "Sorry, man. I didn't mean to press ..."

"It's okay. But I—yeah, I do need to get home." And when he apologized again, I said, "My girlfriend is pregnant."

That stopped him. Robert caught me in a strong hug, then clapped my back and pretended to scold me for letting him drone on about irrelevant ancient history, when I had actual, honest-to-God news.

And on the subway home, a part of me realized I'd told him, because I wanted the baby. I shouldn't have shared. I hadn't told Susan or Don, but somehow because Mom had sensed the baby, it felt like hiding Caitlyn's pregnancy—even this early—like that wasn't an option.

Because he knows, too.

Chapter Seventeen

As days clicked by my chest-knotting countdown came into focus around the image of that thin, dangerous man kneeling beside Don in our old entry hall. The way he tapped Don's face to show the entry point for an icepick lobotomy. *If* he was real, *if* he was still alive, he was waiting in Kentucky. My grandfather's recording said he could collect the first-born children, like Abby. And Dad's brother, Donald, who we never acknowledged. And the baby in Caitlyn's womb. All we had to do was avoid Kentucky.

Until the countdown ended, and we boarded a flight at John F. Kennedy airport to Louisville Muhammed Ali airport for Thanksgiving. Out of time. At Thanksgiving dinner with Mom, Don and his too-young girlfriend, everyone gushed over the turkey, mashed potatoes, mushroom gravy, and spicy cream corn. I did too, but I saw the way Caitlyn eyed me, when I complimented the food. She knew I still couldn't taste anything. The Tyler Lane House in Kentucky had been updated, but I tried to stay in the kitchen. No avoiding the rest of the house, though, when I got up to use the bathroom during dinner and crossed through the living room. Our old TV and Dad's recliner had been replaced by a new gray sofa and matching loveseat. In the hall, I stepped around the same ancient smudge on the carpet. *Don't look at it.* I walked past my old bedroom, now a workout room with a stationary bike and flat screen TV. In Don's old room across the hall, Mom had set up a sewing machine, surrounded by frizzy quilts and half-finished scarves hanging from wooden racks. On the way back to the kitchen, I avoided the front window and the spot where I'd died on the floor.

As I sat again, Don asked Caitlyn why she wouldn't have a bourbon with us. This was Kentucky, after all, he said. Caitlyn finally sighed and told everyone about the pregnancy. Don's girlfriend screamed and hugged her, freaking Don out and making us all laugh. It wasn't a perfect greeting card evening, but for a moment, it was pretty damn close. Close enough that I eased into my seat, as if this house were like any other. As if the walls didn't make me want to bolt. For just a moment, I could breathe, one arm around Caitlyn's back. There was no chicken man or demonic debt. Of course there wasn't.

When it got late, Mom went to bed, and the rest of us sat around the kitchen table to play cards. Caitlyn and I were staying in a hotel down Bardstown Road and Don's apartment in Old Louisville wasn't far either. A couple games in, Don started dropping cards when he shuffled, laughing and talking too loudly. How many drinks did he have? I hadn't counted.

"Dinner was delicious," Don's girlfriend said. "Didn't you like it, Mark?"

"His taste buds don't work right now," Caitlyn said. "We aren't sure why. The doctors are still trying to figure it out."

Except Dr. Laymon, I hadn't told anyone else about that, but okay. Fine for them to know.

"It's just stress," I said.

"It's nothing to. Worry about," Don said, quietly dealing. "I had it too."

The room was still, except for the faint electronic buzz of the microwave and appliances. *Is this a joke?*

"You had it too? What are you talking about?"

"When we were kids. You know that."

What the hell was he talking about?

"No, I don't. You didn't have *this*, Don."

He was avoiding my eyes. "Sorry I brought. It up. Can we just play?"

"Good idea," Caitlyn said.

I reached for my drink, then stopped to keep it on the table. I wasn't looking at my cards. I watched Don. Weeks of him not eating, losing the bulk in his face, his cheeks hollowing. I'd been blocking it out, but the childhood memory was there, waiting. That was real. In my mind, he flashed into a thin, teenaged kid again.

"Talk to me," I said. "Explain."

"Fine," he said. "I had no. Taste in my mouth. For about a week. Or two. Until the big snowstorm."

Until that night. *Don't think about it.* I could already feel sweat on my back, tightness in the air. *Slow breath in, then easy out.*

Don's girlfriend said, "Maybe all you need is some snow, Mark. Shock to your system?"

"Yeah, maybe," I said. "Maybe that would bring back Calvin, too."

The words slipped out, before I could catch them. A frustrated burst, aimed at Don's shrug. His silence every time I brought it up.

Don looked at me like I'd just shoved him. He set the cards down and folded his hands, no thumbs. "Calvin? What happened. To Calvin, Mark? Tell us."

I heard the slide of bourbon in his voice. His voice was too low, daring me to push him again. The pull in my belly from his sudden call back felt ingrained, like I'd rehearsed this scene a hundred times growing up. I had.

But I said, "What do you think?"

"He was just. A dog, Mark."

I felt heat behind my eyes. *Just a dog.* And if I looked out the window, *that* window, into the backyard, would Calvin be there, waiting to come in? Past the backdoor window, I saw the pale outlines of trees in the darkness, barely visible. Don knew better. So what if it was childish. I didn't care. Calvin loved me, and I should have found him. It was so long ago. But I stood, heading through the living room and out onto the front porch. Mom still had two potted plants flanking the welcome mat. *Right here. The chicken man stood right here the first time he knocked.*

I heard Caitlyn come out behind me. "Ready to go?"

I nodded, and we went down the lawn to the car. I should say goodbye, but I didn't.

In the car, as we pulled away, Caitlyn said, "Is it possible—I'm just throwing this out there—that maybe you're overreacting?"

I started to say that Don knew better. *The snowstorm*, as if his taste buds got better at all. The snowstorm was when he lost his fucking tongue.

I said, "I'm sorry. You're right. Happy and healthy."

She let it go, and the next day, I told her I needed to apologize to Don. So while Caitlyn took Mom to brunch, I cornered Don on the front porch of his place in Old Louisville. It was cold and clear out. Perfect for today.

"I knew that. Was coming," he said when he saw me. "Like our great-aunt, the nun said. You can never let. Something just be."

"No, I can't," I said. "So talk. When did it start? That's why you stopped eating, when we were kids, isn't it?"

It started after the chicken man's first visit, he told me. He never mentioned it before, because, as kids, he didn't want to make things worse, with Mom and Dad fighting. And he expected it to go back to normal. Just like I did now.

"When I dreamt that Grandma Elizabeth was in my apartment, she told me it was because I was marked. That's what Abby told Caitlyn too."

"Not Abby," he said. "We don't know if. It was her."

I led him down off his front porch toward my rental car parked on the street.

"Fine, maybe it wasn't her," I said. "But that's what they both said. And Sister Maria Theresa said that about you too, remember? You were fucking *marked*, and now I am somehow. We should go."

He didn't argue, and he didn't ask where.

At Holy Cross, I parked in the lot outside Brescia Hall. The lobby was cleaner than I remembered, with new chairs and no TV, but they still had the same crucifix on the wall. The front desk staff let us through without questioning. It was the holidays, after all, and there were other families visiting with balloons and flowers and prepackaged desserts. Sister Maria Theresa was in a different, smaller room than when we were kids, without bookshelves, and she was dozing with an oxygen mask on, hunched in bed, her head shaking involuntarily just a little bit. Her mouth dangled open, teeth discolored black and streaky brown, and there were sores and dark spots on her neck, forehead, under her left eye, and along both hands.

She started when I knocked and held up her hand, just like she did all those years ago. No plastic rings this time, though.

"I'm glad you're here," she said. "How did you know?" Don and I started to approach, and she snapped her hand up again. "No, just stay there."

"We're still germ factories?" I asked.

Her face kept jittering involuntarily, but her expression didn't change. Her voice was stronger than I expected, sharp too. She shifted the oxygen mask over her nose and mouth to take a breath, then pushed it down again.

"You are," she said. "Because of *him*. He's doing this to you, just like he did your brother, until the debt is due. So you won't cause trouble. It'll go away, when he collects. You will be you again. There's your answer. Happy?" She chuckled, and it turned into a wet cough. "You already knew that, didn't you? Did you bring me something?"

I took out the candy bar I'd brought, and she smiled, her face bright despite the obvious sickness all over her. For an instant, I saw the younger version of her, from when we were kids, with a round, white face.

She said, "That might literally make my stomach explode, but thank you. Have your brother give it here."

I handed the candy bar to Don, and he went over to drop it in her palm, as if she were an oracle. Maybe. She made him unwrap it, then took off a piece at the end in a chewy brown trail of chocolate and caramel. She closed her eyes as she ate the bite. She moaned a little, enjoying the candy bar, then turned her head away from us and spat it out across the bed in a chocolatey slobber.

"*That* was nice," she said. "Do you know I would be 97 years old next year."

"We can come visit," Don said. "For your birthday."

She gave him an irritated look. "You weren't this stupid before. If you have any brains between the two of you, you'll move on."

"Why?" I asked.

"You just want to hear me say it, don't you?" She closed her eyes, as if she were trying to remember. "Poor old Doctor Waller, who helped your grandmother after her surgery. Did you know that he disappeared on a state highway outside Hartford in 1955? They never found him."

She opened her eyes again, frowning at me, as if I had Dr. Waller hidden outside.

"And why? It wasn't *his* debt, was it? But still, one day, just like *that* ..." She snapped her fingers. "... Doctor Waller wasn't there anymore. Wasn't anywhere. Just like the little blonde girl who lived on the street right over there, not a block away. Remember her?"

Rachel. Jesus, I hadn't thought about Rachel in years. She moved away a few months after everything happened. On the last day of school, she told me she was going to Texas in the summer and probably never coming back. During afterschool pickup, she said she wished we had more time. I never saw her again and remembered thinking, at the time, that she probably just felt sorry for me, because of what happened to Don and Dad dying.

"Did you know that she wrote our little Casanova here a letter, all the way from Houston?" Sister Maria Theresa asked. "I know that, because *he* showed it to me. He thought it was funny. She got his attention, because of *you*, Mark. He was watching you and your family like a hungry dog, and along comes this nice little girl, who looks like a meal, and even though she's not on the menu ... well, she's not here anymore. She's not anywhere. Understand?"

What did that mean? Was this supposed to scare me? Some girl I knew briefly back in middle school was supposedly dead or taken away and disappeared? This was a mistake. We shouldn't have come here.

"You can't kill him," she said. "If he asks for your child, you give him your child. Remember, he's just the collector. And anyone who is gone, you'll never get them back. Ever."

Not even Abby, if we went to Dudweiler? Sister Maria Theresa was just an old woman, didn't know what she was talking about.

I looked at Don. We were wasting our time.

But he said, "Our sister called. From Dudweiler."

Sister Maria Theresa paled and fidgeted with her hands, breathing in her oxygen mask again. "It wasn't her."

Of course not. All of this time, I knew, really *knew* it couldn't be Abby. *But what if?* What if she'd just been away somehow? Or, worse, what if the chicken man and all of it were real, and she needed our help? What if she was the tortured woman behind the red door?

"Listen to me. It may seem like it's just a quiet little town in Germany ..." She took a slow, shivery breath. "How do I put this? If something wants you to go there, it won't want to let you leave again."

She said 'something,' not 'someone.' *Something* wanted us to come to Dudweiler, and she knew enough to warn us. The room was very still, only the sound of her raspy breathing.

"After Grandma Elizabeth died, there were *things* at your sister's grave—animals, demons, whatever you want to call them," I said. "I saw them in the middle of the day, in broad daylight."

Don frowned at me, as if I'd just made a bad joke. Wouldn't that be nice?

Sister Maria Theresa closed her eyes. "I'm sure you saw what you saw," she said. "Why should they be afraid of sunlight?"

Behind me, the chicken man asked, "Skin cancer?"

Chapter Eighteen

The chicken man stepped into Sister Maria Theresa's room, a casual smile fixed on his unshaven face. Same gray suit, and although his hair had thinned a little and prickly stubble lined his cheeks and chin, he clearly hadn't aged. He was holding a big, white, plastic bucket in one hand and had his black duffel bag slung over the other shoulder. As he came in, the door and window were gone. The room was suddenly dark, so that the bucket seemed to glow. The wall was bare paint where the window that looked out on the parking lot should have been. Don was tense, and Sister Maria Theresa breathed faster in ragged gasps. My guts spasmed, and I could smell my own sweat stink out of the neck of my shirt.

He's real.

"My ears were burning." He extended his free hand to me.

I couldn't look away from the bucket.

"Mark, it's good to see you again." His hand hovered there, waiting for me to shake it. He noticed I was staring at the bucket and said, "Oh. Right, sorry about that. I guess that's a little tacky, isn't it? It just seemed practical, rather than running out to buy a new one. But I totally sympathize with your reaction. I should have thought about that, my bad."

Still, he was waiting for me to shake his hand. I didn't, just let my hands ball into fists. What would happen if I hit him? He was a real person. Ordinary and standing right here. I was breathing fast, the burn of stomach acid in the back of my throat.

"Well," he dropped his hand, stepped past me toward Sister Maria Theresa. "Here we all are."

Her head shook more violently, as she watched him. Don stepped between them protectively, and the chicken man set down the bucket.

"Hello, Don. You're looking well. I'm glad to see that. Do you remember our last conversation?"

"I'm not. A kid anymore," Don said. "Not afraid of you. Mother-fucker."

"I need you to go to that corner over there and get on your knees, facing the wall. Then I need you to pray." He smiled at Sister Maria Theresa. "You'd like him to do that, wouldn't you, Sister? Don, go pray for our dear sister here to keep her safe."

Don didn't move. "Get. Away from her."

"Don," the chicken man said slowly, "if you don't do that, I'm going to tear out your tongue with my bare hand. For the second time. Are we clear?"

Don started to say something else, and Sister Maria Theresa snapped her fingers at him. "Go. Do it."

Don looked at me, and so did the chicken man.

"One tongue is better than none," the chicken man said. "Right, Mark?"

The adrenaline terror squeezing my stomach made me cough when I tried to speak. *What if it happened again?*

I said, "Just do it, Don."

He covered his face with one hand and went to the corner.

"On your knees, please," the chicken man said. "And let's hear some prayer. Don't be shy."

Don dropped to his knees, murmuring, "Our father, who art in heaven ..."

"Like I was saying," the chicken man set his bag on Sister Maria Theresa's bed right beside her, unzipped it. "The bucket was insensitive, and I'm sorry about that, Mark. And thank you, too, sister, for bringing them both here, especially this one." He nodded to me. "This isn't exactly killing two birds with one stone, but it's close. More like killing one bird to prove a point to the second bird. Mark, you're into birds now, aren't you? I never could get excited about them. Ironic, right?" He shrugged. "This was going to happen anyway, you knew that as soon as you started talking to these *fine gentlemen,* so it shouldn't be a surprise."

He took a metal hammer out of his bag and placed it carefully on the bed beside Sister Maria Theresa's covered up legs.

He was half-turned away from me. I winced as I swallowed and forced my hands to open, flexing the fingers. Maybe I could grab the hammer.

"Don't," Sister Maria Theresa said. She must have seen me watching the hammer.

"Don't what?" the chicken man asked, and then he followed her stare to me and laughed in a sudden high-pitched spike that didn't match his voice, like a hyena. "Oh don't worry. Mark is done playing James Bond. Aren't you, Mark? Do you see that crucifix on the wall over there, right where your brother is praying? Nice job, by the way, Don. Keep it up. Do you see how they position Jesus's hands, nailed as far out as they can go, and the feet, one on top of the other? You know, in the Bible, it says that people laughed at Jesus as he was crucified. Crucifixion wasn't a sad, pitiful death, it was *fun*."

He took a long metal blade from his bag—the icepick. Shit. What was he going to do to her?

My whole body was slick with sweat. I felt it in my hair, clinging on my torso, and in my palms.

"Stop," I said.

Sister Maria Theresa was frozen, watching him.

"But you don't get the humor with these crucifixes, do you?" he asked. "Who is going to laugh at that? I mean, I suppose some sick asshole might laugh, but really, it just looks pathetic, doesn't it? Do you know what the disconnect is? Simple. Crucifixion didn't look like that."

He set the icepick beside the hammer and took out another long spike of metal.

"You see, way back when, they used to arrange people's arms and legs in different positions, sometimes just to make it as ridiculous as possible. An arm nailed up by the person's face, the other down by their ass, legs kicked out in different directions or hunched over or nailed on both sides of the pole even. You get the idea. The Romans were creative people, Mark."

Don glanced over his shoulder at me.

Without looking up from his bag, the chicken man said, "I don't hear praying, Don. Face forward. Thank you."

He took a third icepick and a fourth from the bag, then sighed.

"I told our dear sister here a long time ago that, someday, I would allow her to taste her own liver. Wait. *Allow* isn't the right word there, is it? But you get what I'm saying. You do—*get it*, I mean. That's why I'm glad we ran into each other here, Mark. It's been a little while. I understand. Memories fade. People grow up. Priorities change, and pretty soon everybody is telling you to pay taxes and save for retirement and think about settling down—*oh shit!*"

He stopped, and all three of us looked at him, the room silent, except for Sister Maria Theresa's gaspy breathing.

"I'm so sorry. I almost forgot. Here." He took a Miller Lite can out of the bag, popped off the top, and offered it to me. "This will help. It's easier to relax into acceptance with a little ethanol in your system."

Don looked away again, said, "...thy kingdom come, thy will be done ..."

"Take it," the chicken man said.

What was this? Was it a trick, poisoned or something?

I took the can, and he gestured for me to drink.

"Go ahead," Sister Maria Theresa said.

I sipped the beer. It tasted fine, like ordinary shitty lite beer. It stung going down my throat, then gurgled in my belly, as if it were curdling.

"More," the chicken man said, "bottom's up."

No. You're not in charge. But, I was already swallowing more, dribbling some along the side of my mouth and chin.

"It was all I had. Like the bucket. But I thought you might need a drink if we saw each other. So. This is real. This is happening."

He grabbed Sister Maria Theresa's left arm and jerked it up, slammed her hand, palm open, against the wall at the head of the bed.

Don't. What was he doing?

I said, "Stop it ..." My voice weaker than it should have been, almost like a child.

He started to maneuver one of the icepicks up, and I caught his sleeve. The chicken man paused to blink at my fingers, closed on his shirtsleeve, as if he didn't understand what I was doing.

Sister Maria Theresa shook her head, frantic. "Mark, no ..."

The chicken man met my eyes, his expression soft and patient, as if he felt sorry for me. "Really?" he said and flicked the center of my forehead.

The red door opened in a burnt swell of cleaning chemical smells that made my eyes water. When my vision cleared, I saw the nude woman with the scabby, shaved head, duct-taped mouth, and severed limbs. Chains clinked overhead. A hunched figure in a surgical mask and stained shirt was scraping up wet slime from the far wall. Bodies hung from hooks on the ceiling. The chicken man said something quiet and ordinary-sounding, and ...

... and now he held the icepick in place with the hand that was gripping Sister Maria Theresa's wrist, so the blade's point was firm against her palm. Then he took the hammer. Sister Maria Theresa pawed at him with her other hand.

I had staggered back into the wall. The chemical-smell room past the red door, I still saw it on the insides of my eyelids.

"I'm sorry," Sister Maria Theresa said, gasping. "No. Please."

"Please?" the chicken man asked. "We are past *please* and right into *thank you.*"

He drove the icepick through her hand, embedding it into the wall, and she screamed like a startled, wounded animal. *Oh Jesus.*

Don jumped up. "Fuck this."

He came at the chicken man.

Move. Act.

In one motion, the chicken man pivoted toward Don, stretched out his free hand, into Don's mouth, and then he whipped it back to rip out his tongue in a shrieking spray of blood that sent Don down on all fours.

A shock of nausea made me grab the wall, cover my mouth. My stomach was coming up. *Fucking real.* Don wailed, holding his mouth, curled on the ground, and the chicken man was already walking around the bed, snatching Sister Maria Theresa's other hand, planting it against the wall over her head, the second icepick and the hammer ready.

The chicken man opened a simple black door to a domed room with a stone pillar in the center. A chain from the top of the pillar ran down to connect with the collar of a naked, bruised boy, cowering on a concrete floor. The floor was scattered with gore. Mounds of bloody meat were heaped across the room, swarming with flies and tiny maggots ...

"See?" In Sister Maria Theresa's room, the chicken man smiled at me, casual again. His hands and face were splattered with blood. "It's like she's making a 'Y'—or is that a *touchdown* signal?"

He slammed the hammer, driving the icepick in. Sister Maria Theresa jumped in the bed, as if an electric shock had jolted through her.

"Goooal!"

I couldn't move, my breathing panting and too fast. Little sucks of air.

"Stop," Sister Maria Theresa gasped, and she screamed, crying, "No more!"

"Two more, actually. Not quite like Jesus. We aren't going for historical accuracy today." And he yanked all the covers off her, exposing Sister Maria Theresa's tan bedclothes, baggy pants and a button-up top that was wet with sweat.

On the ground, blood flowed out of Don's mouth. He struggled to get up, then slumped down again, into a red puddle, his face, chest, arms, all soaked. He was going to pass out. I heaved and vomited against the wall and in a splatter across my chest, shoes, and the floor.

Back in the domed, meat room, something hopped by the far wall, past the stone pillar. Moving on stalks, like a stork, it rooted through the bloody meat, tearing a section apart, then straightened to look at me. The top half of a boy's face was planted on its head like a mask. A mask of skin. Someone else's skin, with a bloody, lizard-like muzzle poking through. Its pink tongue cleaned tiny, sharp teeth. 'Does he know where he is right now?' the stork-thing asked and hopped closer. Its head cocked at me, it gestured with human arms and hands. 'Is he awake?'

Sounds from Sister Maria Theresa's room clipped in.

Open your eyes.

I did, and the chicken man still stood over Sister Maria Theresa's bed and exposed body.

"Let's be clear," he said. "*This*, what I'm doing now, is only sort of about you, Mark."

He tried to move Sister Maria Theresa's right ankle to the edge of the bed, and she kicked and struggled.

"Stop that. It's annoying." And he hammered it down, just like that, the icepick in through her ankle into the wooden frame at the edge of the bed. Again, she screamed and writhed.

I wiped tears from my eyes, spat out the vomit, beer, and bile taste. *Move. Stop him. Do something.* That fucking white bucket was planted right in front of me, and I was still holding the Goddamn beer. My body shook uncontrollably. The chicken man walked back around the bed toward me, took her other leg and pulled it over so she was spread eagle.

"Last one. You may feel some pressure here." He positioned the icepick, raised the hammer. He slammed it down. "Not for the faint hearted. You don't have to worry. Stronger men than you have barfed at weaker things than this."

Don wasn't moving on the floor, and more blood pooled around his face, pumping out of his mouth. Why couldn't I act? A part of me said that I was collapsing. My brain was shutting down, snapping back to everything inside the red door eighteen years ago. Impossible things that left guts feeling town into a quivering, sweaty mass. *Please. Stop.*

The chicken man took scissors, a long shiny saw, and a knife from his bag. Then he opened the bucket. It was empty. Sister Maria Theresa was crucified to the bed, whimpering softly.

"Not yet," the chicken man said. "You can't go anywhere until I keep my promise. Your liver, remember? High in potassium and tons of protein and vitamins. It really is a wonderful organ."

He cut her open. I started to reach for him, and my stomach lurched up again ...

... and a second stork-thing wearing the face of a girl hopped around the shivering, naked boy who was chained to the pillar. 'Meat meet meat,' a smiling voice said.

Stop.

I forced my eyes open. *Turn and face him.*

The chicken man said, "I always find it easier to concentrate on this—what should we call it, *surgery?*—with music."

And then the tiny sound of a song playing through bad cellphone speakers: a lilting guitar and flute—*the same fucking song*—started up mid-way through. A man's voice, with an Irish accent:

"… As she was walkin' through the fields
She heard the deathbells knellin'!"

I heard surprised, frantic moaning, a slow wet gurgle.

"And every toll they seemed to say
Hardhearted Barbara Allen!"

Then rough sawing sounds, sloppy pulling noises, and as the song kept going, he said, "Open your mouth. I said … *there*. Good. Now chew. See? It's pretty good."

I sagged into the wall, tears down both cheeks. I was crying. Like a reflex, it was already happening before my mind processed it. I smelled vomit and coppery blood. I heard wet things plopping into the bucket, then the top going back on. I heard his bag shifting around, then zippering closed.

"O mother, mother, make my bed
O make it long and narrow!"

The whole fucking thing—everything under the Cadillac Club—was there when I focused on it now. My mind blipped it into frame. The first, chemical room, and a second room, with impossible creatures, and the naked boy whose face split into a terrible grimace when he saw me. A dark gap in his mouth, past stained teeth. Don's face, without a tongue. His hands were bandaged where his thumbs should be, and the girl-stork-thing chewed on something small and fleshy. With a fingernail.

"Mark, you're missing the big finish," the chicken man said. "Take a look."

But my legs were too soft and unstable to move. I still leaned onto the wall for balance. I heard the click of a lighter, smelled cigarette smoke.

The chicken man had put everything away and was smoking, contented. Sister Maria Theresa wasn't crucified anymore. She was a blood-drenched carcass that had exploded open in the snapped ends of ribs and raw, pink-veined muscle. Somehow, she was still alive and shuddering, blood sputtering onto the floor. The chicken man doused her in water in the sign of the cross, like a ritual.

I made myself move. One step away from the wall, two, my feet awkward lumps, but I didn't fall. I smelled lighter fluid. *Not water.*

I'm going to kill you, I wanted to say. *I'm going to end you right now, whatever terror you are.* But the chicken man turned to me, bopping his head, blew another puff of smoke, and raised his cellphone to eye level so the song was louder again:

"Sweet William died for me today
I'll die for him tomorrow!"

That was Dad's name. William.

"I know," he said, "the sound is pretty terrible. But then again, I guess it's supposed to be a phone first and a stereo second, right?"

He pocketed the phone but didn't turn it off. I could still hear the faint rhythm. Then he took his lit cigarette, positioned it on his thumb to flick, and stopped.

"You know the first child doesn't belong to you. You understand, right? We've had this conversation before, haven't we, Mark?"

Yes. In the third room beneath the Cadillac Club, at a table surrounded by five plastic buckets. 'Sometimes in the old days, when a debt was due, I collected actual chickens. But *you* are the best currency.

A child. If I put you in a shipping container, I can send you to any part of the world, where you can be traded like *that.* Highly *liquid.*' In that underground room, he had leaned in, as if eager for me to smile at his comment. He told me my dad was there with us, but I didn't understand. He told me I had a choice. *What choice?*

Now, in Sister Maria Theresa's room, the chicken man said, "There really is no reason we have to see each other again. I'm a reasonable guy. Just doing my job. None of this is my idea, Mark. You understand that, right? Keep your window dark, stay out of trouble, and everything else will be fine. Clear?"

Keep my window dark.

A choice, he'd said. The memory clotted back into shape. My dad played a game, the chicken man said. Thought he could outsmart the boss. Instead, he lost: both him and Don.

But what about me? I'd asked, 'Can I play the game?' The only way to get my brother and father out—I still didn't know where Dad was. 'And if you lose,' the chicken man said. 'You'll owe two *chickens,* not one.' He'd been smiling then, too, waiting for me to back down. But I didn't. The shock of entering those rooms and the blizzard outside, weeks of anxiety—here was a way to fix it. *Get my family back.*

"You should get going," the chicken man told me, in Sister Maria Theresa's room. "Here. I'll make it easy."

The door was back, and so was the window. I heard people talking quietly out in the hall. I leaned down slowly, barely aware of the movement, as if I were watching someone else take Don's arm and pull it around my shoulder. I heaved with both legs to stand him up. The second time I got him out.

Don't look back.

The first time, the chicken man had waited for me to back down, and when I didn't he drove a knife into my left hand. Now, my steps faltering, Don unconscious and bleeding against my shoulder, I dragged us toward the door.

"It really isn't as bad as all that," the chicken man said. "See for yourself. There's a reason they laughed."

And then I heard the rush of fire as he threw the cigarette on the bed. One last moan from Sister Maria Theresa, and when I reached the doorway, I looked back. The entire room was on fire—the bed, the back wall and curtains, the furniture, even the carpet. Yellow flames enveloped the black mound that had been Sister Maria Theresa, my aunt. The chicken man was gone. Smoke swelled out the open window.

People rushed to us in the hall, grabbing Don, taking my arm and pulling me away. There was shouting and then sudden, immense torrents of gray and white smoke.

Soon, I was sitting on a bench outside. The entire parking lot was crowded with people and the chaos of firetrucks, paramedics, and police. Don was already gone. They had rushed him into the first ambulance. My stomach and throat still hurt, but it was distant, fuzzy. I tasted the beer, alcohol, no surprise there. And the vomit and bile. He let me taste that, too.

Let me. I clamped the thought down, but it wouldn't stay away. Fucking happened, because I let it happen. I didn't stop it. He took me through those rooms eighteen years ago to prove that he was still a human being. He wanted to let me go back then. Instead, I pushed him. Got Don out. After I saw what could happen, somehow I played his game and won. The thought didn't settle my stomach or ease the pain in my chest. *Won what?* No, I didn't win. Or, if I did, that was still buried in my skull, but he left me there on a cold curb with my brother and the wreckage of my father's corpse.

And now?

My phone buzzed: Mom.

I didn't answer. They were probably finishing brunch about now, Mom and Caitlyn, wondering where we were. Everything smelled like smoke, and my clothes were stiff in the cold, heavy with coagulated vomit and blood. Paramedics examined me. They said I should go to the hospital, too, but no, I didn't want to do that. All I wanted to do was sit. Shut off my brain. Stop the trauma rush somehow and go back to forgetting. Across the parking lot, the Virgin Mary statue at the pond was totally mossy green and a lot smaller than I remembered it.

A policeman offered me a cup of Starbucks coffee. I took it and watched the steam rise from the little opening on top. *Don't think about it.*

"I'd like to talk about what happened, if you're up for it," the cop said. "Easiest to remember things as soon as possible. Do you mind if I take this as a statement for my report? And a description of the suspect. Really best if we get all of that ASAP."

He said 'ASAP' like it was a word.

"Sure."

He helped me up and gave me a clean shirt and jacket from the back of his police car, and then we drove to the police station. Numb and a little jittery from the coffee, I couldn't focus on the ride downtown, and inside, the station was more clinical, less exciting than I expected, setup with cubicles, phosphorescent lighting, and a kitchenette, like any office. Back in a room he shared with three other policemen, all their desks arranged on different walls, we sat at a table in the middle. My phone buzzed a few more times with calls from Mom and Caitlyn.

"Do you need to get that?" the cop asked.

Yeah, I should. Tell them not to worry. Except that would be a lie, wouldn't it? Maybe they should worry. We all should, because the chicken man was real. I was marked, and he wanted our unborn child.

"Not yet," I said. *Put it off.* I told the policeman about the chicken man. No choice. He killed my aunt in front of me and set the God-damn room on fire. A police report meant it happened.

I finished my coffee. The policeman ordered me lunch—tomato soup and a salad from a local place—and he kept coming up with more questions, little clarifications. 'What time would you say the suspect arrived?' 'What color was his coat again?' Until finally, he brought a new stack of papers to the table.

"Good news," he said. "It sounds like your brother is stabilizing."

Jesus, I hadn't even thought about the possibility that Don might not make it. There had been a lot of blood.

"I have to see him."

"He's still in surgery. But they told me they're pretty confident. They said he's not out of the woods, but it's looking good."

I got up, already working out how I would call a taxi—my rental car was still at Holy Cross—and find Don at the hospital.

"Mark, there won't be anything for you to do while he's in surgery."

Wait.

"You don't want me to leave?"

He swiveled a set of papers on the table so I would have to sit back down to see. "Mind helping us just a little more?"

I sat and looked at the documents: print-outs of black-and-white surveillance camera photos from the end of Sister Maria Theresa's hall. There were eight of them, each with a time stamp and some technical codes underneath.

"Those are the people recorded as entering that floor in the two hours before the fire. I wanted you to have a look at this."

None of them were him. There were six women, a photo with Don and me, and an older father and child in the last one.

"He's not there," I said.

"And I wanted to get your two cents on that." The cop was watching me. "What do you think, Mark?"

What did that mean? I wasn't a detective. Did his tone change on that last question, with a little drop at the end? This was an interrogation, wasn't it? He was still nodding, like we were partners working this out together, but he was trying to prod me into mixing up my story somehow

"I don't know," I said. "He could have come in the window." The same window that disappeared, while he killed Sister Maria Theresa. Just like the door. Just like Don's bedroom eighteen years ago.

I got up, and this time, when I moved for the door, he stood slowly, an arm's length away, like he wanted to be ready, if I tried to run. What the hell was happening? Don was hurt. I had to leave.

"I have another question for you, chief ..." He called me *chief*. We were buddies now. "... and don't take this one wrong, but are you on any medications? You been drinking today?"

The chicken man was real, and this cop wanted to talk about me? I swallowed, arms shaking until I crossed them.

"No."

"Do you mind taking a Breathalyzer real quick? I know ..." He sighed, as if all of this were out of his hands. "... but otherwise, you run the risk some lawyer brings this up down the road."

What would happen if I refused? Nothing good. *Be quick. Go along with it. Just get through the next five minutes.*

"Sure, no problem," I said.

"Perfect." He shuffled under the papers. There it was. Ready to go. He held up a little plastic white box so I could blow into a tube on the side. Then, he watched the results quietly. "Huh. You know, let's take this again."

So we did it again, and this time, he turned the box to show me the results: 0.07%.

"You know the legal limit in Kentucky? Point-oh-eight." He laughed and set the Breathalyzer on the table. "You squeaked through, my friend. You can go, but I'm sure you're probably planning to stick around for a few extra days anyway?" He handed me a business card. "If you do have to leave the state, give me a shout first, deal?"

Back at the front entrance of the station, I got back my dirty clothes in a transparent plastic bag from a guy behind a bulletproof window. The wall above the window was crowded with pictures of uniformed police. I hadn't noticed before, but now ... a grainy photo high up showed a buzz-cut guy with a half-smile and steady, blue-gray eyes. The cop from the *Cadillac Club*. I couldn't make out the name, but a square at the bottom read:

Killed in the Line of Duty, Nov. 1, 1977.

Jesus.

And there, above the window:

Memorial to Louisville Metropolitan Police Department Fallen Officers.

Get out of here.

On the street, I walked fast in the cold. It was a quiet neighborhood of rehabbed apartment buildings and old houses with skinny, newly-planted trees along the sidewalks. 1977 was the strip club fire. November 1st was my anniversary and All Saint's Day.

Goddamn it, that wasn't him. You're imagining things.

I called Caitlyn.

"Finally," she said. "There you are. Are you okay? Mark, what happened? We just got to the hospital. Where are you?"

I kept moving. The momentum felt good in my legs. I passed a corner convenience store, with a blotchy white wall, clearly painted to mask graffiti. The picture at the police station wasn't real. I was just shaken up.

"The police wanted me to give a statement at their station downtown," I said.

I heard loud talking in the background.

"They told us the whole building is on fire at Holy Cross, the sprinkler system wasn't working," Caitlyn said. "Where are you?"

I didn't stop, passing a gaping hole inside a construction site, a boarded-up house, and a clean, yellow-painted apartment complex with 'For Rent' signs on the lawn.

"Just leaving the police station."

"What happened, Mark? Did you see it? Were you there?"

Did I see it? Was I there?

"Yes. Look, I'll tell you about it when I get there." Maybe somehow I wouldn't have to. Maybe the police would discover another explanation, and I was delusional about all of it. "I'll be there soon."

We said a little more, then hung up, and I stopped walking. Where was I? If I called a taxi, I would need to tell them ... I had stopped in the middle of the block by a spikey fence that surrounded an Antebellum-looking mansion. The library. And the gate was open. I watched a young woman with a backpack go up the steps and push through the front entrance.

Call a cab. Why was I just standing here?

I went in through the main doors of the library. It was quiet, softer than outside. In here, the main desk hadn't changed, but they had a new security turnstile, and half of the main reading room—an area that had been tables with squat lamps, when I was a kid—had computers now. The room still had the same high ceiling, but all the walls were shinier than I remembered, like they'd been polished. It was mostly empty, except for the woman, an older man in a sweater and tie, and another bearded guy dozing on a couch in the back, where the microfilm machine used to be.

A young Asian woman with an easy smile watched me from the front desk. "Are you a member?"

"I just came in to call a taxi."

"Oh I'm sorry. Cellphones aren't allowed in here." She sounded like she was genuinely sorry.

But I didn't move. I just stood there, staring at the room. Why didn't I go back outside? What was I doing here?

She asked, "Can I help you with something else?"

"What did this building used to be? Before it was a library?"

"I'm not sure," she said. "I know it was originally built as a house, before it was renovated and moved."

"Moved?"

"Yes, the whole thing ..." She walked me to a wall near the front doors. What do you know: an old black-and-yellowish-white photo of the library surrounded by big, blooming magnolia trees, with no other buildings anywhere around. A little box below the photo read:

'1947, Nun'Yunu'Wi.'

"What does that mean?"
The girl looked flustered.

"I'm not sure ..." She called to the sweater-and-tie guy, "Tom, can you help us out here? When was the library moved?"

"Mid-twentieth century," he said and quickly sized me up, as if he were debating whether he should beg off as too busy. "What's the question?"

"What did the library used to be?" I asked. "Before it was a library."

"A house," he said, as if I were a moron. He came over, looking skeptical, with his arms crossed. "It was built as a private residence, near Danville before the Civil War. Was a field hospital during the Battle of Perryville. And then I think they moved it, because of flooding. And then it was a lodge for awhile, back in the '60s, before the first big remodel."

"It was a *lodge*?"

"Right, for the Elks or the Masons, I'm not sure which."

I stared at the photo again. Just a southern plantation house, straight from *Gone with the Wind*, plopped down here. Why did this place matter? It didn't. Except for the bull, from Saarbrüken—near Dudweiler.

"I was here as a kid, years ago," I said, "and there were things in the basement, like an inscription and a bull's head ..."

He laughed, and the girl started shaking her head.

"Oh, I'm sure there's nothing down there like that," she said.

"And if there *were*," the guy, Tom, said. "I doubt anybody knows what it is or where it came from."

I was here now. I hadn't thought about that day in years, tried not to anyway. But somehow, I stood here now, and when would I come back? Maybe never. My grandfather brought the bull's head here after the war, didn't he? Standing here, it felt obvious. Too much of a coincidence to be anything else. Which meant the bull connected to the whiskey lamp, the chicken man—and whatever demon pact he made in Germany.

Don't. Walk away. Easy to thank them and leave, really no need to push this. *Just go.* But I didn't.

"The bull's head," I said, "can I see it?"

Now I had his attention. Concentration shifted in Tom's expression from whatever he'd been thinking about to me.

"Where was this?"

"In the stacks, in the basement. I'll show you," I said.

"It's slow up here," the girl told Tom. "Do you mind if I tag along?"

And so we went down, back to the stairs and into the basement passage with restrooms and a water fountain that hadn't changed at all, and into the stacks. No desk down here anymore and the overhead lights were new, but the stacks looked exactly like I remembered. Impersonal and dark. I led them back to the rear wall, while the girl told me they usually didn't do this, but it sounded interesting and it was a holiday weekend. Tom kept quiet. Around the rear wall, the shelves had been rearranged. There it was. The bull's head, mounted exactly where it had been eighteen years ago. I stopped.

Tom and the girl went in to examine it, but I didn't move. The empty black eyes were the same. I was an adult now. I wasn't afraid of this thing that had toyed with me as a kid. Maybe with everything happening, Dr. Laymon would say this was me trying to exercise control over *something*. Prove that there was one thing, a small fear that I could actually face. Not like the chicken man or the dead cop, this was just a taxidermy bull's head.

"Is that all it was?" Tom stood with the girl close to the bull to inspect the metal plate under it, with their backs to me. "Just a dumb bull's head?"

I felt a chill. I was still holding the plastic bag with my dirty shirt and jacket in it. I'd been carrying it around the whole time, except now my hand relaxed, opening to let the bag drop. It hit the ground and tipped over, so my shirt, with all the blood and filth on it, peeked out. The black eyes on the bull were empty marbles. I couldn't look away.

The girl looked back at me, smiling. "This is cool."

Tom crouched to inspect the Latin on the floor. *"Quod erat demon-strandum.'* It has been shown.' I think that's what it means, something like that. I remember that from a college math class. Very interesting."

"Why is it here?" the girl asked.

Tom shrugged and stood back up.

"Who knows? Maybe a donation." He noticed me staring at the bull. "Everything okay?"

"Here," the girl said, "you dropped your bag."

She knelt to pick it up but didn't. Her hand went to my belt. I felt her carefully pull the leather end out, adjust the clip, and unbuckle it. Her fingers touched the button of my pants and adjusted it through the hole.

Tom was just standing there, waiting, his face vacant.

There was something behind the black in the bull's eyes, red and brown flecks moving.

Stop it. What was happening?

The girl unzipped my pants, her hand sliding in, but I caught her wrist just as the tip of her fingers brushed my cock through my boxer shorts. She looked up at me, friendly and still smiling. *The fuck?*

"You should taste more than dirt," she said.

She tried to press her hand in, but I still held her wrist to stop her. And I was hard. For the first time since all this started, I felt the familiar, animal warmth in my erect cock.

Tom asked me something, but I didn't understand. It was in German.

"I said," the girl said, "that I know you, Mark. I am waiting for you."

The bull was still watching.

"You think it's watching?" Tom asked. "It's only a dead bull without eyes. A totem. Come see me, Mark, so I can give you your own light."

The girl tried to reach for my cock again, but still I held her back.

"Don't you want to feel again, Mark?" she asked. "I know you do. Because I can help you. Find me, and I will."

I tried to look away from the bull, but it wouldn't let go.

"Stop," I said. "Please ..."

"Stop?" Tom asked. "Oh, you're still thinking about the bull. If it's important to you, I'll give it eyes. That's how much I love you."

He pinched his left eye with one hand, then dug out the back with the other and pulled, blood streaming down his cheek, as the eyeball came away—still connected to the gaping, bleeding socket by a tissuey cord.

"Find me there," the girl said. "In the church."

Dudweiler.

And she shoved away from me, shouting. Tom slumped and fell, cupping his still-attached eye in one hand. He wailed, his whole body ratcheting in shock.

"What the fuck!" the girl shouted. She scrambled backwards across the room away from me, and then she saw Tom. "Oh my God, what's happening?"

Chapter Nineteen

I ran. I didn't stop. I didn't help them. I bolted for the door, and up the stairs I closed my pants, tied my belt, and rushed for the exit. Another guy at the front desk saw me coming, started to say something.

"Downstairs," I said. "Call 9-1-1 now."

I jumped the turnstile and was outside, stumbling down the stairs and through the fence onto the street.

Jesus fucking Christ.

The bull, the Goddamn bull. What the fuck was that? Dudweiler. It wants me there. Was that real? Was that possible? Yes, I still felt the blood-rush heat fading from my Goddamn cock. It was fucking real. It happened. *Get out of here. Get away from the library.*

How did that happen? What was that?

I followed the sidewalk away from the library, farther from the police station and tracked the Ohio River east, away from downtown. It had been years since I'd been down here, and everywhere there were new housing developments. What should have been a lot with a warehouse and boarded up buildings was a construction site with a huge crane poised overhead and a picture posted out front promising a vaguely cartoonish modern hotel, coming soon. Nobody else walking on the streets, and none of the passing cars seemed to notice me.

As I walked, I told my heart to slow down. No good. Everything was breaking now. The bull wanted to show me that it could 'help,' was that it? Was willing to control people, sacrifice people, if only I would make a pilgrimage to Dudweiler. *No, not a fucking pilgrimage.* Like Mom said in Chicago—the opposite of a sacrament.

On these city blocks, the river city grime and brick factories I remembered growing up had been replaced by coffee shops and colorful street art, bourbon distilleries, and ... *wait.* A parking lot across the street led to a curling condo tower, with windows that wrapped around like twisty fingers on a hand tilted to the side. Through the first-floor windows, I saw people exercising in a gym and lounging on lobby chairs. A new hipster restaurant, a florist, and something like a combo bicycle shop and pet grooming station flanked the place. This could have been a corner of Brooklyn, but it wasn't. It was right here, right where the *Cadillac Club* used to be. The lobby doors were in the same exact spot, even if the old building was gone.

Good. That fucking place had been erased. But my pulse still throbbed. Why didn't seeing this help? *Because it doesn't matter.* The chicken man was still here. Whatever the *Cadillac Club* was, plowing over it with condos hadn't set anything right. No, this made it worse. *He* was here, without the *Cadillac Club*. He didn't give a damn whether it made sense. Now, the worst things could happen anywhere.

I called a taxi. A few minutes later, there were sirens behind me, in the direction of the library. In the yellow cab, I didn't talk, just let the driver take me back to Holy Cross for the rental car. It was going to be fine.

A man tore out his fucking eye, and a random girl at the library tried to grab my cock. And it wasn't her, wasn't either of them. It was that *thing*, the bull's head, demonstrating that it still cared about me. Still wanted me. I couldn't outrun it or will it away.

I closed my eyes and listened to the bumps and rustling of the drive.

When we got there, I gave the taxi driver a big tip. There was still smoke coming out of the windows on the third floor of Brescia Hall, still fire trucks, police, and people watching from the parking lot. But I went straight to the rental car in the lot and reached into my pocket. Nothing.

Fuck.

The keys were in my jacket. This coat belonged to the cop, and mine … was in a bag in the basement of the library. *Okay, stay calm.*

I walked away from the car and crossed back to the pond, as if I were hiking back to school. As if I were young again.

At the Virgin Mary statue, I stopped.

Think this through. Call Mom and Caitlyn.

The thought of Caitlyn made my insides go hollow. That girl in the library—no, it wasn't just that. It had been working. I felt something for the first time in forever. Whatever had been dragging me down, making it so I couldn't taste or fuck for the past month, had been gone in the library. The bull helped me.

I approached the pond statue. It wasn't the same. It was much smaller and completely covered in moss, still in the same pose, though. She had her hands folded in prayer, looking up at the sky. The layer of moss was a thick second skin that made the features indistinct. It was a child. That was new.

What the fuck was this?

I tore some of the moss away from the face, then more and more, then pitched backwards when I saw the face.

Rachel was crying.

***

On a bench by the pond, I called another taxi. Careful not to look at the statue again, I studied the pond. No, that wasn't Rachel. I had the strangest urge to throw in a rock or maybe step in myself, to kick my feet in that black-ish water.

They had my rental car keys at the library, and I blew a 0.07 at the police station. How? That Goddamn beer, the one the chicken man gave me. I'd forgotten about that, but my bloodstream hadn't, even if I threw it up. That's why he gave it to me. So my story wouldn't be trusted.

A cab took me to a sprawling suburban hospital, and I found Mom and Caitlyn in a family waiting room decorated with plastic, multi-colored Christmas ornament globes and paper snowmen, hanging from the ceiling. Children's names and dates were scrawled on the snowmen. Babies born in the hospital, dangling around the walls of the room, like puppets. *Stop it.* What if our baby was born here someday? Maybe named 'William,' after my Dad, or, for a girl, something pretty and different, like 'Josephina.'

Nurses worked quietly at a station alongside the waiting room, chatting with doctors and staff in the hall. We had all the chairs to ourselves. Caitlyn held me for a long moment, but when I hugged Mom, she stood limp

"He just got out of surgery," Caitlyn told me. "They said he's going to be okay."

"Okay." Mom sat and picked up a gardening magazine. "*Okay.*"

"Do the police know what happened?" Caitlyn asked.

"There was a fire in Sister Maria Theresa's room," I said. "She's dead."

Caitlyn squeezed my hand, rubbed the scar on my left hand, as if that were a secret anti-trigger to calm me down. Mom flipped her magazine.

"I'm so sorry, Mark," Caitlyn said. "But why were you guys there, I thought you were just going to apologize to him for last night?"

"Mark lied," Mom said, without looking up.

"I wasn't lying. I went to talk to Don. When we were kids, Don—something happened to his sense of taste, like what I have now. And back then, Sister Maria Theresa *knew* what was wrong with him, when no one else did."

Caitlyn let go of my hand. "I don't understand."

"Why don't you tell us the truth?" Mom asked.

The truth. The word sounded like a joke, as if there were a short-hand explanation for all this. As if I knew and were hiding it.

She curled her magazine into a hard tube, as if she were going to swat me with it and glared up at me.

"You couldn't leave it alone," Mom said, "all your father's non-sense."

"What does that mean?" Caitlyn asked. "What's she talking about?"

Don't. Just make something up. A spark from the radiator caused the fire and Don tripped in a freak accident that made him bite off his tongue. Behind me, I heard the murmur of voices from the nurses' station. Maybe an alarm would go off, like on a TV hospital show. An emergency would interrupt.

"We went to see Sister Maria Theresa. She said that my first-born child—*our child*—is going to be taken from us by the chicken man.

That's why I can't taste anything and won't, until that happens." Caitlyn started to speak, and I held up my hands. "Just give me a second. I'm trying to explain. I don't understand all of it, but there's some kind of debt in our family. That's why my sister, Abby, is gone. It's why my dad's older brother was taken when he was a kid. I've been trying not to … I don't know. I hoped it would go away. But *he* was there. He made the door and window disappear in Sister Maria Theresa's room, just like Don's bedroom when we were kids. He killed her."

Caitlyn stood very still. "Oh Mark …"

No ringing sounded. No desperate screaming from the quiet people in the hospital behind me. I was alone. *Shit.* They didn't believe me. Of course they didn't. I barely did.

"He did," I said, my voice jagging a little too much. Desperate. "I saw it happen. He hurt Don."

"And that's it?" Mom asked.

The library, the Goddamn library. *No, don't talk about that.* But they had my things. And it happened.

"Then—look, when I was a kid, I went to the library downtown. And in the basement, I saw something, a bull's head, mounted on the wall. It says 'Saarbrüken,' the same part of Germany my grandparents came from."

"Mark, I want to understand this," Caitlyn said. "But …" She shook her head, expression soft and pitying. "Why would you go to a *library* after what happened to your aunt?"

"When I was a kid, that bull's head at the library convinced me that I was really an old man in a nursing home with dementia."

Caitlyn said, "Mark …"

"It was still there," I said. "I think it brought me back. The bull's head if linked to the lamp and—"

Mom got up, took a deep breath, and then slapped me hard across the cheek. The sudden hot pain almost brought tears to my eyes. I stepped back, touched my cheek. *The fuck.* She gave me a long, disappointed look.

"Just like your father," she said. "You have a responsibility now. Stop it, Mark. Just stop."

Then she walked away, back into the hospital.

"She shouldn't have done that," Caitlyn said quietly. "But she's not wrong. I don't want to know any more about this—any of it. Not right now, okay?"

"Caitlyn, this bull made people ..."

"Mark." Her voice stopped me, and now I noticed an unsteady shake in her legs. She shifted her weight, like she wanted to move. Retreat from the hospital. "Someday, okay? Not right now. Whatever you think happened or *is happening*, right now, in this hospital, with your brother just out of surgery—please just don't."

Don't. Don't tell her about the girl or the man who balled his own eyeball in one hand. Or the soothing voice in my head, calling me to Dudweiler. The chicken man was coming for our child, and that thing in Germany wanted to protect us. Mom was right. Just like my dad. Whatever this was, I couldn't wish it away or wait until our time ran out.

"The police called me," Caitlyn said, watching me closely, as if I were suddenly testifying. "It sounded like ... Mark, they weren't clear, but it sounded like they think you're a suspect in the fire. That's your aunt's murder."

She said it like I didn't know.

"And then you're here." Caitlyn turned away, rubbing her face, with a frustrated smile. The way she'd looked last night when she was dealt the wrong card. One away from a royal flush, and now she had nothing. "You're talking about disappearing doors and this *chicken man* and ..." There were tears in her eyes when she looked up at me again. "Mark, I'm really worried about you. And us." Her hand dropped, probably unconsciously, to her stomach.

'Us' didn't mean me.

"I'm okay," I said, but that sounded weak. "Really. I think I am. I think I'm starting to see what's happening—what hit me as a kid."

Stork-things wearing children's faces in a room of meat. I shivered and rubbed my arms. Fuck. What if I was insane? Fifty percent chance, at least.

"Caitlyn, I love you."

When I reached for her, she took my hand, nodding. "You, too. But I'm going back to New York."

"What—now?"

"Yes. My office called, and there's a problem with some casework, and ... I have to think about this. This whole thing." She dropped my hand. "I do, you know. Love you, too, Mark."

The work excuse was probably legit, but could she have begged off? Told them about a family emergency over the holiday weekend? Yes. Now, she wanted room to breathe and see if I would come up for air, too, enough to take care of myself. And our family. I couldn't be her ward, that's what this meant. I couldn't be the wounded, alcoholic man-child imagining monsters, if our lives were meant to work to-gether. Except she loved me.

"Okay," I said.

Caitlyn met my eyes, the frightened tears gone. She nodded again, as if I'd just said all that out loud and we had an agreement. "We'll talk more tonight."

Tell her you know none of it's real. It was a bad joke. Stress and the flash of the fire made you say crazy things. She might stay. If I pre-

tended, she might believe me—because she wanted to think I wasn't a lunatic—and we could go back together.

But I was past that now.

We hugged again, then I walked Caitlyn to the elevator, and when she was gone, I found a nurse who agreed to show me Don's room. Down the hall, his room was on the right, and my legs locked in the doorway. He looked terrible. His jaw swollen and stuffed with bandages and white tape, his eyes heavy and squinting, an IV in one arm. A curtain partitioned the room in half, and I heard someone wheezing on the other side. Don blinked and smiled a little when he saw me. The nurse gave him notebook-sized whiteboard with an erasable marker, then left us alone.

"You look good," I said.

He wrote: *'Thx. I know.'*

I didn't go in. "Sister Maria Theresa is dead. *He's* gone again. I don't know where."

He stared at me, waiting.

"I told the police," I said.

'What?'

I couldn't stay here, had to fix this somehow. Sitting at Don's bedside felt like giving up. I had to make this right, before I stopped moving. Couldn't rest or close my eyes now that *he* was back.

"I told the police and Mom and Caitlyn what happened," I said. "They didn't ..."

He wrote: *'Of course not.'*

And the rest. Tell him the rest. "I went back to the library. I didn't mean to, but the bull's head was still there, the one I told you about in the basement ..." I leaned on the doorframe and kept my breathing steady. "It made one of the librarians rip his own eye out. Told me to go."

He wrote: *'Where?'*

"Where do you think? I'm going to."

Don shifted, wincing as he sat up.

'Me 2.'

"No, look at you. Stay here. Mom's losing it. She doesn't want to hear any of this."

'Like before.'

The nurse came back down the hall to tap my shoulder. "Sir, I told you it had to be quick. Your brother needs to rest."

"Just one minute." I finally went in to stand beside him. More softly, I said, "I'm going to deal with this now. You tried the last time. When you went to the Cadillac Club, why couldn't you stop him?"

'I missed.'

I tried to picture teenage Don firing a gun. An image of the video game screen on TV turning red as I was shot, then going black.

I held his hand. His fingers were soft. "Thanks for looking out for me, Don. Back then, I never said that. You tried to deal with it, so I wouldn't have to."

He wrote: *'So dramatic.'*

Behind me, the nurse made an impatient noise.

'Drive,' he wrote. *'Take my car. Then fly.'*

Get out of town, then hop on a plane to Germany. He was right. It was safest. He should be coming with me. Don saw things I didn't. We were in it together again, but this was on me now. No way around it.

He wrote: *'And take the lamp.'*

CHAPTER TWENTY

By 3:00 PM, I was on the road, in Don's Ford Taurus, headed northeast on I-71 along the northern edge of Kentucky toward Cincinnati. What about the lamp? I should leave the damn thing in our Brooklyn apartment or chuck it in the East River. At least a 12-hour drive back to the city. Caitlyn would probably be back there before I arrived.

Tell her I'm coming? Leave the lamp or take it?

I saw an exit sign for Cincinnati / Northern Kentucky International Airport coming up. I could let the car follow the curve of the road, and get on a flight now. *Just go to Germany and resolve this—finally. Prove there's nothing there. Or? Face down the bull. Kill it.* It wanted to help me the way it had at the library, my grandfather's evil still moldered in Europe somewhere. But I didn't. I kept the wheel steady and crossed a rusty suspension bridge into Ohio, continuing north through Cincinnati. When I stopped for gas and sandwiches in Pennsylvania, I noticed missed calls from Caitlyn and a voicemail from Mom on my phone. Lots of patches of dead air with no cell signal between Kentucky and New York City. I dialed on and heard Mom's voice. Maybe she was going to apologize ...

"Mark, the police came by," Mom said.

Not an apology.

"... I told them I didn't know where you are, because I don't. They're looking for you, Mark. The police said you were involved with the fire and an incident—that's what they called it, *incident*—at the library. What did you do? Whatever it was ..." She paused, heavy, strained breathing on the line. "... you know I love you. Please, just leave it alone. Don't go."

The message ended. *Don't go.* Too late for that. I got back in the car and switched on the headlights, flipping radio stations, as I pulled back onto the Pennsylvania Turnpike. I tried to put Mom's voice out of my head and called Caitlyn. No answer, so I stared at the darkening road. It helped. There was a meditative quality to the pace of this highway at night. All I had to do was watch for red brake lights and adjust as cars merged or revved past me.

Hours passed in near-total darkness, until I got closer to the city. Even in the middle of the night, as the interstate grew wider, it attracted a busier flow of traffic: cross-country trucks, night-shift workers, drunks swerving between the lanes, and more police. By the time I saw the lights and glass towers of Manhattan, it was already after 4:00 AM. The sky was a dark blue, not black anymore, when I got to our apartment. The street was quiet, but I found a parking spot two doors down. A minor miracle. I would have to call Robert, too, explain that I needed time off for a last minute emergency.

Of course, I didn't have my keys. They were still in the plastic bag, probably in a police locker in Kentucky. If Caitlyn hadn't flown out immediately, our apartment would be empty, and I would have to call the super. Out of the car, the night air woke me.

At the locked glass entry doors to our building lobby, I punched the number of our apartment and heard the buzzer ring on the intercom. No answer, so I did it again, and by the third time was ready to give up, when a muffled voice—Caitlyn—asked, "Who's there?"

"It's me."

She said, "Mark? I don't understand."

She wasn't going to be happy about my fugue-state plan to fly to Germany to search for my grandfather's Nazi demon bull. Not even a little. What if she called the cops? The police in Kentucky were looking for me. Would my name pop up in a cross-country system here in Brooklyn?

I said, "I'm not staying. I'll be two minutes."

"It's 4:00 AM, Mark."

But the door clicked open, and I went up. Through the lobby, I took the elevator, and Caitlyn was already waiting in our doorway at the end of the hall, dressed in her blue robe, her hair flat and matted from sleep. She looked ready to block me.

"I can't believe you're here," she said. "What about your brother—and the police ..? Didn't they say not to leave the state?"

As I walked past her into the apartment, I felt her tension amping up, as if the adrenaline were clearing her mind.

"Mark, what is this? Are you a fugitive now?"

I crossed to our bedroom and the closet, where I found my black rolling suitcase and quickly shoved in a change of clothes. I had my passport already, but I found an envelope of emergency cash in a folder with important documents. Just a couple hundred, but I took it all.

"No," I said. "Don't worry."

I finished packing, then went back into the living room and found the whiskey lamp, still in the box from Grandma Elizabeth. The Goddamn thing was going to be pressed in with my clothes, but no time to worry about that now. I took the suitcase into the bathroom, grabbed a toothbrush, deodorant ...

"Where are you going?" She came into the bathroom doorway. "This feels manic. How did you get here? Have you slept since I saw you?"

I zipped up the suitcase. Whatever I didn't have, I could get somewhere else.

"I don't want to argue."

"Me neither," she said. "Just tell me what's happening."

I'm going to find a demon in Germany, because of a bull in the Kentucky library and my grandfather's cassette recording. Because the chicken man told me to keep my window dark. Because I have to know what this means.

I rolled the suitcase to the door. "I love you."

She watched me from across the kitchen.

I said, "I'm going to get better."

Her expression softened a little. "Are you checking yourself in somewhere?"

"I have to go."

I opened the door and left without looking back.

On the front stoop, I stopped. Someone was watching. I scanned the early-morning neighborhood. A biker passed, then a guy in a reflective vest walking five poodles. The hair on the back of my neck and arms felt charged. *No one here. Stop it. You're tired, and Caitlyn is right—a little manic.*

Focus.

I forced myself to pull up a travel website on my phone. I should have done this earlier, but I hadn't known how long the drive would take. Dudweiler was a small town, near Saarbrüken. I had $250 in cash and probably about that amount in my checking account, another

$50 in savings, and the $1,500 on the credit card. It would have to be enough. There was a flight to Saarbrüken, Germany, via Lisbon and Munich, leaving in three hours. Altogether, with the connecting flights, it would take eighteen hours and cost almost $1,000. I put a one-way ticket on my credit card and drove to JFK airport.

No way to pay for that credit card bill when it came due—or for the apartment, after Caitlyn moved out. *Don't worry. Not important right now.*

Back in the car, I texted Robert:

> *'I'm sorry. I probably won't be in next week. Family emergency.'*

Before I could put the phone away, it buzzed with a response. He was already up. His text:

> *'Call?'*

Shit, I didn't want to do this, but okay, I owed him a conversation after that message. I tapped to dial Robert, and he answered with a caffeinated smile in his voice, "Hey Mark, early riser today! What's going on, man? Talk to me."

"I have a family ..." The sentence withered in my throat. I was too tired to organize a bullshit story or dodge his questions. "I have to go to Germany," I said.

"Germany," he repeated. "Like what we talked about? Right now?"

"Yeah. It's complicated, and hopefully won't be long ..."

"You know I thought you were an ass when you told me about your Nazi granddad."

I swallowed, my right hand already squeezing the steering wheel. I hadn't started the car, was still in the parking spot by our apartment. I could just stay here. Let it go, like Mom said.

"Yeah?" I said at last.

"Oh yeah. What kind of guy tells his Black boss that 'oh by the way, my family were Nazis' just a few days into a new job? I'm serious, Mark, that's not something you want to hear. Understand me?"

"Yeah," I said again. I'd never heard him talk like this. The same easy cadence in Robert's voice sounded harder now, almost threatening.

"Still," he said, "here's my answer to your Germany ancestor trip: fuck you."

My mouth went dry. "What?"

"I said, 'fuck you,' Mark. You want to find your roots? Well, my family were picking cotton eighteen hours a day for no wages in Alabama, while your granddad was doing whatever Nazi shit he was doing. And before that, we were *chattel*, Mark. Fuck you for having a granddad who did whatever he did. I know it wasn't you—I know that—but I can still be angry and irrational a little. And do I think you should have to atone for atrocities that happened before you were born? I do indeed. It's not pretty, but it's the only way any of this world we're left with can make sense. I told you about the Romans who built cave temples to a deity we no longer acknowledge, in the same place where your little town of Dudweiler was founded. Why do I care about that? Why does anyone study it? Because if we don't—if we don't take seriously all those people who came before us and the damage they did, deal with that in our lives, not just shrug it away as 'the past'—then we dishonor them *and* ourselves. Their lives don't mean a damn thing outside our own heads. Which means ours don't either."

A muffled silence. His words sounded practiced, like a classroom lecture, but they still bit. I realized I was holding my breath, didn't want to answer with the wrong thing. Not just because of the job.

"Okay," he said. "End of rant." And laughed. "Bet you didn't know I'd get this wound up before 6:00 AM, did you? You know why, right? Because I want you to come back from Germany in one piece. You've still got to finish wiring my fuse box."

This flip from frustration to caring took a moment to register.

"I will," I said.

"Oh, you sound *real* sure. Something happened to you since we last saw each other."

Not a question. He probably read it in my voice and impulsive, maybe self-destructive travel plans.

"I think maybe my sister is there," I said softly. "In Dudweiler." The part I hadn't wanted to say out loud, because it meant hope. Hope that Abby called Caitlyn, when all this started—no, when it *restarted*. Because as long as the whiskey lamp and bull head—and the chicken man—as long as they existed, it wasn't over. "I told you, it's about family," I said. "Not just my grandfather, but ..."

"Okay," he said again. "I believe you have a good reason. Or think you do at least. So my one piece of advice? If things *don't* turn out the way you expect, hit the dirt. Just leave. Fair enough?"

I agreed, and he wished me safe travels, made a joke about how Germans didn't have a sense of humor, and then the call ended. And I was alone again. Time to go. I texted my friend, Susan, too, told her I had to be away, and started the car.

At the airport, I sent a message to Don from a shuttle bus to apologize for leaving his car parked in a long-term lot 730 miles from his apartment, then went to check-in in Terminal 1.

"I'm sorry, sir," a woman at the airline desk said.

Lufthansa had no record of my ticket. Luckily, I still had it on my phone, so I showed her.

She stared at the screen, confused. "Is there a way to make your screen brighter?"

I looked at it. The phone screen was totally normal. But I flipped through a couple menus and upped the brightness setting.

Still, she couldn't read what was onscreen. "Sir, if you wouldn't mind, we do have other guests waiting."

"The ticket is right here," I said. "Check again."

When she did and still couldn't find it or make sense of my phone display, I asked to speak to her manager. I knew I looked tired, disheveled, and my eyes were probably still bloodshot from the all-night drive. My hair and clothes, somehow my hands, still smelled like smoke. A large, bored-looking man came over to give me a hard time about the ticket, too, and when I showed him the phone, he also pretended he couldn't understand it.

Finally, I had to stand aside, so other people could check-in. What the hell was happening? I checked my phone. It seemed fine. There was the ticket, right there, and on the monitors, it said I still had an hour and a half before the flight to Lisbon was scheduled to leave. It was a computer glitch. That was all. I wanted to sleep or drink or find coffee. Instead, I pushed my way back to the airline desk.

The bored guy called over, "You'll have to step away, sir, or I will call security."

"I want my ticket," I said.

"You don't have a ticket, sir."

"Then I'll buy another one right now."

This was stupid and would max out my card, overdraw my bank account. This was eviction in a month, ruined credit when I couldn't pay, and maybe other things too. But they relaxed when I offered to buy a new ticket. The bored man got everything ready, then swiped my credit card for part of the total. The rest would have to come out of my bank account.

"I'm sorry, sir, this card isn't going through," he said. "Do you have another card we can try?"

"Try it again."

He did, and it didn't work.

This time, I backed away before he could lose his cool again. Something was wrong. I had to find another way onto the plane. I watched out the main terminal doors, where police were directing traffic and people waved down cars, popping open trunks, or rushing to catch their flights. The monitor said I had one hour and twenty-five minutes before departure. I wasn't going to be able to buy a ticket, was I? Not for Saarbrüken anyway. The card didn't work. But I still had cash. I checked the envelope of emergency cash: two hundred and thirty-five dollars. Whatever was happening, I had to work around it somehow.

At the check-in desk of a different airline, I waited in line, then asked where I could go one-way for two-hundred dollars. At first, the guy at the desk didn't understand, but eventually, he put me on a flight to Boston, leaving in two hours. Once I got past security, I would find a way on the Lisbon flight. I handed him a small stack of cash, and he checked my passport and typed for a while on the computer.

"I'm sorry. There seems to be a problem with our system. Your ID is not coming up." He examined my passport again. There was some back-and-forth with a few other people, and then he looked at me hopelessly. "There's really nothing I can do."

"I can't fly anywhere," I said. "That's what you're telling me?"

Was it the police? Was I on a travel watch list, after fleeing Kentucky? Must be.

He gave me back my money, and I went to sit and watch people file through a security checkpoint on their way to a wall of restaurants and stores by the terminal gates on the other side.

One hour and five minutes left.

What was I supposed to do? Go back home? Try to find my ticket again? Look for a Goddamn boat to take me across the ocean? There had to be a way through this. Without really thinking, I put the cash back in the envelope and unzipped my suitcase to wedge it deep inside, so nobody would be able to grab it out, and my hand brushed the whiskey lamp. I stopped. It was just a lamp. A lamp that electrocuted me as a kid and made me see things that weren't there, and that had some deep, fucked up tie to Dudweiler. And the chicken man was afraid of it. *Keep your window dark.* Dad lit the lamp to keep us safe, because he believed, just like my grandfather, in a sunken lady. The lamp and the bull.

This was crazy. Completely and totally nuts, but I took the lamp out of the bag and got back in line at the first airline desk. What did I expect to happen? Even before I got to the front, the bored guy spotted me and grabbed a white phone from the wall, watching me as he spoke into it. Calling security. I got to the front and approached him. He still had the phone in one hand. There was a power outlet right here, conveniently on my side of the counter.

Someone tapped my shoulder. "Sir?"

I spun. A cop in a full-on flak jacket, with an assault rifle slung over his shoulder, stood there. He held the leash of a friendly drug-sniffing dog. The dog's leash was connected to a 'Do Not Pet' neon orange doggie vest. "Could you step over here for me, please?"

I wanted to say no. The dog was sniffing around, watching the line of people behind me. Clearly, I wasn't a drug mule, but the cop took me aside, right by the power outlet. "Can I see your ID, please?"

I gave him my passport, and he clicked a walkie-talkie mouthpiece that was attached to his shoulder. "Yes, that's right." Then to me: "Mr. Morris? Did you recently visit Louisville, Kentucky?"

I stared at him, started to answer … and say what? This was about the fire, Sister Maria Theresa, and the library *incident*. Why did I think I could get on an international flight? *I wanted to run, trace this thing back to its roots and try to pull the whole curse—whatever it was—out of the dirt in Germany.* But that was insane. All of it.

"Sir, are you aware that you're now a person of interest in at least two separate investigations in that state, in Kentucky? They've asked us to hold you here. Do you have a lawyer, Mr. Morris?"

I shook my head.

"Can you tell me …" He smiled a little, as if the situation were absurd. It was. "… where are you headed?"

Nowhere. I glanced at the outlet, still holding the whiskey lamp in one hand. "Germany. Do you mind if I plug this in?"

I half-expected him to tense up and ask me to step away from the counter, but he shrugged. "Go ahead."

I plugged in the lamp. It lit up, but nothing changed.

He tapped the handle of his assault rifle. "Little late for Oktober-fest, isn't it? What's the occasion?"

Stalling me. He was waiting for other people to show, wasn't he? Probably the 'deal with this guy so me and my drug dog can get back to busting smugglers' squad. Maybe even U.S. Marshalls. This was a national issue now, wasn't it? I should have thought this through.

"Family," I said.

What was I forgetting about the lamp? Something I was missing. The first time, I broke a glass, spilled water, before I touched it, and again at our apartment when I saw Grandma Elizabeth without the whiskey lamp, I dropped another glass—*blood*. There was blood every time.

The cop's radio crackled, and he looked past me, scanning the room for his squad, whoever was going to—and I saw them: a big guy with a red beard and a fast-moving Hispanic woman, staring hard at me. They were both wearing white and blue uniforms, not regular police, but they were armed. My ride.

Standing over the lit lamp, I pinched my left palm hard, digging in my fingernails into the scar. The pain was sharp, but no blood.

"All right, sir, let's step away from the desk." His dog was suddenly poised, watching me.

Stop. Call a lawyer or Caitlyn. What do you think is going to happen? The two security agents were ten meters away and closing, pressing past an Indian family with a huge cart full of luggage. The cop touched my shoulder, his fingers hard but loose. This felt like a practiced, professional move, so he could twist my arm behind me, knock me down, plant a knee in my back, if he had to.

"Sir, step away."

I squeezed my palm harder and a little line of blood smeared onto the side of my hand. It dripped, splattering on the lamp—the glass, the wood, even the leather skin.

The cop's radio chirped again, and the two other security guards stopped abruptly, chatting with someone else.

"Apologies, sir. Looks like there's been a mistake." He waved over the guy at the airline desk. "Everything okay here? He has a flight to catch."

The bored guy watched me eagerly, waiting. "We're fine. Let's see if we can't check you in, sir."

Even the dog relaxed, and just like that, the cop wandered away. The two security guards did, too. There it was: my ticket, already purchased. They didn't have to look at my phone. I kept the lamp plugged in by my feet the whole time, until I was holding my passport and the ticket. Then I unplugged it, half-expecting the cop to spin around and charge back over with handcuffs the moment the light went out. He didn't. I still had fifty minutes until the flight left, and it wasn't far. Plenty of time.

Whatever was happening, go with it now. Don't stop to think or question this, just carry the lamp through, all the way to the gate. At the security checkpoint, I waited until it was my turn. My passport and ticket checked out, and I took off my shoes, emptied my pockets into a plastic tub. I was still holding the lamp, but in a second, I would have to drop it on a conveyer belt, along with my suitcase, so they could go through the X-ray machine. Then I would step through the metal detector and get them back on the other side. Easy. But I hesitated. When it was time for me to put it down, I held the lamp tighter.

The TSA people were waiting. In another moment, there would be questions. I had to make a decision.

No.

"I'm sorry," I said. "I forgot something."

I grabbed my stuff and went back out. It would only take a few seconds for the whiskey lamp to go through the metal detector and then I would have it back. But it wasn't lit.

In the main area, I found a spot to plug it in—that reassuring yellow light inside the bourbon bottle again—and I started asking random people for help.

"I need a battery charger for this lamp, to keep it lit."

The third person I asked—a harried guy in a suit—had one, and he gave it to me, no questions asked. When I tried to pay him, he said that he had to run and didn't want to miss his flight. I had it plugged in, tucked under one arm, the electric light glowing as I got back in line at security. Only thirty-five minutes until my flight left, but in less than five, I was through. I carried the lit whiskey lamp all the way to the gate. They were already boarding. I needed more batteries. No telling how long this would last, but there wasn't time.

I got on, found my middle seat, and stowed the whiskey lamp under the seat in front of me, with the little light shining. I should have stayed awake to watch it, but I didn't, and hours later, I jolted back awake as the plane touched down in Portugal. Out the window, wide-leafed trees lined the airport runway, and uniformed workers waved us on with white neon sticks. The sun was already going down again. My mouth was dry, and somehow I felt worse, more exhausted from the rest. But there was the lamp, still glowing by my feet.

The flight to Munich was the same. I drifted in and out of cramped sleep, until we landed. Through the airport, waiting by the gate, and the entire time we were in the air, the lamp stayed lit. Again, I didn't have time to find spare batteries, but that hardly mattered, when the plane landed in Germany. I was practically there.

We were sitting on the dark runway. No sense of what time it was. My body felt ragged from travel, not enough food, and just a few cups of water and coffee along the way. But I didn't care. The plane pulled up to the gate. Another short flight to Saarbrüken, then Dudweiler. My mind was bleary so that everything, not just my vision, my *awareness*, was soft around the edges. I dragged my suitcase out of the plane, with the whiskey lamp in my other hand. The lamplight was out. I stopped outside a restroom in the clean, chrome-colored terminal. I was here now. It would be fine. I found a departures monitor and sat in a chair near a power outlet. The airport was crowded and loud, but nicer than I'd expected, like a high-end mall.

The power outlet didn't fit. *Shit, of course*—it used a different type of plug, with two circle holes, not the twin vertical lines and roundish hole underneath of American outlets that had always reminded me of a tiny face in shock. A 120V supply voltage. The German outlets were type F 230V supply sockets. Even if I bought a simple converter, unless it was also a voltage adapter, it would fry the lamp. Of everything, *I* should have anticipated this.

I wasn't thinking clearly. I was too tired, had been hustling for too long without a break, all the way from Kentucky. I found the flight to Saarbrüken on the screen. It was leaving in about an hour, and then it was only an hour and five minutes in the air. Saarbrüken was right next door to Dudweiler. I was almost there.

Careful with the whiskey lamp, I got up and went to look for Terminal 2. I was in Terminal 1 now. I had plenty of time. I followed a steel-looking corridor past the terminal gates and several chain stores selling clothes, a MacDonald's, past an elaborate jewelry kiosk with multi-colored tassels dangling from the slots of window beams over-head, past more stores ... and back to the place where I had started. Now I had 50 minutes to make the plane. Somehow, I had just wan-dered in a circle, a neat loop around the terminal. But that didn't seem possible. The entire terminal looked like it was cut in nothing but straight lines, even the functional chair I'd sat in a minute ago.

Many of the signs in here were in both English and German, but nothing seemed to indicate where the other terminals might be. So I walked it again, slower this time, careful to watch for side passages or direction signs. There were the clothing stores, the MacDonald's, and at the jewelry kiosk I stopped to ask for help. A couple was chatting in German with the staff. I waited, and as time clicked away, I felt the familiar tug of adrenaline in my arms and chest. Still, they were busy.

Finally, I interrupted. "I'm sorry. I need to find Terminal 2. Can you tell me where that is?"

A guy working there stopped just long enough to say, "Sir, I am busy with a customer. Please wait." And then he launched back into the German conversation.

This wasn't helping. I started walking again, checking the signs, watching the walls for any hallways I might have missed. But no, there it was directly in front of me: the same damn chair and screen, the gate I had come out of when the plane landed from Lisbon. *Calm down.* I had 30 minutes left. They were probably boarding. I went up to the airline counter, where I sidestepped another line and waved to get the attendant's attention.

"I was just on the flight from Portugal, I have a flight to—"

"Please wait at the back of the line, sir. Thank you," she said.

"Terminal 2," I said. "Where is it?"

She frowned, then pointed back the way I had just come.

I kept moving. *Not random.* This wouldn't work without the whiskey lamp. I needed a battery. At a store with magazines, drinks, and snacks, there was another line, but I called to get the cashier's attention, "Batteries? Do you have batteries?"

"No, sorry."

I stared at a display of electronics by the checkout: cameras, phone chargers, earbuds … maybe I could wire a makeshift 120V battery, if I had more time. With the right tools, I could crack open different components—except my credit card wouldn't work without the whiskey lamp. Nothing would. I ran to the next store, just clothing, and the next—a store with soap and fancy candles, incense—and back to the jewelry kiosk, where the couple was still having the same Goddamn conversation.

Find a way out of this somehow.

This couldn't be real. *You're tired. Stop and rest or find a cup of coffee, or someone to help.* This was impossible. Whatever I was seeing wasn't real. I was wandering back and forth, delusional.

Or the lamp went out, and something didn't want me to go to Dudweiler. Something was trying to stop me. *Him.*

I looked at the lamp. Years ago, the chicken man harassed my father for lighting it, and he'd warned me to stay dark. This damn thing got me on the plane in New York. It made no sense, but it did. And why should that be any stranger than anything else? But even if that were true, there were no batteries or voltage converters or lights to fix it. No way forward.

Unless I was thinking about this wrong. Too much in electrician-mode. What did Mom say—it was a wicked relic, created in a living hell. I only had a few minutes left—and who knew how far Terminal 2 might be—but I went back to the store with all the bath soaps and incense and bought a package of candles.

Who said it had to be an electric light?

I bought them with cash, overpaying when the female cashier tried to refuse my U.S. dollars. She dropped a box of matches in the bag, and I ripped open the package. Frantically, I yanked the electric cord out of the whiskey lamp.

"Sorry," the cashier woman said, "you cannot light those in here."

I fit one of the candles in so it rested on the wooden base under the bottle, covering the hole where the electric cord had come through. The old whiskey lamp, the original bottle, had been charred, scored and streaked black—not by electric light but by fire.

The cashier woman hurried over to stop me. "Sir!"

I struck a match and lit the lamp.

"Can I help you with anything else?" she said.

I left and immediately saw a new sign: directly over the jewelry kiosk there were directions to Terminal 2. They had been there the whole time—and a new passage on the opposite wall that was crowded with people on moving walkways. The lamp tight in one hand, suitcase bouncing as I dragged it behind me, I charged through the crowd.

"Sorry," I said, "my flight is leaving!"

I hurried through a series of connecting corridors with checkerboard floors into Terminal 2. There was the gate. The door was still open, and an airline attendant saw me coming, checked her watch, and then waved me on.

"Hurry, hurry!" she said. "You almost missed it. Mr. Morris? We paged your name in the airport over the speakers."

I panted as I dug out my ticket. "Thank you."

"You are lucky," she said. "Only one thing: you cannot bring that lit candle onto the plane. You'll have to put it out."

She waited, and I stared blankly, probably looking as scattered as I felt. No, I was here. The plane was right there, and I had the lamp working again.

"English? Do you understand?" She gestured at the whiskey lamp, said something in German.

Probably 'blow it out, moron.'

"I can't," I said. That confused her, so I spoke fast, pleading: the whiskey lamp was helping me, even if it was evil. It belonged to my grandfather, I felt safe with it, was terrified of flying without it ...

"My answer is 'no,'" she said simply. "Now I have to close the doors. What would you like to do?"

"How far is it to drive to Saarbrüken?" I asked. I didn't want to say Dudweiler, as if someone were listening.

"Four or five hours," she said.

Get on the damn plane and go. I made it. Somehow, I had found the way, despite that funhouse bullshit at the other end of the airport. I was here. Blow out the candle and get on.

Except I was only here because of the candle. What if the plane fell out of the sky or got redirected to another country without the whiskey lamp lit? I still had the matches. I could always light it again, if I really needed to, couldn't I? I imagined flight attendants wrestling me to the ground as I tried to strike a match. Goddamn it.

"All right," I said. "I guess it sails without me."

Chapter Twenty-One

Despite the whiskey lamp, they wouldn't let me rent a car at the airport without an international driver's license, so I converted my cash to Euros and hid the lit lamp in my suitcase at the bus terminal. Maybe my clothes would ignite, but a direct bus from the airport to Dudweiler was leaving in ten minutes. No sense chancing it, if they refused to let me on with the candle burning. I boarded on a concrete walkway in the chilly early-morning sunshine and found a window seat near the back. The sky outside was pale, overcast, and when we were off, I took out the whiskey lamp again. No problem. Blocky neighborhoods passed. Except for German advertisements plastered over the bus doors and along the walls, the glass apartment towers and walled-off subdivisions didn't look so foreign. When the first candle started to burn down in the lamp, I switched it out for another one and kept it on the seat beside me.

Across the aisle, a young guy with glasses and a prematurely gray beard saw me adjusting the lamp and called over something in German.

"I'm sorry," I said. "I only speak English."

"American?" He smiled and scooted closer. An older woman a few rows ahead of us glared back at him, as if this were a 'quiet' bus. "Where are you going?"

"Dudweiler."

"For the conference?" He was excited. "And what is this lamp, an antique?"

"I'm not ..." My head was still foggy, hard to organize my thoughts. I needed to sleep. "What conference?"

"About what we owe the past for the current generation. You're not a scholar, no?" He asked it in the blunt way people sometimes talked when they weren't using their native language—or maybe this was just how Germans spoke. Then he offered me his hand. "My name is Friedrich."

"I'm Mark. Yes, I'm American. The lamp belonged to my grandfather."

"From the war?"

He watched the candle burn inside it, and I resisted the urge to pull it away from him.

"Yes," I said. "My grandfather was in the war."

"You look German," he said. "He was part of the Reich, your grandfather? I thought so, and this lamp of yours is something that he stole or that gives you guilt about the things he did? This is exactly the purpose of the dialogue today. My family, too, many of them were in the army during the war. And I grew up ashamed of the things they did. But today, I think there is a new stage in the discussion. Why should we carry this burden? You were not here. You don't even live in this country. All of these things that happened before you and I were born, why should we struggle under that weight?"

Like a shadow of my call with Robert back in New York, this felt too obvious, like a dream. The old woman a few rows in front muttered something, and Friedrich perked up and shouted back at her in German.

"Because," the woman said with a thick accent, "you *are* guilty. We all are. The land is, forever."

"That is bullshit," Friedrich said, smiling. "My American friend here, Mark, should apologize for something that happened thousands of kilometers from his home, 50 years before he was even born?"

"It is sin," the woman said, and then more in German.

"She says we are ignorant," Friedrich told me. "But she is old and will die soon." He said it more loudly, so the woman could hear. "And who will make the hard decisions next? Is *she* going to preserve our culture?"

He muttered something else in German, with a knowing smile, as if he knew I were pretending not to understand. Something ugly, all of it, as if we were on the same team. I tightened my grip on the whiskey lamp. Whatever Robert or these people thought, I wasn't here for a generational reckoning—not really. I was here because of the call from Abby. And the bull, and because my grandmother's skinned corpse murmured the name, 'Dudweiler.' *You're here with a fucking Nazi heirloom, and you're losing your mind.* Clipping the pieces into a neat, explanatory line did make this trip feel not just impulse, but delusional. Dr. Laymon would be disappointed to see me in full-on relapse mode—unless this was a means to flush the mental toxins from my system. Prove that Dudweiler was just an ordinary place, and the rot inside my brain ... past the eyes, just like my grandmother ...

"Sorry," I said, "I'm tired."

"No problem, my friend." He patted me on the shoulder and moved away to a window seat on the other side of the bus. A moment later, he said more quietly, "I recognize that type of lamp. You are not alone."

Still holding the lamp, I closed my eyes and rested my head against the glass, pretending to sleep. Was it possible he actually knew about the lamp? What was I walking into?

I dozed, until someone poked my arm: the old woman from before. Friedrich was gone. We had stopped. Outside, there was a narrow road with old stone and brick buildings and a development of newer-looking, green-and-beige condos a little farther up a hill behind them.

"Dudweiler," the woman said. "We are here." I started to thank her, and she cut me off. "You should stay on the bus. Do not step out with *that*."

She indicated the lamp.

Did everybody in Germany know about the whiskey lamp or only the people on this bus?

"Why not?"

She walked away.

I grabbed my bag and the lamp, and followed her out. "Wait."

"*This*," she said, and notched her hand into an 'L' right next to the lamp base and stand. I didn't get it, so she sighed and held up her other hand next to it. In line with her hands, the lamp stand formed part of a swastika. I'd never noticed it before, but the foundation of the lamp itself must have been cut from a dismembered wooden swastika. *Throw the damn thing away.*

"I didn't know," I said.

She snorted and walked slowly down the road.

The woman was headed toward the hotel, so I followed along beside her.

"Do you live here?"

"I *clean* here," she said. "Did you bring that lamp here for the war conference?"

"No, I came to find my sister."

And other things.

"There is nothing in this town but tourists and graves," she said. "I don't stay after dark ..." And then more in German.

I was too drained to press her on that. I was still walking, but my legs ached, and now I felt random snags in my back, muscle aches from the flights. I needed sleep.

"If you are not here for the conference, there won't be any room," she said.

The parking lot was packed, but worth a try. Inside, the hotel lobby was loud with people checking in and laughing, talking excitedly in German. They were all overdressed but rumpled, like academics.

"Come with me," the woman said.

I followed her up a staircase to the third floor. She swiped a card, then took me to an unmarked door at the end of a drab red-carpet hall, right by the ice machine. She handed me a key. "This room is for hotel workers, if we are snowed in or if the road floods by the river. You can stay here tonight."

"Seriously?" This was for me? Not possible. "Thank you."

I reached to hug her, and she backed away.

She said something nonchalant in German, and left, down the same stairs. Maybe it was the lamp, maybe not. Didn't matter. I opened the door to a simple room, without a TV or window, just a bed and a bathroom and scuffed carpet. I collapsed on the mattress. After switching out the candle for a new one, I set the whiskey lamp on the floor by the head of the bed. No furniture, except a table on the opposite wall, with a brownish fern, and the pillow was musty and thin, like something from a hospital ward in another century. But none of that mattered now.

On the planes, I'd had restless, intermittent bursts of sleep that only made me more exhausted. I would be useless without resting. And now, mercifully, I did—then woke with a start from a dream.

There were faces on the walls. I felt a startled chill. They were watching me and moving their mouths. People's heads extended out of the wallpaper in a random configuration like insane wall art, their lips and jaws making hushed clicks and snaps.

Sit up. I did and grabbed the whiskey lamp, aimed it directly across from me. The faces were behind me too, on every wall. The closer the lamplight got to a section of the wall, the more I saw. One of the nearest heads—a young woman with broken teeth and crusted lips—shied away from the candle. She moved her mouth to shout, but I couldn't hear it.

Fuck this. I flipped the light switch on: the faces were gone. How long had I slept? No clock in here and no windows. I checked my phone. Nothing. It wasn't working. Out of battery. I must have been dreaming. The faces on the wall were part of a dream. No big deal. In the hall, a long line of closed doors and cluttered room service trays led to a dark window at the far end. I'd slept through the entire day.

Okay. Worse than ordinary jet lag, my brain felt like my senses had been incoherently smudged. *Those faces weren't real. Deal with it.* I needed food, and I needed to figure out what the fuck I was doing here.

I started back downstairs, following the sound of people laughing and talking, clinking glasses and silverware in the main lobby. A buffet banquet was set up with a long, orange-ish heat-lamp selection of meats and steaming things that looked like potatoes and green beans. For a moment, I forgot about my broken taste buds. My mouth watered in anticipation of rare roast beef and buttery potatoes. Balloons were tied to the furniture around more German signs. No sign of Friedrich.

When I approached a group by the front desk, the whiskey lamp caught their attention and illuminated a large, skinny shadow man behind them. The yellow candlelight cast a soft glow everywhere else but polarized this invisible figure, showing long, thin legs and a formless torso. Both of the shadow man's arms were stretched over the people like a puppeteer holding strings. Not strings, black hooks that curled down into each person's back. It maneuvered the ends of the hooks in its hands—they disappeared when the light shifted away, returned when I raised the lamp higher—and the shadow man's face was a reflective oval mask. But it didn't reflect my face. It showed Caitlyn, gagged and sleeping.

Not real. Serbian puppet theater is different than regular puppet theater ...

Nearby, people were watching me. They didn't see the shadow man, and I had stopped, fixated on the empty air behind them. A man asked me something in German. I backed away. The shadow men were everywhere, holding each person with an invisible hook.

I stumbled out into the cold, panicked heat rising from my sweaty neck and forehead. Two women were out here smoking.

The first one gestured at the lamp. *"Wahrsager?"*

I said, "The church—do you know how I get to the church?"

"That way." She pointed away from where the bus had dropped me off. "You can't miss it."

There were faces in the road, melted into the pavement between uneven cobblestones. They were alive and begging softly. And as they did, shapes walked between them: small fish men, just like the demon parade at Grandma Elizabeth's grave. The fish men carried bags and used sharp pokers to skewer ragged hunks out of the bags that they dropped into the open, desperate mouths in the ground. One of the fish men led someone by a chain collar toward me, an ugly little hatchet in its other hand. As they passed under a street lamp, the fish man's head glittered a vibrant purple. The person was all bleeding muscle, except for her head, where a face and neck—cut out in a ragged tear around her collarbone—had been dropped on like a mask, so it sat crooked, the eyeholes dark, the lips dangling off the grinning bare flesh of her jaw. Grandma Elizabeth.

I didn't need the lamp to see any of this. It was happening in the open, where the people at the hotel behind me should have been able to watch. But no one seemed to notice. The fish man brought Grandma Elizabeth closer, then stopped. Blood dripped off her bare arms and sluiced in a slow trickle down her thighs and legs to pool around her feet. *Impossible.* The cruel absurdity of this felt far away, but no more unreal than the disruption of a foreign time zone.

"Explain," the fish man said in a high voice, as if it were mocking Grandma Elizabeth, like a parrot.

She cocked her head so the skin mask of her face shifted to fit her wide eyeballs into the socket holes. I recognized her eyes and even the tilt of her neck was familiar. From the nursing home, from the funeral. A corpse, but it was Grandma Elizabeth.

"You came." Her voice gurgled, as if she needed to clear her throat. "You brought the skinny lamp. Good."

"Explain," the fish man said again.

It jerked her collar, so Grandma Elizabeth hunched. Her skin face-mask shifted. I couldn't see her eyes anymore, just bloody muscle through the eye holes. *Help her. Stop that creature.*

"They keep the faces," she said. "For the dragon, so we aren't forgotten."

"And ..?"

"And for the hungry ones, the blacklegs who sleep in the stone."

Not the first time I'd heard about the dragon collecting people. My mind was still muddy, hard to focus.

The fish man was watching me, waiting.

Grandma Elizabeth said, "She spoke to you, didn't she? In the library that isn't a library, you felt her, didn't you?"

"I'm here to find my sister," I said.

"Would you like to meet her?" Grandma Elizabeth asked.

"Where is she?"

The fish man started back down the street, stepping around the faces in the ground, pulling Grandma Elizabeth behind it. She tried to turn and say something but was dragged on.

Slowly, I fell into step behind them. The quiet street smelled like evergreen trees. The whiskey lamp in front of me, not looking down, except to be sure I was following the stones. We turned a corner onto a road overgrown with black vines. And it wasn't just the street. The buildings, streetlamps, sidewalk benches—all of it was completely covered, as if it had been abandoned for generations. At the end of the street, a simple wooden church—like something from pioneer days in America, with unpainted, slapdash boards—was planted in the center of a square, away from the overgrowth. I followed the fish man and Grandma Elizabeth onto the brambles, and my shoe tore. *Wait.* This wasn't foliage. These vines were sharp, metal wires. In the glow around the whiskey lamp, fingers moved under the growth, probing against the black vines, as if they were trapped.

And the vines were *growing.* The end of a narrow point split around my foot into new segments, like a stop-motion plant budding. It blossomed into barbed wire, digging into my sole.

I kept on. *Don't think about any of it.* A part of me said that I was still asleep, and this was all a ridiculous, tortured dream. It couldn't be real.

At the church door, there was a plaque, with German words, and then English underneath:

On this site in 1939, innocent souls perished.
And the garden grew.
Quod Erat Demonstrandum

"I can't go inside," Grandma Elizabeth said.

I hesitated. It was a simple wooden entrance, with a brass ring knocker that had been used so many times the shine had worn to rough green. Behind us, I heard a scraping hum, like a hundred knives dragging against pots. The vines.

What did I expect to find here? *Not this.*

"Is this real?" I asked.

The fish man pulled Grandma Elizabeth away, back onto the overgrown road.

"She has to sing now," it said.

"This will be real someday," Grandma Elizabeth said. "Still, tell him I love him."

Stop the fish man. Save her. But they were back on the vines, and the thought of crossing through those blades again—the metal shredded her exposed feet like raw steak.

The church door opened. My grandfather smiled at me from the other side. In the pictures, when he was much younger, he had a handsome straight jaw and short, slicked-back hair. Now, he looked worn, dressed in a black military uniform that didn't fit him, because he was too thin. It was him, though. I knew the dimple in his chin, stern blue eyes, and high forehead.

"Mark?" he asked. "I'm happy to meet you. I'm here to take you down to her."

He spoke with the same stocky German accent from the tape. Impatient and precise. Behind me, the fish man and Grandma Elizabeth were gone down the road. A dream. My grandfather was dead. This was all a surreal fantasy. My grandfather held the door for me. When I went inside, his clothes were moving, shifting with something underneath, as if he had mice or lumpy insects crawling on him. I smelled his thick mint aftershave, with that lingering rubbing alcohol scent, same as before.

The church was overgrown with more black metal vines and inky lichen that covered mounds in the pews, people-mounds, all of it bristling with tiny razors and barbed wire. Not statues, the people-mounds were moving, struggling. As I followed my grandfather down a clear central aisle, pale fingers slipped through the vines on my right, splattering blood, as they dragged against the blades. Whoever was trapped inside knew I was here, was reaching for me. I went over and tried to pry back the vines from the figure's face. Sharp points dug into my palms and the pain made my mind spot clear. *Good.*

The black metal flexed against my hands. I saw brown eyes through a gap, pulled harder, blood trickling through my fingers, down the backs of my hands. I could see the top half of a bloody face, the skin gone from a veiny meat forehead. Her fingers grasped for me, but as I strained, the metal vegetation snapped back into place. I yanked my fingers away to keep them from catching in overlapping razorblades, and the person was covered again. Black vines spread over her fingers, making her a trembling mound again. There were so many of them.

The woman's fingers had skin. It was only her face. They cut it off. Someone took it, just like Grandma Elizabeth.

"You were—*this*," I said to my grandfather. "I can't listen to you or trust you. Did you do this?"

He paused in the aisle ahead of me. "It's hard to explain. The whole world was a broken bottle that we had to light. We didn't think about next year or the year after. We thought about the Ice Age and past extinctions and the lifespan of a civilization. We believed in a creation to last beyond the end of the world."

I was breathing hard from the pain and sweat and cold outside. Real or not, fuck this. *Fuck him.*

"You helped kill these people, didn't you? The massacre at Dudweiler—that's what happened. You took their faces."

Their skin.

"I didn't know they were people," he said.

What did that mean? *Walk away from this, even if it is a dream.* Nothing good was coming. *Get out of here now.*

"That's convenient," I said. "Or maybe you just hurt and killed a lot of people, because you wanted to. The worst, mass murder cliché, right—following fucking order?"

"No. I wanted to protect my family, all of you, from our debt. You'll see."

He went past the vine-mounds to the back of the church. Where the altar should have been, there was a hole with black stone steps that went straight down. *I shouldn't be here.* I stepped beside him. Cold air with the stink of dust and sewer rot wafted up. I couldn't see the bottom. The hole seemed to go deep under the church, into an old crypt.

"Which one of these people did you cut up to make this thing—this *skinny lamp*?" I asked. "That one? Or was it this one over here?"

"I'm glad you brought my lamp," he said. "Has it helped you? The blood worship—I first joined, because they were teaching us how. The only way to stop the dragon. No benevolent, divine God could be real and allow the things I've seen. We are left with the many, older gods, Mark. Put your faith in her. Our true goddess."

Listening to him, I rubbed the wet holes and cuts in my hands. One sliced directly across the scar on my left palm, like I'd lined it up with the vine razor. Blood oozed and smeared down my hands, and when I curled my fingers tight, I felt the wincing clarity of the pain again. Gods whose names we could barely remember, whose rituals were long forgotten—like Robert said. Is that what this was?

"I don't care that we're related. You're unforgivable," I said. "I would probably try to kill you right now, if you weren't already dead."

"Someday, you'll understand." Then he started down the steps and paused to look back, when I didn't follow. "This is where I found her. Many years ago, when she gave me the light. Come down or go back, while you can."

The air from down there tasted like sickness. Old foamy sweat, urine, and disease.

"This place feels like ..."

"Like Hell?" he asked. "Yes. But it isn't. It's the future. Come."

The pain in my hands helped. If my blood was real, then I could still fight whatever my Nazi grandfather's ghost threw at me. He led me into a passage of black rock with narrow shelves on the walls full of gray, mildewy bones in rotting clothes. We didn't stop, and I tried not to look at them. Just an ordinary crypt, something from the Middle Ages or maybe older, when people had hidden bodies under sacred sites. Nothing to it.

The tunnel opened into a cavern with a dead black tree in the center and a stream of fast-splashing water right behind it. A small hole in the rock ceiling cast shadowy twilight across the fissures and juts in the walls and floor. The sickness smell was gone. In here, the air tasted like wet earth and sex. Strange. But I recognized that human, tangy smell. Deeper into the cavern was a bull's head on the other side of the tree, facing the water. It wasn't a big stream, but it was fast and loud.

"It's a garden." My grandfather stood by the tunnel where we'd come in. "She plants it, and it spreads. Someday, it'll be the world."

She who?

"Where is she?"

"I'm here, Mark," a woman's voice called from the tree.

I raised the whiskey lamp and crept closer. The bull's head was different than in the library. This one had red and brown patterns painted on its face, around the eyes, and its horns were solid black. It wasn't nailed to the tree. It came out from *inside* a knotty gash that ran down the center of the trunk, like it had been struck by lightning and then tried to regrow up around the wound. Below the bull's head, in the shadowy bowels of the tree, was a naked woman's body, with pale breasts and flexing stomach, and legs and arms that disappeared into the wood. The bull's head covered her face.

"Thank you for coming," she said.

The sunken lady. That was what this was. I squeezed my hands again, but the pain only made my vision spot. I felt heat in my groin, when she spoke.

"You're not my sister."

"No, love. I'm not. I wanted to see you," the sunken lady said. "I said I was her, but your sister is gone."

It was the same voice as the library. It wasn't, though—the bull hadn't spoken to me there. But there was a concentration behind that *incident* and in this tone that was identical.

"You can set the lamp down now, Mark."

I didn't. "Why am I here?"

"I want to make you a new light," she said. "A new agreement. I want to help you. There are blood trails in the air around your family. They are flowing out of Caitlyn's womb right now and attracting predators. When your child is born, the animal will say she belongs to him."

The same deal my grandfather made. That was what this was about? I glared at him, still watching from the opening of the tunnel. What did he want me to do, believe this thing? Trust a woman who wasn't a woman? None of this could be real, but here it was—happening.

"You're talking about the chicken man," I said.

"The animal in the deep is not a man," she said. "He is the weak point in a star, a miserable, diseased *thing* that should be sleeping in the stone."

"Who are you?" I asked.

"I am everlasting life," she said, "and I will be the world someday."

She was talking about my unborn child. 'She belongs'—a girl, the sunken lady said the baby would be a girl.

"What do you want?" I asked.

"The light you are carrying now is mine. That's a part of me. I gave it to your grandfather, so that if anyone touched him—as long as he kept it lit—they would be touching me. And they don't want to touch me, Mark. Because my light can burn away lies to show what's underneath. I can keep you safe. But that light is old. It won't last much longer. I will make a new agreement with you, if you ask."

The lamplight got me here. Even if this was wrong, the whiskey lamp worked. She was against the chicken man, whatever she was. And now she wanted me to sign a contract, because of course she did. A blood oath with an ancient, nameless god.

"What agreement?"

"Your life for your child's life. You will belong to me when you die, but while you live, my light will protect you and your child from the animals."

The smell of sex soaked over me, and I felt warmth in my groin, my cock hardening. I shifted, looked away from her, at the stream. *She's doing it so you can't think. Like at the library.*

"What are you?" I asked. "What is this place?"

"I am the future, Mark."

"I heard that before. What does it mean?"

"Someday, I will be all that is. It will take time. I know that. Maybe so much time that there won't be any people left, when I'm through. But if there are, I will love them the same way I love you. I will remake the world without the animals or death."

Couldn't be real, of course, but here I was, with the faceless thing that my grandfather dug up generations ago. The source of the whiskey lamp, the sunken lady hated the chicken man or whatever *animal* he worked for as much as I did. And all she wanted in return was me. Just me. And she was growing to cover the world. I imagined sharp black vines crushing the landscape, swallowing skyscrapers and hillsides.

"Do I have a choice?" I asked.

My grandfather shifted a little. Was he nervous? "This is how you save your child."

Maybe. I felt my heart beat harder, the swell of my cock pressing at my pants. But I waited, and the woman's body moved, squirming and naked inside the tree. I watched the water, not the bull.

"Do you want more, Mark?" she asked. "My light can show you the threads of the world. It can make you well again."

The red-robed mole-man thing at Grandma Elizabeth's graveside spoke like this, too. He'd been colder, more transactional, but it was the same. That vision and this one. She wanted to own me. Whatever the sunken lady was, she shouldn't be here. Was only here because of my grandfather's desperation.

"No."

The sex stink was gone, the cave just deep stone and mineral water now. The stream tinkled and gushed in the quiet. My erection faded. That familiar unsteadiness in my legs, I recognized that from the library. It was instinctive. *She* did this.

"Why would you say that, Mark?" the sunken lady asked softly. "I love you. I'm giving you a choice. I'm not slipping my fingers into the folds of your brain."

The cavern was still. *How nice of you. Not to reach into my mind. I imagined a metal point sinking into my eyes where it met the nose. Just a tap. No more tears.*

"You don't understand, do you?" she asked. "I am sewing a picture of the world. The whole world. I know this is confusing. But I can feel the shaft of your penis and the empty ache in your stomach, the squeezing pulse of your heart. I am inside you, in every part, and I love you."

My grandfather said, "Believe in her, Mark."

That was why he brought me here, as a trap? But he was a ghost, what could he do? I looked at the solid shape of my grandfather, still blocking the tunnel. He was here. Whatever was happening, we were both really here. *Make a deal.* I had to agree to this or I was done, never going back. And maybe it was the right thing to do anyway. Maybe she really would protect us.

"Come stand close to me," she said. "I'll show you what to do, love. I'll guide you every step of the way to your new light."

I could always run, couldn't I?

I went to the tree.

"Oh, thank you, Mark," she said. "I knew, since I first saw you."

As I approached, the sunken lady swayed slowly inside the trunk. The bull's head was a part of her, and her hands and feet weren't hidden by the tree, they *were* the tree, flowing into it, the skin mottling to striated wood. I stopped close enough to touch her. The air was staticky here, fizzy and charged. The tree, the sunken lady in it, smelled like wet bark. The insides of her thighs were slick with something dark.

"Kneel, Mark, love," she said.

She didn't have me. I could bolt, when I needed to, but that felt distant now. I dropped to my knees on the rock floor, the whiskey lamp still in my right hand.

Anyone who stepped into this place was trapped. The sunken lady wasn't a bull. What was she? A god, monster, some kind of demon? Did it even matter? *You're here now, kneeling to save yourself and your child—your little unborn girl—from the chicken man, just like your grandfather did.* The whiskey lamp *was* her, a link to keep the other monsters away, even the chicken man. I didn't have a choice, but wasn't that what the worst motherfuckers always said? I had to. No choice.

My grandfather came over to stand behind me.

"Why did you do this?" I asked.

"It's okay," the sunken lady said to my grandfather. "Mark is here now. Tell him."

"There was no other way," my grandfather said. "You see, I loved beetles growing up, insects that were here before the last extinction. Somehow, they survived the great dying, these little marvels in different shapes, colors, and sizes. Have you heard of the Zopherus, ironclad? Black with white speckled markings on their shells, not very large, about the size of a nail. They don't live in Germany, but I found one in the woods. When I touched it, the ironclad fell limp, so I took it home for my collection. But my metal pins could not pierce the ironclad's shell, no matter how hard I pressed. Finally, I went to find the sharpest knife in the kitchen. But when I came back, the beetle was gone. It hadn't been dead, only pretending and waiting for its escape. I never found it again. Later, I learned that people use electric drills to pierce the ironclad shells—that's how hard they are. But do you know what also works? The pincers and claws of other beetles. In the wild, that strong shell can be cracked by tools made from the same source."

He wasn't talking about bugs. He was talking about the chicken man and the whiskey lamp, wasn't he? Whatever the chicken man worked for—the dragon—it wasn't human. It was unnatural, something *other*. So my grandfather had reasoned that the only way to stop it was to find another unnatural thing *in the wild*. Something he could use like armor.

"Hell is very real, Mark," he said. "The sunken lady, our goddess, has given us a light to keep the darkness away. A shell. She will protect your child, if you let her."

I tried not to think about the faces I'd seen in the hotel and in the road outside, the shadow figures and fish men and everything else at Grandma Elizabeth's grave. All connected to the sunken lady, too, somehow. Maybe not Hell, but it wasn't far off.

"I think I understand," I said. Only a beetle could stop another beetle. A tool made from the same source.

"We will need some of your blood, Mark," the sunken lady said. "A new wound."

My grandfather was holding a knife. Did he have it the whole time? It was a small black switchblade with a sharp point, rusted at the edges. This was wrong. This fucking knife might be the same weapon he used on those people upstairs. But I took it from him. Still, I kept a hand on the whiskey lamp.

What came next? The tree roots under the stone would swallow my blood? Was it a symbol or did it activate some gore-driven mechanism? I lowered the knife blade to the soft skin of my wrist. It pressed in, didn't cut. If I dragged it along, the skin would tear open. I felt the sharp, narrow pressure of it.

Thinking about my grandfather, it had been easy to explain away his imagined atrocities from the deep past, because *I* would never do that. Until I'm kneeling where he knelt, facing the same choice: protect my daughter by cutting my skin. But there was no living with this. I wouldn't be me anymore. Not if I stopped questioning and gave into belief. *Surrender yourself for your family.* It was what every father was supposed to do, wasn't it?

My grandfather said, "It'll only hurt for a moment. It'll be a release."

I didn't need a release. I needed a way out.

I whipped the whiskey lamp around to smash it against the tree. It shattered in a spray of glass, wood, and candle wax splashed up the trunk, swelling into a sudden burst of flame and white smoke. The sunken lady screamed, and I shoved backwards. *Run—get out.* I raced for the tunnel.

As I ducked into the dark passageway, the sunken lady shouted, "Pain, Mark! Pain!"

I glimpsed my grandfather at the stream, grabbing handfuls of water to douse the fire that spread around the base of the tree.

Back down the crypt passageway, I ran to the stone steps and up into the church—the vines and people-mounds were gone—and then, finally, winded, I stumbled out on the front steps. *Happened so fast. Keep moving.* All the black metal wines and overgrowth out here were gone, too. *Back to the hotel. Get your suitcase and go.*

Past the next intersection, the cobblestone street was normal again. No faces in the ground, no fish men or any sign of my grandmother. *Losing my mind. Don't stop.* I crossed the road, all the way back to the hotel, where the banquet was wrapping up. All the food had been put away, and a few people lounged in chairs with drinks, but no shadow men. The first woman I'd seen smoking earlier waved to me from a small group.

"You lost your lamp?" she asked.

I didn't answer. My jaw was clenched. If I stopped, all of it would come back into focus and have to fit somehow. I walked up to the third floor. I still had the knife. Jesus, I was still holding the switchblade. My hand shaking, I carefully clicked the blade back in and put it away. She was right. I didn't have the lamp anymore. I had to get out of here. I had to grab my things and go—right now. At the end of the hall, I opened my unmarked room.

A voice inside said, "Mark, we have ourselves a problem."

The chicken man was waiting on my bed, with the severed head of the old woman, the nice lady from the bus who had given me this room, on the pillow beside him.

Chapter Twenty-Two

I didn't go in, just stopped in the doorway, one hand in my pocket, on the switchblade.

"Why are you here?" I asked.

The chicken man frowned. "I thought I made myself pretty clear the last time. I hoped we were past this 'finding your roots' exercise. Get it—*roots*? When I heard you were here, I said to myself that must be a mistake. Not Mark. Mark is the smart one. Maybe your brother, Don, trekked all the way to Germany carrying his family's antique Nazi lamp. That sounded like a *Don thing* to me, not a *Mark thing*. And it was so last minute, not even a direct flight. This little shit town doesn't have an airport, and you wouldn't believe the last-minute hassles. Or, I guess you would, actually. Next time you have the urge to do something that's going to get nice people decapitated, call me first, okay?"

He patted the old woman's head. Her eyes were open and glassy, staring up into nothing, and her skin was already a rubbery gray, her lips blue-ish black. The pillow under her was soaked dark red. My stomach was on fire. Not nausea, it burned, felt swollen and empty. I was still shaking.

"Here, we can bring her with us." He wheeled my suitcase over, opened it, and carefully cleared out a section in the middle where the whiskey lamp had been. Then he set the head inside, wrapped it in my clothes, blood already soaking out, and zipped it up again. "Let's walk and talk."

He offered me the suitcase handle, then followed me into the hall, his duffel bag over one shoulder.

"I don't like being here, Mark. This little town doesn't improve my subjective well-being. I have a history here, you understand. It's too close to home."

We went downstairs, to the lobby.

"We both work in a skilled trade, so you know what I'm talking about. Autonomy, control, respect—all the things that give you a sense of purpose from your profession. I have that all the time, most days. And do you know why?"

We walked right through the lobby without anybody noticing and went out into the parking lot. Why was I following him? *Turn around. Scream. Call the police.*

"Because I work remote. Thousands of miles away from my employer's home office and at a safe distance from my own deep, dark past. But right now, Mark, right now, I'm basically working in my old high school, surrounded by memories of the captain of the football team and the prom queen who never went out with me. Do you understand?"

We stopped by a blue Volkswagen, and he beeped a little rental car keychain so the doors unlocked. The chicken man was full of lies, but he was real, and he murdered Sister Maria Theresa—and the woman from the bus. And Dad. My breath tasted hot. I was going to hit him, finally fight him.

"Hence the head." He frowned at me, across the roof of the car. "Do you think I like sawing off a nice, old lady's head? Do you know how much work it is, with the crying and screaming and carrying on? Neck bones and vertebrae are pretty tough. Don't let anybody tell you otherwise. *And* there's the blood. Look at this suit—spotless. That took a lot of effort. But I did need you to know that I'm serious, *so* she had to die. Really, that's on you. Who else was I going to kill? The wannabe brownshirt on the bus?"

He shook out a cigarette, found his red flip lighter, and lit up, relaxing a little when he puffed out his first breath of smoke.

"Nope, this was the only sensible murder. And the point is this: once again, you have a choice to make. Let's talk in the car. It's cold out here."

He shoved my suitcase and his duffel bag into the backseat, then got into the driver's seat. *Run. No, stab him in the neck.* I had the knife. Wait for the right moment, then drive the fucking blade into his throat. I got in beside him. He pressed a button to start the engine and turned the heat up all the way.

"Here's the choice," he said. "You can be punished and things can go back to the way they were. Or you can roll the dice and probably make them much, much worse."

"Why did you follow me?" I asked.

"Really? After everything, I thought you got this. But fine, if you really need me to spell it out, it's about trust. And you've broken mine."

He rubbed his hands together and held his fingers up to the heating vents. Sister Maria Theresa said he couldn't be killed. Told us not to fight him. I squeezed the knife handle.

"Did you know," he said, "the human brain can stay oxygenated for around twelve seconds without being connected to the circulatory system? Do you know what that means? During the French Revolution—that's what they call it now—with the guillotine, they used to pick up the severed heads and show the crowd. Some poor aristocrat would walk up, put their head on the block, the wood thingy would lock them in—so they didn't try to make a break for it—and then there was a *snap*."

He squinted out the front windshield, as if hoping to see it set up farther down the street. *Stab him. Do it now.*

"I remember the sound seemed to happen first," he said. "The blade dropped so fast you couldn't even really see it, until it had already fallen. Then your mind would kind of go back and convince you that you'd seen it fall. And the head would already be in a basket, the body jerking around, spouting blood everywhere out of the neck hole. And then some asshole executioner would pick up the head and show it to the crowd, so they could all cheer and laugh. Except here's the thing, Mark. Nine times out of ten, those heads were still alive."

I was going to do it. *Right now.* I shifted, my right hand tight on the switchblade, arm tense, and he turned, locked eyes with me. A long silence of our breathing.

"The jaws *moved*," he said quietly. "The eyes *looked*. I remember one time, the executioner was holding a woman's head that had just been cut off and decided to slap her cheek. And do you know what happened? She gave him this indignant look: 'fuck you buddy'—this glare, just like she would have done if he'd slapped her in the street."

The chicken man kept staring at me. His breath smelled like cigarettes.

Do it.

"The crowd didn't laugh or cheer or anything that time. They gasped and went quiet. What I'm saying is, twelve seconds is a long time." He turned back around to adjust his seat, not looking at me. "Try counting it out—that's how long those heads stayed alive. See, I knew that when I decapitated your friend back there, so I kept talking to her, you know, easing her into death *after* the head was off, for a good twelve seconds, at least. I figured it was the least I could do."

He shifted gears and slowly backed up.

What if he couldn't be killed? I was only alive now, because he let me go. *Maybe. Or maybe it's because I'm a coward. Still afraid of the icepick.*

He drove us out of the parking lot and onto the road, away from the church. We bounced toward the center of town, past the bus drop-off. If I was fast enough, straight out of my pocket with the switchblade, could I hit him? Could I land it in his throat? What if I missed? What if Sister Maria Theresa was right? But hadn't Grandma Elizabeth said all those years ago at Dad's funeral that I *could* kill him? And that funeral was because of his plastic buckets.

The chicken man was talking about how this was a pain in the ass, such an inconvenience, and he was such a nice guy. *Yeah, always ready to tell a story loaded with dark, scary tidbits.*

"Why are you talking like you were there, at the guillotine?"

He barked a high-pitched, startled laugh.

"Ha!" he said. "You got me! Somebody was paying attention, guilty as charged. Nope, I wasn't there, Mark. I didn't see it for myself, that was narrative license, is what they call that—making something more personal with first-hand embellishments."

He pulled onto the curb. We stopped in front of an ancient-looking stone castle spire, with a cellphone store and a supermarket on either side. Everything around us was quiet and shuttered for the night. As we got out of the car, the air tasted frosty and moist, like snow. The sky was a barren black, too deep for the sun to ever come up again. With his bag slung over one shoulder, the chicken man went up to a low, medieval-looking door in the stone spire and knocked.

"What are we doing here?" I asked.

"I told you," he said. "Penance or chance."

"What is this place?"

"You know how there are miles and miles of tiny anthills and mole tunnels under our feet right now? There are ant colonies bigger than countries, but you only ever see them come out of a few holes. This is one of those holes."

I thought about my grandfather and his beetles, glanced up the empty road back toward the hotel and church beyond. We weren't far. I was losing control, following him because he told me to. *I'll stab him.* But what about the tremor in my arms and that fucking stomach cramp?

"Oh, come on," the chicken man called at the door, and he slammed his fist against it again. "Open up. Swordfish!"

The door clicked, then creaked open just enough for me to see the sliver of a young woman with dark hair and bright blue makeup around her eyes, a soft orange glow in the room behind her.

"I'm not going all the way down," the chicken man told her. "Relax. This is the one I'm here about." He nodded to me. "Mark, grab your suitcase. Don't leave it in the car."

I got it out, hesitated. He was waiting with the girl at the door. She wore a red and black velvety robe, but her skin below her face was completely black, as if her neck and the rest of her body, even her fingers holding the door, had been painted over. Like a face propped up on a shadow. Another version of the Cadillac Club, with different people in another country. One of his 'anthills.'

"What if I don't go in there with you?" I asked.

"Again with this?" The chicken man came back toward me.

I was ready.

"What are you going to do instead? Go back to the hotel or maybe call a cab and rush to the airport? Back to New York or Kentucky or Chicago, or maybe someplace new you've never even been, like Egypt or China? You make it there, but then it occurs to you: 'Oh wait, you aren't alone in this world, and didn't the mean old chicken man kill your aunt right in front of you, couldn't he do other unpleasant things to people you love?'"

He finished his cigarette and tossed it, crossed his arms.

"So, bring the suitcase in with you like I asked, okay? And stop saying inane things. You're smarter than this."

Fight him or go with it. If I tried and couldn't kill him, he might hurt me—okay—but what about Caitlyn and our daughter? He still wanted to take the baby when she was born, didn't he? *Find another way. There has to be something else.*

I followed him into a country western bar. The walls were old stone, the kind of masonry that fit irregularly before the invention of cement or edging. Deer antlers, cowboy hats, lassos, multi-colored throw rugs hung from the walls, with a huge, electric antler chandelier dangling over the center of the room. Down here, the air over the pool table, booths and sticky card tables was thick with the smell of beer and cigarette smoke.

A circular bar in the center was stacked high with liquor, three old boxy TVs playing different sitcoms overhead. The bartenders were women in robes, bodies painted black, their faces a little too pale and with harsh, exaggerated makeup. The men at the tables all hunched forward, faces downcast, wearing rough clothing smeared black around the joints. The chicken man took me to the bar, and as we passed a booth, I noticed the men all had black smears around their noses and mouths, eyes, and even their ears, as if they'd been breathing soot.

"Coal." The chicken man sat at the bar. "That's from the mine, Mark. That's why they look like that."

Some old pop song played in the background. I didn't recognize the sitcom on the TV directly above me, either, but it looked familiar: a wide shot of a family eating dinner, two boys and—*shit*. I couldn't look away. That was our old kitchen in Schaumburg, right before we moved to Kentucky. The sound was turned off, but there were closed captions on:

Dad: … as simple as that. Anybody who's really your friend will stay in your life. And the others you won't miss.

Onscreen, Mom reach over to spoon more pasta out of a bowl onto her plate. Don and I—I was facing away from the camera, my face hidden—were both eating.

Mom: I wouldn't put it like that. Don, what your father's saying …

I looked at the bar, away from the screen, but it was still there, just at the top of my vision.

"What is this place?" I asked.

"I told you. It's a hole in the ground. But fortunately, we don't have to go down any further, not like the last time. Have a seat. Oh, and take out the head."

I slowly eased myself onto a stool. A dream, some kind of trick.

"What?" I asked.

"The old woman from the hotel. I'll do it …"

He unzipped the bag, and I tasted the raw, wet stink of the head. Everything in the bag, all my clothes, were bloody, soaked through. The woman's scalp shifted, the skin slack when he lifted her out. Keeping the face angled away from me, the chicken man gently set it on the bar between us.

No one noticed. I scanned the room. Not a single person looked over, as if the head were totally normal, boring even.

There was a second TV, farther down. This one had a different program—*no, not a fucking TV show.* The camera was tracking close to a face, *my face*, lit in the white glare of phosphorescent lights, staring blankly ahead. Onscreen, I smiled slightly, my eyes distant, and as it panned out, I saw a clean, clinical room, like a muted hotel. Or mental institution. No one else there, just me sitting on the plain bed, smiling, because none of this was real.

A bartender with a nose ring and short hair dyed green pointed at me with a black hand. It was a disconnected gesture, as if she weren't controlling her arm. Like another puppet.

"Did you do that?" she asked me.

The chicken man leaned onto the bar. "Did *he* do that? Don't be like that. I know I've been gone awhile, but I'm not a tourist. Now, let's deal already."

Her dark body was too fluid as she came over, like a plastic bag gusting down the street. "Is he payment too?"

She meant me.

The chicken man looked at me. "She wants to know if I want to trade you. What do you think, Mark? Your face is really the only part they care about now."

Before I could answer, he made a sarcastic, frustrated sound.

"Does he look like he belongs to me? Take a *good* look this time."

She came a little closer, squinting, then snapped back, blinking, as if I'd just tried to kiss her or pulled a gun. I still saw the two TVs behind her, and there was a third one, too, off to my left. I'd have to turn to see it, though.

"I'm sorry," she said. "I didn't know ..."

"Get us bourbon," the chicken man said. "Leave the bottle."

"Yes, sir," she said. "I really am sorry."

Bowing, she picked up the head and took it away, disappearing around the backside of the bar, then came back with a bottle of Woodford Reserve bourbon and two shot glasses. She wiped off the bloody smudge on the bar where the head had been. After we both had shots, the chicken man raised his glass.

"To life," he said.

I touched the shot glass. What the fuck was this?

"You see the TVs?" I asked.

"Yes, Mark, I see the TVs," he said. "Take a drink. It'll help."

I picked it up. *Fuck it.* We drank, the whiskey hot, burning down my throat and empty stomach like raw, curing acid. I coughed, a taste that scored the insides of my mouth. But it felt good. He was right. It helped.

"You realize, I have to hurt you for making me come all the way here and using that stupid old lamp again," he said. "What did you do with it, by the way?"

I covered my brow with one hand to block out the two TVs. What about the other one?

"I broke it," I said.

"Good. You know, that lamp always felt like cheating at cards. Like you were carrying a pocketful of Aces, because it wasn't *your* power, was it? You didn't get those cards in an honest deal. No, your Nazi grandfather made an arrangement with the dealer to cheat. All the scary energy bottled up in that lamp never belonged to any of you. And, no offense, but you never could have kicked my ass, not even with that pocketknife you're carrying. If you had pulled that on me in the car, I would have taken off your nose and part of an ear. But *her?*" He rolled his eyes and did a fake, theatrical shiver. "Like I said, the lamp wasn't fair. Smart to get rid of it. I appreciate that. So option A is you get hurt enough that you remember it, and then we all go back to what we were doing before, problem solved."

"Hurt how?"

He poured us both another drink. "This is why I asked for whiskey, Mark. Hurt like I cut out a piece of who you are. A few taps with a hammer into your eyes, that kind of hurt."

I picked up the shot glass and stared at the full brown liquor. My stomach and throat still hurt. There was an answer here. I was alive after the last time. "Like with my grandmother."

"Like that, yes. It could help with your drinking and depression. Learn to laugh every now and then. When's the last time you did that?"

I wanted to turn and look at the last screen or see myself again in Schaumburg. See Dad and Mom, steady and loving. Don from before. Dad was alive on that screen.

"What's the other choice?" I asked.

He shrugged. "Option B is we play the game again. You don't remember the last time. I know you don't. But it's the same game. And if you lose, the stakes get bigger."

"And if I win?"

"Same thing, you pick. The last time, do you remember what we were playing for?"

Fuck you. The last time. When you murdered him. When you tortured Don, broke us all apart. Like we didn't matter.

I downed the second whiskey and poured another, wincing hard. *Shit, that hurt.* "You had my brother and my dad. You let them go, because I won."

Won what? Dad was already dead, and Don permanently scarred.

"I guess it made an impression," he said. "Yes, that's right."

I held the shot glass tight, the side smeared brown from the dried blood on my fingers. My hands were still raw but not bleeding from the black vines anymore.

"If we do it again, what happens?"

He gave me an unsteady look, as if he were flustered and impressed but trying to stay casual. His usual routine was starting to fray around the edges, wasn't it?

"You won't win," he said. "I should tell you that, so it's fair. I want to be a nice guy here."

"Okay," I said, "but what happens if I do?"

He started to object, and when I pressed him again, he said, "If you play and you lose, we continue from the last time. That means Don and your dad are gone again, along with your children. Kids numbers one and two. That's *before* the new stakes. If you lose this time, I take everyone. All of them, along with your mother, Caitlyn, and the little piece of you up here." He tapped me right between the eyes. "You lose everything, Mark. I told you. You don't want to play."

I almost hit him, my arms tight and trembling. Almost did it. The whiskey cleared my head. I could focus. Some of this was real. He was and maybe this place, maybe even the animals waiting to gobble us all up. But the rules? Those were his bullshit rules, weren't they? Maybe the chicken man had to follow them, because of his boss, but they weren't a law of physics. They could be snapped. Fuck what he said. I wasn't living with this anymore. No more *taking.*

"And if I win, this debt is over," I said.

He smiled, shook his head. "Can't do it. That's out of my hands."

That was your chance to live. Back out of the debt. Let me go free.

"Then if I win, you help me put the whiskey lamp back together."

He laughed in a ratcheting shriek. "Oh, that's funny! That's what you want? To watch me grovel and make your shitty amulet whole again? Do you really want to consider this? If you lose—"

"I understand."

"You're a grown up. You probably do. This game is older than me, but it's really the *only* game there is."

I swiveled to glance at the third TV. It was a still shot of me, the outline of my thin body—dressed like I was now—frozen in mid-step, mouth open, eyes wide and desperate. I was trapped inside a solid stone wall, with hazy rivulets of darker rock around me, clouding out other shadows. Onscreen, I wasn't moving.

I looked back at him.

"I don't care," I said. "No more. Are we playing or not?"

All the laughter and smiling dropped out of his face. "Put your hand on the bar."

And as I did, a new bartender came around from behind the center of the bar, completely dark everywhere but on her face, like the others. She carried beers to guys at the booth. When she noticed me staring, she turned. It was the old hotel maid from the bus, alive and smiling again.

The chicken man grabbed the switchblade out of my pocket and slammed it into the center of my hand.

***

We were back in the car, and it was snowing. The engine wasn't on. Snow clouded the air around us, melting on the ruddy windshield, making the houses and streetlights on the narrow road outside blurry and indistinct. The chicken man was in the driver's seat beside me, holding the wheel and staring off into nothing. Pain throbbed in my bandaged left hand, where he'd stabbed me. Again.

"Why did you do that?" the chicken man asked.

Do what? Was it over? Did I win? Same as the last time, I didn't remember anything. One moment we were inside drinking whiskey, the next we were here. And again, it was snowing. I still felt the heat of the bourbon in my stomach and felt a slight swirl, when I shifted my vision. We hadn't been long.

"I won, didn't I?"

He watched the snow out the windshield. It was accumulating on the road, too.

"Do you want your sister back?" he asked. His voice was a little shakier. "I can do that. He has her, still alive. How about it?"

Don't listen. No more Goddamn tricks or games. Except mine. Get him to the lamp.

"We had a deal," I said.

"Where is it?"

"I'll show you," I said. "Start the car."

He did, and we drove away from the dark stone turret. Was I ever going to know what happened in his *game*? What the hell was this? Maybe nothing happened, and it was a joke. Maybe he was planning to hurt me anyway.

There wasn't much snow, but it was coming down hard, and no tracks on the street. We were alone.

"The game isn't mine," he said. "I just carry it."

We passed the hotel onto the area with the cobblestones, sliding a little around a turn in the road, and I made him pull onto the side road toward the wooden church square. All the vines were still gone. This was just an ordinary snowy road at night now.

"There." I pointed to the church. "We're going inside."

We got out, and he took his bag. I left my suitcase. The air tasted clean and wet.

"I've got to tell you, Mark. I'm getting a tingly feeling," he said. "You know the feeling you get when somebody is treating you like you're a moron and planning to screw you over somehow? I'm getting that right now."

I walked up the church steps and waited. *Don't talk to him. Make him move.* "So? Are you coming?"

"What's in there?"

"A hole down to an old crypt. That's where the lamp is. I dropped it there, and it broke. I came here looking for my sister," I said. "But I guess you know she wasn't here."

He sized me up, searching for any sign I was lying. I wasn't, though. It was here.

"And all the other parts of that story you aren't telling me?" Slowly, he came up to the church. "I'm guessing you set some kind of trap? Listen to me very carefully, Mark. If we walk in there, and you pull some James Bond bullshit, I won't just hurt you, I'll go back for your mom, Caitlyn, Don. Anybody I think of, okay? We made a deal with the game, and I have to honor that. I don't have a choice. But if anything fucked up starts to happen down there in your little crypt, I'll show you I'm serious. There's a reason I rented a full-size car."

Why, so he could drive faster? Strange thing to say. I glanced at the Volkswagen, the tail pipe still steaming in the snow.

"The lamp is down there." I reached for the door. *Please, let it be unlocked.* "What are you afraid of?"

The door opened.

"The balls on you," the chicken man muttered, as he followed me inside.

The church was very still. It was probably cold, but I didn't feel it through the whiskey buzz steadying me. We walked past the pews, and the hole was right there, with black steps going straight down.

The chicken man opened his bag and took out a small flashlight, clicked it on. "Go ahead. You first."

I started down, and at the bottom, the air got tighter and musty, closer around me. The chicken man flashed his little light on the shelves, lighting crumbly skeletons. He whistled.

"You weren't kidding," he said. "This is *so* cool. I mean look at all these old dead people you found. Is this the big reveal or—ooh, is that a *cavern* at the end of the tunnel? I wonder what's inside?"

We entered the cave, and there they were, the black tree and splashing stream. No sign of my grandfather. No movement. I would have to walk a few steps around to see the bull's head. *Don't hesitate. Go.*

"Beautiful," the chicken man said, as he came in after me, flashing his light at the tree, the distant cavern walls, all the way up to the hole at the top. "This is so *neat.*"

He followed me casually, closer to the tree. That flash of shakiness I'd seen in the car was gone.

"When we get back, let me tell you what's going to happen," he said. "First, I'll break your fingers, cut off a few of them, we'll see. Oh, there's your broken lamp over by the tree. *Then*, I'll tie you up in the car and show you who's waiting in the trunk ..."

The full-size car. What was he talking about? I stopped, turned to face him, as he came closer. The bull's head was in view now, but he was still grinning at me.

"... and I'll take her out, and I'll hurt her in front of you, Mark. You see, I've been nice about it until now, but I'll show you what's possible. I'll pop on some music—*oh Barbara Allen!*—and take off her arms and legs. She doesn't need those to give birth, does she? I'll probably shave her head, too. I like to see reactions, you know, get feedback."

He was watching me, waiting for a response. *Wants me to lunge or curl into a ball. Closer, you motherfucker.*

"And *then*, it's icepick time. When you wake up, you won't have a care in the world. Should I get your lamp for you, fulfill our bargain?"

He stepped past me toward the tree, then stopped, his flashlight aimed at the bull's head. He whispered, *"Fuck me."*

"It's not his light anymore," the sunken lady said.

The chicken man was locked in place, staring at the bull's head, and very slowly, he let his bag drop. "I know you."

"You do?"

I couldn't see her, only the bull.

"And how do you know me?"

"It's been awhile," he said, then more in German, much softer. It almost didn't sound like him. "Mark, I can't believe you did this."

"Mark knows I love him," she said.

"He's important to you?" the chicken man asked.

"Mark found my totem in a library in the limestone south. He can help me bring love back to that borderland of fossils and smoke. I will give him a light to protect him and his daughter from your owner, just as I did for his grandfather. And he will help me to remake the world."

My pulse was loud, throbbing in my left hand. No need to wait. I was remaking it right now. But what was this?

"Do you remember me?" the chicken man asked quietly.

"You are the broken instrument of a dragon."

"No, do you *remember*?" His voice cracked, sad. The chicken man stepped closer to her, arms slack. "Your face is—"

"They took my face," she said. "They traded it."

"I didn't know they did this to you. I really didn't." Slowly, he approached until he was close enough to touch her. He tilted his head and hummed a song, then sang low, *"In the merry month of May, when the green buds..."* Was he crying? His shoulders shook, and the chicken man covered his face. "Well damn. You were always my Barbara Allen, anyway. You know that, right? I tried to find you. I'm so sorry, Jana ..."

Jana?

The chicken man made a slow, wheezy noise like the huffing of air out of a balloon.

"There, broken man," she said. "*There*, find peace. That is not my name anymore. In this place, I am all that is. Someday, I will be the world."

Tree branches looped through his armpits, and the chicken man was hoisted up. He slumped sideways in midair, then twisted, arms and legs dangling as he came to rest in the dead branches. He stopped moving.

Jana, from my grandfather's cassette tape story? The woman who went missing and was killed by the dragon, the wife of the chicken man, before he became that. The sunken lady.

I had to get out of here. His bag. *Just go. Leave it.* No. Hadn't Don said Abby was in the bag? I went to grab it.

"I am glad you came back, Mark."

When I looked up, the sunken lady was unchanged, the broken parts of the whiskey lamp right where I left them. The fire had left a dull ashy smear around the base of the tree, but it hadn't done any damage.

"I never stopped loving you," she said. "I'll give you a new light, Mark, to carry my love to America."

The chicken man was slowly turning into wood where his body touched the twisted branches overhead. Along his neck, arms, stomach, and legs, his clothes and skin were blackening, hardening into dead branches, flowing into the tree.

Caitlyn, was she really in the trunk of his car? That was what he meant.

"I have to go," I said. "Right now."

"No," she said. "I love you too much to let you leave again. We have too much to do."

I turned. My grandfather blocked the tunnel entrance. What was he going to do? Catch me on the way out? I had to try.

I started for the exit.

"Don't make me do this, love," the sunken lady said.

As I neared the crypt tunnel, my grandfather shifted into my path. No way to slip past him.

He said, "You'll be okay. Listen for a familiar voice. Remember that."

Behind me, the sunken lady called, "Stay, Mark, please ..."

Above her, the chicken man was gone, leaving a gnarled tangle of tree branches in the vague shape of a man.

When I tried to duck past, my grandfather grabbed my wrist.

Chapter Twenty-Three

I stared at a reflection in a closet mirror of a thin old man in a blue Chicago Cubs sweatshirt and baggy sweatpants. The clothes looked too big, the man shrunken and sagging on his plastic-metal walker. He didn't have much white hair left and trembled, unable to stay still. Sometimes, the elderly stopped looking like themselves and started looking like husks, corpses waiting to happen. That was him. *Me.* When I looked down, my neck ached, and pain spiked like flashbulbs along my spine. My fingers were dumb, heavy claws, and my legs felt stiff and asleep. It was exhausting to stand here and stare at myself.

"You see," a man said behind me. "Same as always."

A friendly Black man waited beside my bed. I knew him, but what was his name? This room was familiar, arranged like Sister Maria Theresa's room at the end, before she died—*was killed*. The window looked out on a misty parking lot and pond, with trees beyond.

"My old school is over there," I said. I didn't mean to say it out loud. I meant to keep it in my head.

"It is, indeed," the man said. A nurse. He was a nurse attending me, but his name was Robert. Not a nurse, no, he taught history at a university. "I think I heard the last bell all the way from across campus a few minutes ago. I know how much you like to watch the kids walk home."

"I used to walk a girl home that way," I said. Again, the words slipped out.

I tried to approach the window, but the walker was heavier than I expected, and my legs didn't respond right away. I had to focus on them, really concentrate to get them to move—first the right, then left.

The man, Robert, came to help, one hand holding my elbow. "Do you know where you are right now?"

That question tickled the back of my mind. A meat-stinking voice in a room. A stork-legged monster asked me that a lifetime ago, as if none of what I saw were real. All of it a delusion, because of course it was.

"This is Holy Cross," I said.

"That's right. Do you know how you got here, Mark?"

"I beat the chicken man."

He walked me to the window, and we stood there in silence for a moment, watching a car pass below.

"What does that mean?" he asked. "That you 'beat the chicken man'?"

"I don't ..." But I did know. I remembered. The knife went into my hand—both times, I remembered them in parallel. The chicken man told me I wouldn't recall a thing until the game was done. And these were the rules, the kind of rules that only made sense to someone who saw the world in geologic time, who could wait for mountains to flatten and cities to shrivel away. Before my first child was born, I had to kill him. Kill the unkillable man, or I would lose. And I wouldn't remember that I had to do it either. I would have to find a way without knowing it was possible. Then I would win, but that was the only way it could work, he told me, because otherwise, he wouldn't have a choice. You see, that was the *only* game, life and death. And so long as he was alive, he was responsible for serving his boss, the dragon. He had a job to do. The only way I could win was if his job ended, and the game was over. The knife was proof of the agreement, blood spilled on his employer's front door, so the boss would know *he*—the chicken man—was serious. We had an agreement and would play the game until my child was born or I ended him.

"That's new. You've never told me that before," Robert said quietly.

"Did I say all of that out loud?"

He smiled, kept holding my arm. "You did, but it's okay."

"When can I leave?"

"We'll talk about that later."

This was my memory ward, Holy Cross. This was where I waited to die. But what about Germany? And Caitlyn? What about my daughter who wasn't born yet?

"Don't worry about those things right now," he said. "You remember the documentaries we watched about folk tales, and that audiobook I bought you by a famous professor, about ancient religions?" He nodded, as if waiting for me to agree. "I think maybe you were so interested in some of those stories that they filtered into your dreams. Happens to all of us."

None of it was real. That's what he wanted me to believe, just the mental collapse of an old man.

"I don't remember how I got here," I said.

"It's okay," she said. "You don't have to remember right now."

Below, I watched a young boy in a heavy jacket step out of the trees by the pond with a blonde girl. They stood by the statue, talking and holding hands.

I felt waves of nausea, chills. Not from anything in particular, this was just what it meant to be alive now.

Outside, the girl walked away, crossing the parking lot under us and out of sight. The boy looked after her, too far away for me to make out his face. *I'm so sorry for what happened to you. What he did to you.* Both of you. Rachel taken by the chicken man on a whim, and me.

"You haven't been up like this in awhile," Robert said.

"Isn't this what people sometimes do right before they die? One last burst of strength?"

He looked away. "Let's go back to the bed, okay?"

He pushed a little too hard, and I had to turn and amble back over, so he could maneuver me around to sit. Then he took away the walker and picked up my thin, useless legs and tucked them under the covers. Every part of this hurt and left my joints aching and sore. I still had the white scar on my left hand.

"Yes, you do," he said, when I was settled in bed again. "A mishap with some chickens is what you told me it was. You were butchering one for the holidays years ago, you said."

Close enough.

"I don't want to die in this room, the same as Sister Maria Theresa. Where is my mother and Don? Where's Caitlyn?"

"It's okay," he said. "Would you like me to bring you some more water?"

And he left me alone.

They're gone, because I lost, didn't I? I didn't win, and he collected. Caitlyn and everyone else were dead. That was why the nurse dodged the question. I sank deeper into the bed. I couldn't feel my legs or arms, and every breath caught in my chest, as if there were a wall of phlegmy skin blocking my lungs. It was hard to keep the air moving in and out. Every breath scratched and made me wince. I would die in this room.

Concentrate on what came after Germany. *How did I get back?* But the pain from breathing was too much, and then it stopped.

No. *Make it go again.* I heaved and jerked in bed to try to jumpstart my lungs. But they wouldn't work.

I sucked at the air like a fish, felt my body panic, as if I were drowning and too weak to swim up. My legs were tingling and kicking, my arms writhing, fists grabbing the sheets.

Where was the air?

Don't die. Breathe. Why? Someone pull me up. For one clear moment, as my body flopped and slowly suffocated, I knew I *could* bounce back. My lungs were giving up, but if Caitlyn were here, Don or Mom grabbed my hand, maybe I could suck the flesh in my chest together to pump another breath. I imagined slipping out again, watching my own body, just like when I touched the live wire of the whiskey lamp as a boy ...

A dog barked.

I craned my head. A fat black Labrador Retriever came into my room, and my vision blurred with tears. I gasped, choking again.

"Calvin ..."

Not possible.

He hopped onto the side of the bed, climbed over my feet, then licked my face.

Good dog. My friend, I missed you. Where have you been?

I was hallucinating, had to be, but now Calvin dropped off again, and waited by the door, his tail wagging. He barked at me. *Get up.*

I rolled onto my side and closed my eyes through the pain, as I hefted my torso up and swung both legs off the bed. Calvin waited by me, his tail rhythmically slapping, slapping, slapping the wall. I got my walker, then was up and mobile again. The pain made me cry out, but I kept going, following Calvin into the hall, to the elevator. When it came, we went down, and in the main lobby below, Robert was chatting with the front-desk staff.

"Oh no, you can't be down here," he said. "And where did this *dog* come from? It shouldn't be here. Go on!"

Calvin looked up at me with a happy, panting smile. He barked at the door. *Go.*

I kept moving, and when Robert stepped into my path, Calvin went for his leg, dragging him—shocked—to the floor. The staff shouted, all rushing to grab the dog.

Go.

I made it by the door, Robert yelling after me, but I was already halfway across the parking lot when he banged out behind me. Calvin darted past, ready to defend me again. My best friend was alive, never forgot me. Not in an alley somewhere. He was here. Waiting for me.

"You're not thinking clearly, Mark," Robert said. "Please come back inside. Don't cross the street. It's very dangerous."

On the other side, the boy was gone, and the statue shrine by the pond was the Virgin Mary again, not Rachel.

"Mark, please! You're confused."

At the edge of the street, Robert caught me, more of the Holy Cross staff behind him. He looked desperate and sad. Calvin was right by my side.

"I'm not going to die in there." I walked to the shrine.

Calvin bounded past me, splashing into the pond, then turned and barked again. I was supposed to follow him in. It was freezing out here.

Robert held up his hands. "I only want to help you. Please don't do this, Mark. Think for a second, just *think*. If you go into that water, you will die."

I dipped my feet into the pond and my toes went numb. He was right. But Calvin was waiting there for me, tail wagging. Ducks paddled away across the water. This was the way.

"You don't have to die today, Mark." Robert came closer, almost near enough to grab me. "You're sick. I want to keep you safe. Please don't do this."

If I let myself fall backwards, he wouldn't be able to stop me. I'd hit the water fast and go under.

"Don't you feel all this around you right now?" he asked. "Don't you know this is real? Take my hand, please."

Believe that you just happened to meet this man in New York City, who offered you an electrical job and could go deep about Roman cults in ancient Germany—or. Or he was a nurse in a memory ward, and the rest, just confusion in my fucking brain.

I should go back in. He was right. I was foolish, delusional. Robert smiled when he saw me release the walker and raise my arm. So easy, just take his hand and let him guide me back, settle into bed again, stop fighting—and Calvin barked, sharp in my ear.

No.

He was here. My dog was here.

Robert said, "Wait, Mark ..."

And I dropped backwards, hit the water hard in a cold shock that made everything go black.

***

Outside the church in Dudweiler, I stood alone in the snow, staring at the chicken man's Volkswagen, with his bag slung over my shoulder. *The trunk.*

"Mark."

My grandfather was on the church steps behind me, the color gone from his face, as if it were washing out, like an old change of clothes.

I started down the steps. "My dog, Calvin ..."

"I kept him with me for a long time," he said.

"What was that? That felt real." I tried to steady my pulse and stumbled to the Volkswagen. "I was old ..."

"She showed me that branch, too," he said.

"What 'branch'? That *happened*."

"No, it *could* happen," he said. "When I was younger, she showed me how the dragon would split the ground to release the hungry ones. She showed me how the world would go quiet and dead. I saw people disappear without her to protect them. That could happen, too."

I fumbled in the chicken man's bag. *Where are the keys?* My beat-up shoes crunched through the snow, then slipped on a bare patch. I caught myself, didn't fall.

"But it didn't," I said. *I'm not dying in a nursing home.* "Was it a dream, fake?"

"No, I told you," he said. "Think of a tree. Branches are possibilities. She sees them all, even if she doesn't know which limbs will be strong enough to survive. She wanted to confuse you to keep you with her. To remake you."

There. The car keys. I clicked them and the trunk popped open. Caitlyn was inside, just like he said, shaking and terrified, duct tape over her mouth, lots more around her wrists behind her back, and ankles. Thank God, she was okay. She was still wearing the robe from the other night. How the hell had he gotten her all the way to Germany like this? I tore the tape off her mouth and held her tight.

"Oh Jesus," she said.

I was fumbling, tearing the tape off her hands in long fraying strips. "I'm so glad you're not hurt. God, I thought—"

"Mark, where am I?"

How did he do this to her? Dragging her onto a plane, keeping her bound all the way to Germany. *Motherfucker.*

"We're in Germany," I said.

"*Germany?*" she said and looked around, frantic. "Where is he?"

I finished ripping the tape off her. "He's not here. He's dead."

"I didn't see him break in," she said. "He hit me from behind, right after I shut the door on you at four in the morning." She collapsed against me, shaking and weak. "I'm so hungry. Is there anything ..?"

We got in the front seat of the car, and I started the engine, then checked the chicken man's bag: icepicks, his Goddamn hammer, more cigarettes, and a Collection of *'Amazing Protein!'* energy bars. Of course he would bring those. I offered her one, and Caitlyn chewed, ravenous.

"Give me a second," I said and ducked out, called to my grandfather, "I listened to your recording, you know. You owe me an explanation, now that I'm in the middle of this." Maybe he wasn't real, but I still needed an answer.

"A dragon was hunting my family," my grandfather said, "is *still* hunting you. I had to do something, find someone who could protect you. I tried to bring the sunken lady to the surface, here and in America. Why do you think her totem, the bull's head, was so close to you there?"

"Because it was connected to the sunken lady, Jana—whatever you call her—wasn't it? You worshipped her." *In those borderlands. Here and in Kentucky.* Was that why Sister Maria Theresa became a nun, as penance? Was that why the chicken man murdered her? "Who was she?"

"During an ancient apocalypse, Jana was a woman. Men sacrificed her to a black tree, with cancer in its roots. They thought the tree could save them. But it didn't. It *became* her. The apocalypse came and went. I found her much later, during the war."

The sunken lady toyed with me, showed me a version of things that may or may not ever play out, and somehow my grandfather saved Calvin. He knew she might do that, so he created a way out. Because that future isn't real. Maybe never would be. I couldn't get my head around it—almost, but not quite. And maybe it was lies. Maybe the whole thing was bullshit peddled by a ruined thing pretending to be my grandfather. *Maybe.*

"That was clever, Mark," he said, "to bring the debt collector to her. You're smarter than I was."

"Yeah, but his boss is still out there. We're still being *hunted*, re-member?"

What did the chicken man say at that stone turret cowboy bar? It was on his employer's doorstep, the hole into an anthill—which meant there was a way down. I looked at Caitlyn, watching me through the windshield. The snow was melting in misshapen patches on the road, just like in Kentucky. *It's not over. My blood carries this debt.*

"Stay away from me," I told my grandfather. "No more mint after-shave or songs or bullshit explanations. We're done."

"You're angry," he said.

"Don't try to talk me out of this."

"No," he said. "Not everyone has to be angry. But if you are, don't apologize for it. Burn the motherfucker down."

Back in the car, I tore open an energy bar and chewed into a burst of sugary chocolate and almonds. The taste was so sudden, a cold thrill shivered the back of my neck, made my eyes tear.

"Are you okay?" Caitlyn asked.

No.

My grandfather wasn't at the church door anymore, but this was enough.

"I love you," I said.

She touched my hand, as I switched gears to pull away. "We have to call the police, Mark. I'm so sorry I didn't believe you in Kentucky, when ..."

"It's okay."

"You were talking to someone over there, by the church, weren't you?"

"Just myself, and imagining what I would say to my grandfather. I think this is where he—where the lamp came from."

Caitlyn leaned against her window, staring out at the snow. My mouth still sparked with the lingering flavors of the energy bar, my focus steady on the slick road.

"It's so surreal," she said softly. "After the police, what do we ..?"

"I don't know."

But that wasn't true either. I pressed the pedal harder. After that, I would find a way to follow my grandfather's advice. *Burn the motherfucker down.*